WAIT A SEASON FOR THEIR NAMES

a novel of
the African painted wolf

by

Alexander Kendziorski

Edited by A. Victoria Mixon

Part One:
Botswana

Oh, my African painted wolves, do not be anxious to claim your pups.
Wait a season for their names.

Chapter 1

The Cape turtledove purred across the clearing at dawn, a steady *kuk-coorr-uk, kuk-coorr-uk*, over the occasional blast of *ha-da!* from the hadeda ibis.

Light crept into the abandoned aardvark den to find the painted wolf already awake, her hazel eyes gazing upon her largest pup as he struggled against her splendid body to suckle, his young face pug-like and mouth a perpetual frown. Her wiry, coarse fur was a mélange of black, white, and gold in which five pups buried their diminutive heads.

"Aalwyn—" A growl resounded from the den entrance, where a gaunt figure cast his shadow. "Have you names for them yet?"

"A name will find each of those, Grootboom—" She winced as her son latched onto her teat. "—who survives the season."

Grootboom grunted, staring. After a moment, he turned and padded to the giraffe thorn acacia that sheltered the rest of the sleeping pack. Four adults stirred as cicada trills receded with the night and crickets sawed into the dawn. The wolves were dwarfed by the vast, indifferent savanna under the rising sun.

Aalwyn had been named for the aloes that grew on rocky outcroppings near the place of her birth, Grootboom for the great tree that had shadowed his mother's den.

Now as Grootboom roused the pack, each wolf rose and yawned to reveal serrated teeth. Each hailed their neighbor with high-pitched twittering calls, a chaotic noise that did not carry far. Subordinates stood shoulder to shoulder with teeth bared and tongues rolled, rubbing briskly past one another.

Grootboom's younger brother Vaalgras sprinted from the clearing and rapidly returned to where Grootboom rose on his hind legs to box him, batting with his forepaws, while their elder brother Sekelbos glared at the disturbance. Aalwyn's elder sister Essenhout dipped her head to Vaalgras, their bodies brushing, while her younger sister Duinemirt was already running with a turn in the air and baying to the others. The high-pitched staccato calls rose in urgency as the greeting passed from one wolf to another. No one was ever left out.

"The hunt is on." Grootboom was tall and slender, his voice dulcet as he called to the others.

He led the wolves on silent feet through sparse mopane and acacia wood. Their twitters were subdued, the excitement of the rallying faded to an uneasy quiet.

"Reedbuck ahead." Grootboom issued terse growls and twitters as the wind shifted. "We prowl by the river." He accelerated from a steady lope to open run. "As we broach the tall grasses, take heed of your surroundings."

"Do reedbuck demand such caution?" rumbled Sekelbos.

"Their horns do," Grootboom answered over his shoulder. "Of greater concern are hidden lions."

His dish-like ears swiveled as he sprinted, straining to separate signals of alarm from the ambient noise. The trees gave way to stunted and dry open grassland. Ruined trunks of acacia and feverberry stood awkwardly amid grass thickets, torn apart by elephants in their aggressive browsing. Before the pack lay the great Chobe River snaking through the arid bushveld.

As the wolves approached the river, the grasses became thicker and coarser, rising high on Grootboom's shoulders. His eyes narrowed, peering for the swish of lion tail. The soil beneath his paws became increasingly wet, and his ears folded back, sensing movement ahead. In the distance against the swaying of grass in thickets, a pair of curved horn tips moved. They canted to the side as the reedbuck ripped a blade of grass and glanced about, chewing the tough cellulose to paste. Her fawn body was nearly invisible against the dried foliage, fading to white underparts, with a tuft of tail leaving little outline. Only her horns and black nose stood out, and even those disappeared as the winds tousled the grass.

She turned and locked eyes with Grootboom.

"Take her."

The wolves burst forth in abrupt acceleration.

The reedbuck turned instantly and lurched away.

"Essenhout—break left and corner her mate!"

As the first reedbuck left cover, her mate did the same, both fleeing toward the river.

The wolf pack formed a horseshoe, Vaalgras and Sekelbos moving to flank the first reedbuck, while Essenhout and Duinemirt gave chase to her mate. Hooves pounded, throwing up mud and water in torrents as the wolves worked their sinewy muscles, closing the distance and rushing toward the Chobe River to drive the reedbuck back to dry ground. The prey divided to escape.

"Duinemirt—stay with your quarry—the rest, follow my lead!"

Grootboom's paws sank deeper into muck with each stroke.

Duinemirt sped after the first reedbuck as the other wolves circled around to rejoin Essenhout. The reedbuck escaped into the river, splashing far out until submerged to the shoulders.

"Why should I allow you to escape?" Duinemirt ran along on the grassy bank.

The reedbuck tensed and snorted, uneasy in the deep blue water.

The surface of the river seethed, and the reedbuck's hooves flew into the air as a coil of leathery skin rolled over her body. The head struggled above water, but crocodile jaws closed over her neck and shoulders, dragging her under. A hiss of bubbles broke the surface.

The reedbuck's mate bounded back toward the brush and forest with Essenhout and Grootboom close on his flanks. His hooves struck the earth in desperation as he bounded with titanic leaps over torn acacia brush, forcing the wolves to drive straight through the tangle. "Sekelbos—head up the side." Grootboom took the lead. "Direct him to the wood edge." He could taste the perspiration of the fleeing reedbuck. *Closer, closer—*

The reedbuck neared the riverine forest edge, his heart pounding and adrenaline coursing through his blood. The wolves' breath was hot upon his flanks. *Too late, too late—*

Sekelbos pushed forward, and the reedbuck faltered against the edge of *Combretum* shrub. Grootboom locked jaws upon the reedbuck's haunch while Vaalgras gripped his shoulder. Essenhout ripped open his abdomen, and Sekelbos closed upon his panting throat. As one, the wolves pulled the animal open, dead before he hit the ground and eviscerated within seconds.

The wolves tore the carcass apart in resumed silence, dispatching mouthfuls with haste. They paused only for brief glances for lion or hyena as they stripped the meat from rib and hip. The vultures had not yet spotted them from the thermals high above.

Without a sound, Grootboom rose suddenly and ran, and the wolves padded after him back toward the den, drenched in blood.

They left the head of the reedbuck resting on the ground, eyes lifeless to the rising sun.

***

Aalwyn waited above ground. She greeted her sisters Essenhout and Duinemirt first, licking their muzzles and prompting regurgitation of thick ropes of undigested meat. This Aalwyn devoured at once, leaving no stain on the ground. The males Vaalgras and Sekelbos released far more meat than necessary, and this pooled bounty was eagerly taken up by the females. Aalwyn retired to the dark of the den, and the pups took their portion through her milk. The pack always ate as a family, every scrap shared.

When Grootboom finally strode into camp, he bore his weight on his foreleg uneasily, the deep, clotting laceration from acacia thorn a common trauma that he ignored. He crawled into the den and regurgitated his entire meal for Aalwyn, and they licked one another's muzzles as he looked over his brood.

"The river rewards us, Aalwyn."

A pug face pulled away from Aalwyn to meet his father's gaze.

"For now."

Chapter 2

The dry season of June winter is a dangerous time. Water sources disappear, leaving only major tributaries of the Chobe River for predator and prey to share. Normally wild dogs obtain their water from the blood of their kills, but Aalwyn had milk to produce.

She hurried along, her paws mute against moist soil that suggested the river. The towering *brachystegia* trees boasted flat crowns of pendulous dark green leaves, the dense foliage concealing seed pods that would explode in the dry season. The stand provided ample shade, but Aalwyn was not comforted. She regarded darkness with suspicion, preferring sun-blasted ground.

She hastened through the copse with her large ears swiveling about. Her nose sniffed the air, scenting only the water and a hint of baboon, over a distant call of *bogom—bogom.* She paused in alarm, knowing that little would frighten a baboon troop.

Her pace increased, ears flattened as though hunting. She altered course away from the baboon calls toward an area of open grasses where armies of ants and insects sawed busily at the tough grass fibers. The sandy soil became waterlogged, making it difficult to walk in stealth, and the tall grass parted to reveal the Chobe River meandering through the arid region. Although its surface was placid, she knew that crocodiles skulked close by. In the distant bend of river stood an elephant herd with the titanic patriarch observing the matriarch as she threw torrents of mud over her back and the family around her bathed luxuriously. Further down the river, waterbuck milled about in the shallower water, drinking while keeping an eye out for danger. A marabou stork glided down at the water's edge, and upon landing tucked away its great grey wings. Surveying the river, its naked red skinned head turned side to side. Satisfied it was out of the range of any threats, it examined the slowly coursing river. A light grey blade of a bill stabbed into the shimmering surface and brought back a small fish, quickly maneuvered to slide down its pendulous throat pouch.

Aalwyn eyed the nearby grass thickets at the river's edge. She listened cautiously as she lapped the precious water. Her heart began to pound before her belly reached its fill. The wind blowing the grasses behind her sounded different, as though blunted or perhaps blocked by a moving object.

She spun about, muscles tensed.

He was the largest lion she had ever seen. His rippling musculature outweighed Aalwyn tenfold, his deep black mane cascaded over broad shoulders, and his massive paws splayed in the sandy soil. His jaws opened to reveal conical fangs that dripped saliva as he stepped cautiously toward Aalwyn with his lips pulled back, releasing a steady rumble.

"You have a litter—" His growl was rising, his language common enough for her to understand. "The scent of your milk carries further than you assumed."

Aalwyn's eyes darted aside. No lionesses accompanied him.

"Your miserable kind presumed to walk the veld I hold." The lion took another step, anticipating her next move. "And you wish to bring even more of your rats into this world to share your misery. Your every breath now is a challenge I answer by feeding your young to the vultures."

"Aalwyn does not yield to—"

"You have a name? Whatever for? Do the maggots that devour you have names?" His rumbling growl resembled a chuckle. "My call troubles the night and finds you wherever you cower. Your fear will not avail you." Another step. "I am the very land come alive with claw and fang… and over it, and you, I hold dominion." His growl rose into a roar that sent a fine electric fear through Aalwyn's spine. "*Moordenaar calls!*"

She bolted as he roared, her hind legs pounding the wet soil. She held low to the ground and ducked under the mighty swipe of his forepaw with his hot breath on her flanks. She dove into the tall grasses, her narrow body parting the foliage like a wedge. All of her life was reduced to these seconds, her claws digging into earth and straining for purchase.

The growl resounded behind her, seemingly in front of her, the air all around filled with the acrid stench of lion.

Her legs were pistons on the hard ground. The river receded as she ran, and the grasses diminished, now dry and less substantial.

Sharp pain erupted as a claw slashed her flank. The strike slowed the lion, and she took advantage, reaching the speed of a car on open road. The scent and sound of lion lessened, but her fear kept her at speed for kilometers, invulnerable to fatigue, until the *Brachystegia* trees were well behind her. Finally, she slowed.

In the distance Moordenaar stood watching her, his growl a rumble.

Chapter 3

Cathedral mopane wood dominated the land further from the river, before transitioning into *Miombo* forest. The mopane leaves outlined an elegant butterfly in vibrant green, capable of folding shut as the air dried to conserve moisture. The vertically fissured grey trunks stood proud and straight, vaulting high above the browsers below. Occasional stands of less mature trees had been felled by elephant seeking the precious foliage. A zebra stallion wandered through the grove alone, nostrils flaring at the powerful bouquet of turpentine in the air. He sniffed a mid-sized mopane tree brought low, its crown a tangled ruin on the forest floor. The bulk of the leaves had been stripped by the elephant bull that had pushed the tree over, and eland had taken most of what remained. Some greenery was hidden in the labyrinth of branches, and he reached in with his long muzzle to pull them free, relishing the astringent flavor as he ground them with worn teeth. He sensed the presence of painted wolves, their musk only partly concealed by the scent of turpentine. Rearing his head only slightly, a derisive snort was released in the direction of the predators.

"Fancy hunting a zebra in the prime of its life, Essenhout?" Grootboom chuckled to himself.

"I hope you are not serious." She raised her brow.

"Even a lone one is a danger." Grootboom dismissed the male. "I doubt it would even run from us."

"Would it fear us in greater numbers?" Essenhout peered at the zebra, noting that it was no longer glancing their way.

"Perhaps. Even so, the risk of losing one of our hunters in bringing him down would be high." They padded through the forest, their black, gold, and white blending with the shadows. A racket-tailed roller flitted just above them, and finding no insects to prey upon, disappeared into the canopy. There were no emperor moths about in winter, the voracious mopane worms already having burrowed underground to pupate. Grootboom sniffed the air and his lips parted. "Ah, perhaps roan is more agreeable to you?"

The wood thinned, and the two wolves passed a lethargic herd of roan antelope. The light broke through the sparse tree tops above, and grass held on in patches as the forest transitioned to savanna. The giant bull took a tussock of grass and pulled it out whole, quickly dispatching it in massive chews. His narrow tasseled ears were constantly flicking about at the flies that were a permanent annoyance. The sun illuminated his reddish-grey coat, his stocky form rippling with buried muscle. He looked aside at the wolves that disturbed his herd, only four cows in this lean dry season. He shook his massive horned head with several tosses. All five of the antelope returned to their grazing, towering over the lithe wild dogs that ambled past.

"Your wit remains a blunt tool at best, Grootboom." Essenhout did not give the roan another look, and continued padding out to the savanna ahead.

Grootboom managed a smile, always amused by her attitude. "I sense you will make a fine alpha when the time comes."

"For now, I am content to serve my sister."

His brow rose imperceptibly. "You have no ambitions to mate?"

"Only when the hunger is sated, and our numbers exceed the land's ability to provide. Then I may break from the pack to find my way." Her voice was flat, as though discussing the dirt. "In any case, there are no suitors of interest."

"Cheeky *bliksem*!" He boxed her roughly, but she only gave him a wider berth.

"We may have an opportunity ahead." She sniffed the air. She paused for a moment to examine a fresh dung midden. Beside it was the milky-white calcified scat of hyena. "Several days old, I suspect. We will not likely be bothered."

"The hunt is coming - can you sense it?"

Essenhout closed her eyes for a moment, and she listened to the forest. The breeze stirred whispers through the wood behind, and across the rustling dried grasses ahead, an ancient language known by all in the wild. "I can indeed, Grootboom." She padded forward, and perceived two common duikers grazing in a clearing. They were shorter at the shoulder than the wolves, uniformly grey in appearance, heads adorned with short but sharp dagger-like horns. They had not seen the carnivores, but sensed them nonetheless. They laid low at once.

"Close upon them." Grootboom burst forth with violent speed, and Essenhout was close behind. The duikers bolted into a swift zig-zagging flight. They isolated the slower partner, and the wolves exchanged their lead each time the duiker changed direction, closing the distance. As the land opened up into wider grasslands and fewer trees, there were no barriers to impede the antelope, but also no obstructions to evade behind. The wolves pursued through the grasses and brush, and to patchy dirt in a clearing ringed by more dense mopane forest. Seeing the trees, the duiker ran flat out in a final desperate attempt to escape.

"The wood edge ahead—it shall falter there!" Essenhout advanced to lead, and prepared for the kill, only three meters from her prey. "*STOP NOW!*" Grootboom bayed in a deafening high pitched call, prompting Essenhout to nearly tumble. Sand flew forward as the wild dog arrested.

The duiker took another stride before it was struck by a gunmetal-grey snake. Hit broadside, it bucked and stood still for a moment in stunned disbelief. The mamba, four meters from head to tail, stood with half its length off the ground, its coffin-shaped mouth wide open. Coiled, with the hood flared out, it struck three more times in rapid succession, each impact marked with a barely audible thud. The antelope lurched away from the last bite, drunkenly trotting from the clearing and into the wood beyond. The shadows of the mopane trees enveloped it, where the duiker would become somnolent, then ceasing to breathe within minutes.

The black mamba turned its attention to the wolves that interrupted its day. The head was chambered and ready to strike again, mouth agape to reveal a pitch-black lining. Its tongue flickered, calculating with precision the attack distance.

"Do you fancy… snake?"

Essenhout did not move, breathing only with reluctance. Her eyes were fixed upon the mamba, and the mamba returned her stare. The tongue flickered, the upper body waved, back, then forth. The wolf was a statue, tendons locked, paws anchors on the soil. After what seemed hours, the snake began to relax, and brought its coiled upper body back to the ground. It resumed weaving apace through the grasses, seeming to fly through the brush. As it vanished into the sedge, Essenhout took a deep breath and turned. She regarded Grootboom silently, dipping her head slightly, a gesture of gratitude. "Another *jag* awaits us tomorrow." He gave a nod to her. Grootboom wondered to himself why she had no interest in mating with him.

"Another hunt, yes." Essenhout breathed deeply, shaken by the encounter. They returned the way they came, to rejoin the rest of the pack on patrol.

***

The standoff in the clearing was interrupted only by the buzzing of a dung beetle. On one side, the young elephant was a thickset behemoth of grey, trunk swaying gently. Although only half the girth of his four-meter father, the yearling elephant was still imposing, his lashes flecked with dust and his amber eyes glaring. His massive ears flapped forward in final warning.

Duinemirt stood with parted muzzle and gleaming teeth as she panted in the mid-morning heat, her coat of black, white, and gold muted with dust. She appeared lax, but every muscle was a coiled spring.

The small elephant charged abruptly. His trunk swung widely, a cudgel to crush a wolf's ribcage, and Duinemirt deftly sidestepped. The elephant turned, trumpeting in anger. He charged again and was just as quickly evaded in a sprint aside.

"Duinemirt—this meal is too rich for you." Sekelbos bayed irritably. "We are on patrol."

"Trees are fleeter of foot than this oke."

"*Eish*, Your restlessness is tiresome. You lack Aalwyn's caution."
The young elephant reared back and around, his interest in the game suddenly lost, and he disappeared silently into the brush on pillow-like feet.

"These patrols are too limited, like the flight of a grasshopper." Duinemirt padded to the elder Sekelbos. "Greater patrols would give us warning of lions."

"Aalwyn and Grootboom give the orders." Sekelbos grunted.

"No need to chafe." Duinemirt looked him over. "Your time will come."

"I have given no challenge to their authority." He glared.

"Nor did you need to. Your glances at Aalwyn are hardly subtle." Duinemirt gave a bark of laughter as she followed Sekelbos under the jackalberry trees. "When our packs joined, Aalwyn and Grootboom seemed to know one another. She had been tracking him for days and would not accept failure." Duinemirt grinned. "Their aggression is alpha, their bond everlasting."

"Nonetheless, I have given no such challenge." Sekelbos bowed his head moodily.

They passed termite mounds that gave the jackalberry roots moist, aerated soil. Where the tiny white flowers had faded and fruit burst forth, antelope had crowded around the jackalberry trees and scattered only when elephants arrived in search of the nutritious leaves.

"Our hunts would benefit from this place—" Duinemirt spoke over her shoulder to the slower Sekelbos.

"Warthogs seem to have made the most use of it." Grootboom sidled up to them from nowhere, Essenhout following.

"We have yet to attempt a warthog hunt," Sekelbos said uneasily.

"For good reason. Such a risk is unwarranted. Their charges shatter bone." Grootboom looked west toward the descent of evening. "Hurry—the sun does not pause on our behalf."

"Why have we not extended our runs?" Duinemirt galloped after him.

"Aalwyn spoke upon that. There is nothing to add."

"She is afraid," Sekelbos panted.

"As well she should be." Grootboom halted suddenly. "Bear in mind how few survived her mother's litter—" He looked to Duinemirt. "Including you." He did not regard Essenhout with this barb, as she was still unnerved by the encounter with the mamba. He stepped toward Sekelbos, ears folding back. "Do not speak of it again." Sekelbos licked Grootboom's muzzle and lowered his head beneath the stare of his alpha. The mood lifted—rarely do ill feelings last between wild dogs.

"She has done well to bring us to the riverfront." Grootboom resumed his canter. "Trust her judgment, as I do."

The trail entered a low forest of acacia in a tunnel carved by the passage of elephants, where the wolves' slight forms were rendered even more diminutive under the gaping cavity that towered around them.

***

Grootboom stood proudly in the clearing of short dried grasses, basking in the diminishing sun. Wild fig trees vaulted to great heights about him, their branches spread wide from central trunks buttressed by roots to the ground. Vervet monkeys collected the sugar-rich fruit avidly, keeping watch on the wolf below.

A pair of hazel eyes observed from a distance, the owner's painted coat blending into the shade.

Duinemirt emerged from the wood edge, glanced about, and slowly advanced toward Grootboom with her tail down. In halting steps, she sidled up and turned to present herself.

Grootboom rose on hind legs to mount her, and Aalwyn burst from cover. She struck them both broadside, sending him spinning.

"Duinemirt—be gone from my sight," she growled in fury.

Duinemirt slunk away without meeting Aalwyn's eyes, and Aalwyn turned her fierce gaze upon Grootboom, her growl undiminished. He glared back for a moment, then turned and padded back to the den where the others gathered under the giraffe thorn acacia.

Aalwyn looked to the sun, now fading behind distant hills. When night comes to the bushveld, it slams home with resolve, leaving the land in utter darkness. From across the savanna came the *whoop* of a hyena, answered by a chorus of *whoops* in kind.

Aalwyn loped off rapidly toward the den, where her pups lay under guard.

Chapter 4

"Are you certain?"

"Beyond doubt, Grootboom." Essenhout paused. "Same wolf prints as before. And no scent markers."

"We are being tracked then." Grootboom grunted, eyes narrowing. "Be aware—there may be more of our kind along the river than we realized." He padded to the den to share the news with Aalwyn.

"What does this *kak* portend?" Jittery young Vaalgras was nervous.

"No way of knowing." Sekelbos yawned, showing white teeth and black gums. "If we are outnumbered and attacked—exile."

As though in response, a hyena *whoop* reached their ears.

"The riverfront grows crowded."

"The oke we seek has a large paw base." Grootboom returned, shaking his head against the tsetse flies. "The wide patrols begin."

***

Their silhouettes were cut against the slight hillside, an uncommon elevation so close to the river that afforded the only decent view for kilometers around. Their ears swiveled and strained for signs of movement against the grass rattled by wind.

"Do you feel that this is wise, Duinemirt, straying so far from the den?" Essenhout scarcely raised her voice, although no other creature was in sight.

"Furthest is best, else we lead something malevolent back to the pups."

"Your concern is for the horizon," Essenhout muttered. "The sentiments of Aalwyn do not weigh upon you."

"Perhaps adventure draws me." Duinemirt grinned in the way of wolves, muzzle parted and panting. "Or her vigilance repels me. I long for the trail ahead—to leave the den behind."

"As evident as your foolish attempt at a second litter."

Duinemirt shrank, still abashed.

"We cannot provide for twice as many pups, Duinemirt. And were we immobilized for another season, disaster would find us. You know that we are safest when we wander." Essenhout paused. "Your time to breed may yet come."

"Your patience is a credit to you." Duinemirt ran down from the hill before Essenhout read the tone of her voice.

A hammerkop flitted overhead, releasing toward the river its call, *wauu wauu—awwwk awk awk*. Evergreen river dwababerry covered the slight elevations, spreading its drooping leaves over old termite mounds in thick sedge. A springhare crossed the path, kangaroo-like with powerful rear legs, a long tail tipped in black, and bat-like ears. It froze fixed for an instant before the towering wolves, then vanished as though it had never been.

"Hold here." Essenhout stopped. She sniffed the air, a familiar musk lingering on the breeze.

Duinemirt halted by her side.

A pair of dish-like ears rose from behind a dwababerry bush, and a strange wolf stepped from cover, regarding Essenhout and Duinemirt with suspicion. A smaller female pup followed—quite young, with a blunted muzzle, short legs, and coat of white and black with no gold, the signs of youth. The black swirls along her sides resembled the West African Coast and Cape.

"Take heed, Olien." The adult issued a swift growl. "Danger is before us."

The young wolf promptly disappeared.

"We intend no harm," Essenhout said in soft twittering tones. Her ears pricked as two more wild dogs emerged from the foliage. More quietly, she spoke to Duinemirt: "On my mark, dash to the south."

"A small group—will they join us?" Duinemirt was hopeful.

Several more left cover and began to close toward them.

"*Mark!*"

Essenhout and Duinemirt shot away, the other pack fast on their heels.

"Why do they give chase?" Duinemirt twittered as she ran. "We mean no threat!"

"We threaten their hunting grounds," Essenhout responded between pants. "Maybe a den. A large pack defends its grounds with vigor." They ran in a broad circle, limbs pumping as they ducked under branches and leapt over brush.

"They will not give way—divide and rendezvous at the fever tree!" Essenhout sprinted down a gully, leaving a cloud of dust in her wake.

Rock ridges flew past her for kilometers, until the twittering behind faded and footfalls diminished from many to a persistent pair. When Essenhout entered a stand of zebrawood trees, she sensed only one pursuer. Her paws dug into the sandy soil, and she turned her muzzle, bared her fangs, and leapt as the wolf stormed out of the brush.

Essenhout fell upon the other wolf before it could react. She rent free a portion of the wolf's ear and spat it on the ground. "Show some gratitude for my gift."

"Gift?" The wolf howled, teeth glistening.

"I am willing to part with you, but only this once." Saliva dripped from her jaws. "I would prefer to sever your mangy head from its mooring."

The wolf paused and backed up. He showed his teeth briefly before leaping into the brush and dashing away.

Essenhout paused for a moment, then headed north.

"How many did you kill?" Duinemirt waited at the fever tree with its bark glowing in the noon light.

"Nearly one." Blood flecked Essenhout's head and neck. "Not enough."

Duinemirt gave a quick bark of laughter.

"You must admit that was a foolish exploit." Essenhout struggled to regain her breath as they trotted through the brush back to the den. "I barely escaped with my fur intact." She took note of a lion print devoid of claw marks in the grainy soil. "Another fight awaits us. One always will."

The wolves picked up speed, their noses moving nervously in the wind.

***

"A sizable pack to the east, and none too friendly." Essenhout twittered to Aalwyn.

"Then the stranger tracking us is alone," Aalwyn answered from her darkened hole, where the ultrasonic calls of the pups rose to audible levels as they mewled for attention.

"The other pack does not claim this territory, else we would have been driven away before now."

"Well done with your escape." Grootboom lay down beside the panting Essenhout. "This gives us a notion of where our borders lie." He rested his head on his forepaws. "I found the tracks of the lone wolf not far from our den."

"Still no scent markings?"

"There are now." A low growl began as Grootboom spoke. "A male. He has alerted us to his presence."

"He may not know we are aware of him."

"I would not presume any enemy that stupid." Grootboom entered the dank den cautiously and touched noses with Aalwyn. "Our pups' hunger grows."

"It will grow greater still." Aalwyn raised her head. "Tomorrow must bring them a meal far more substantial."

From under the thick cover of the giraffe thorn acacia, black eyes regarded the den. The scent of pup around the den was unmistakable, and their mewling could be heard even at a distance.

Chapter 5

Although Aalwyn had left the den before, this time the pups sensed a profound change. She turned her muzzle back toward the den entrance from outside and issued a low murmur between a twitter and a growl—an invitation.

While the pack watched and listened, the pups' bodies made muted thumps as they attempted to climb the sharp rise to the opening, lost their footing, and tumbled into a pile below. The largest pup managed to leave first, his white and black coloration stark against the dust of the clearing. He opened his mouth to yip and was knocked over by a small sister crawling across him, followed by the other pups.

The denning area erupted in a cacophony of twitters and whines as the adults overwhelmed the pups excitedly, seizing hold of each one and licking its face clean with such force that the little figures were knocked over with small paws in the air. Each belly was licked clean, the adults nosing the pups back and forth. Grootboom bounded to and fro, muscling the other adults aside and smashing into Vaalgras. The wolves rolled into a heap, lapping and nuzzling the pups, who tumbled dizzily from one adult to the next, bathed in lavish attention.

"*Ag,* shame." Aalwyn stood back, a warm feeling rising within her as she watched her pack celebrate the litter. "At least now they are ready, should we be forced to move."

"Has this one a name?" Grootboom sent the largest pup reeling with his muzzle.

"No." Aalwyn met his eyes. "It is still too soon."

***

Grasses stirred in the slight breeze in a clearing between stands of squat bushveld saffron. The reddish brown wood was obscured by clusters of rich green leaves, thinned by the constant browsing by antelope. An Egyptian goose ambled through the shorter grass, nibbling on tender shoots and seeds with its narrow, duck-like bill. Its webbed feet crunched the vegetation as it walked, pausing to take note of its mate's location. Distant cracking of branches reached them, and the large geese paused. They swept their broad wings forward, brilliant white with a rear band of darker green revealed from under its brown back. Their bills parted as they shared a a glance, seeming to hold a breath. With an abrupt snapping of the saffron bush branches, they took flight with a blast of loud grunting *HONK! HONK! HONK!* They called repeatedly to one another ensuring they remained together as they fled the clearing. Twin loose spirals of horn emerged from the thick brush, crowning a drab, brown sitatunga. Its mouth was agape, gulping panic breaths as it leapt into the clearing. Its front hooves struck ground followed by its powerful hind legs, planted to leap again as a storm of black, white, and gold fur roiled out of the sedge around the antelope.

Sekelbos gripped the flank, and the massive hind legs of the brown sitatunga antelope scrambled for safety, its horns no defense at this range. Essenhout rounded the front and locked her jaws upon its snout, as Grootboom ripped open the abdomen. Vaalgras dove in to unroot the heart, while the wolves seized limbs to begin the final pull. Before the bulk of the body gave way, the pack was stricken by a lowing call.

Whoop!

"*Bliksem.*" Grootboom looked up, blood matting his fur from ear to shoulder, toward spotted hyenas pacing a short distance away. "*Bliksem,* one and all."

Essenhout raised her head from the body cavity in response to his curse.

The hyena pack rapidly swelled to over a dozen as the low-pitched call echoed through the riverine forest, bringing more to the kill. One hyena dashed in close with its teeth bared. The wolves leaped away from the carcass to bark and bay, and more hyena rushed the dead sitatunga antelope.

"Abandon the kill!" Grootboom called. "There are too many of them."

The wolves ran back, giving the sitatunga a wide berth as the hyena swarmed in. Their acidic stomachs would digest every shred of meat, bone, and hoof.

Grootboom turned and padded furiously in the direction of the den, growling all the way. This rose to cut off any attempts by the others to speak. The hours passed slowly as they returned to the den with empty stomachs.

Aalwyn greeted each of the hunters upon return. As she licked her mate's muzzle, she sighed her disappointment as no meat was provided. The others twittered to her about the hyena theft.

"Not a short run away, mind you." Vaalgras was nervous. "Their numbers are considerable. We cannot fight."

"Nonsense." Grootboom towered over Vaalgras. "We shall fight until their blood coats the forest."

Vaalgras folded back his ears and lay down in supplication.

"Nonetheless, it is time the pups were weaned," Aalwyn interrupted. "They are ready for meat, and we have nothing to show for the day." She looked to the pups tumbling around the feet of Essenhout and Duinemirt.

The largest pup trotted to her and rooted at her belly.

"We shall manage, my son." Aalwyn stepped away from him. "One way or—" Her voice cut off abruptly as she glanced aside.

The acacia brush parted around a figure so lean that he was almost a silhouette in the sunlight. Tall for a wild dog and broad across the shoulders, he had dark black and gold coloration—a northern trait—his wiry coat weathered and worn through in places so that he appeared ghostly grey. One rounded ear was partially torn, and his eyes, unusually, were obsidian black. His build was gaunt, but his bearing defiant and his gaze calm, without yielding.

"What creature approaches seeking death?" Grootboom advanced with fangs bared between the stranger and the pups.

The grey wolf slipped backward into the acacia.

"See him off." Grootboom's growl rang out.

Vaalgras started after him, then paused, and the stranger reappeared at a distance staring at the pack.

"You heard me!"

The pack gave chase. Aalwyn and Grootboom stood over the pups listening to a loud twitter arise in the distance, then sharp yips, then silence. Aalwyn and Grootboom looked at one another.

Grootboom sprinted off and found Sekelbos, Vaalgras, Duinemirt, and Essenhout with their heads buried in the carcass of a reedbuck, its throat torn open and abdomen laid wide. The grey wolf stood to one side, and he dipped his head in greeting. This close it was now apparent the old wolf's head was spattered with dried blood. Grootboom bolted down his share and hastened the wolves back to the den.

At the sight of the blood-drenched adults, the pups yipped with excitement. The wolves released onto them the salty, rust-smelling meat, and the pups forgot about nursing as they dove into the feast. In less than a minute, the clearing was clean of all but the smallest patches of blood.

"Presented as a gift!" Essenhout was ecstatic. "I cannot remember ever before consuming a kill that was not our own."

"*Ja,* we were fed once by humans long ago." Aalwyn paused. "Before we came to this great river and joined Grootboom and his brothers. You surely remember, Essenhout—a vehicle roared up to where we rested and pitched off sections of freshly-killed antelope. They stood and waited for us to eat. Strange, that." While they consumed the carcass provided by the rangers so long ago, Aalwyn tore into a plastic blister that had been inserted into the muscle. She and her sisters had consumed the packets of rabies vaccine whole with the antelope. "It never happened again."

Grootboom strode up to Aalwyn and regurgitated his meal for her. As she bent to take her share, she glanced up at the grey wolf on the edge of the clearing. He stood closer than before, his expression blank. Grootboom threw himself down to play with the pups with his eyes on the stranger.

Chapter 6

A red-eyed dove called into the evening with a steady dirge of *coo-coo, cuk-coo-coo*. The sound of cicadas rose as the light faded, and Grootboom returned to camp glaring at the ground.

"Reedbuck growing too clever?" Aalwyn noted the wolves' fur untouched by blood.

"The hyenas have become persistent." Grootboom lay down beside her with a whine. "Just as we cornered another sitatunga fatigued by pursuit, they appeared." He managed a grin. "They seemed angry at us for allowing their feast to run away." He grunted, muttering.

"They are welcome to their own labor."

"Why do you suppose the stranger yielded his kill to us?" Aalwyn scanned the periphery of their denning area.

Grootboom shot her a glance and was on his feet again. He paced their clearing restlessly, urinating copiously and squatting to defecate.

"He appears to mean us little harm."

"I intend him great harm if he approaches my pups." Saliva dripped from Grootboom's muzzle, his lip wrinkled to expose a fang. He lay down again.

"I recall our first meeting." Aalwyn smiled to herself. "The veld was alive with your scent."

"And yours as well." Grootboom's features softened. "I was not long in finding you."

"You were taller and more savage in appearance than I'd expected."

"You flatter me."

"I thought you a hyena."

"Insult me further, and I feed you to the pups, my *bokkie*." He gripped the ruff of her neck with his teeth and shook his ears against mosquitoes.

"You are welcome to feed them anything you like, should you ever learn to hunt." Aalwyn gave a swift kick to his midsection with her hind leg.

Grootboom licked her muzzle, she rubbed her cheek to his, and restful quiet resumed between them.

On the edge of the clearing, the grey wolf watched from beneath a knobthorn acacia tree.

***

Weeeeee-kow-kow-kow! A mating pair of fish eagles glided gently on the morning wind, scanning the river for fish or carcass. This time of year was the most active, when the Chobe River flowed with sweet, fresh water. The fish eagles alighted on a dead tree denuded of bark leaning over the water and noted the wolf pack on the move.

As the wolves threaded through the scattered acacia brush and blue grass thatches, the brothers Sekelbos and Vaalgras sniffed for scent markings of other wolves, while the sisters Essenhout and Duinemirt raised their noses to the air in search of rot.

"Just ahead—" twittered Essenhout. "The lingering reek of carrion." Grootboom nodded, and the females broke toward the south to slip through a forest of Natal mahogany, brown trunks holding aloft dense crowns of glossy green over ground streaked with yellow fruit capsules in the leaf litter. When they emerged onto a flat of herringbone grass, periodic hoots sounded again overhead, and beyond the next ridge they spied a pack of spotted hyena strolling with their sturdy build and high shoulders. The alpha female chewed the femur of an antelope corpse, the muscles of her head and jaw contracting, straining, until with a sharp *crack* she severed the ball of the hip joint and swallowed it whole. She looked up at the wolves and began a lowing call to her pack.

"Make yourself known, Duinemirt," Essenhout hoo-called.

The effect was galvanizing, as the hyena leaped after Essenhout and Duinemirt on their leisurely trot away from Grootbroom and the hunt. Out on the veld, the male wolves picked up speed upon the grass, ears flattened and hazel eyes boring through the foliage.

"To the river with us." Grootboom called in high-pitched whistles that did not carry far.

A powerful red lechwe bull stood on a tributary of the Chobe River, his curved horns regal. His high-set hindquarters tensed as the wolves approached, and he bolted, his herd of thirty following swiftly in their ungainly lope. Once they reached the muddy riverbank, the high vertical leaps of the red lechwe gave them a powerful edge, and they were quickly up to their shoulders in water.

"Hold here." Grootboom padded along the river with his nose in the air.

The wolves slowed as he cautiously moved forward and sniffed. He peered into the tall grasses near the water and moved away from the river, ears straining above the swish of blue grass in the wind. A tuft of grass wavered to reveal a bushbuck, short and fawn-colored with white splotches melting into the foliage. The breeze picked up, and it ducked.

"Wall off the river!" Grootboom launched himself after the bushbuck, twittering with urgency.

The wolves raced toward the Chobe River in a line as the bushbuck evaded in the other direction.

"Ring the flanks—I will close the chase!" Grootboom was almost upon its hooves, Essenhout and Sekelbos working ahead on either side.

The bushbuck pounded the earth, its eyes large and black and its hind flanks pumping to carry it over an acacia thicket. The wolves tore through the bush—Sekelbos nearly throttled on it—as the bushbuck extended its lead to bound around feverberry trees. Grootboom had pushed to his limit, but the bushbuck was faster. Grootboom was turning to call off the hunt when a black form appeared from the *Combretum* brush and struck the antelope head-on. The fawn body twisted in midair, and jaws locked onto its foreleg, holding it just long enough for the wolves to mob the bushbuck and end its life swiftly. They crouched silently to swallow the meat and offal.

"You followed us all this way?" Grootboom pulled hide off the reedbuck, eyes on the grey wolf.

"You are not difficult to track." The grey wolf's voice was low and resonating in the thicket, every word a tortured growl.

"Do we require the assistance of an interloper?" Grootboom rumbled in his throat.

"It would seem so." Vaalgras swallowed his mouthful of liver.

"*Voetsek*, before I lose my pleasant demeanor." Grootboom growled.

"There is enough to share." Vaalgras ripped loose sections of muscle. "Six hunt better than five."

"What are you called?" Essenhout dragged entrails from the abdominal cavity.

"Blackthorn." He tossed his head, grey ruff shaking. "From a world entirely different from yours." He nodded to Grootboom in subtle deference. "And from that world, we find a kill in common."

***

One of the smaller pups swung from Aalwyn's ear, lost its tiny grip, and hit the dirt, shaking its head up at her with its perpetual pug-faced frown. Aalwyn touched noses with it, panting in the afternoon heat, and glanced around quickly. She grinned at the sight of her pack approaching, bellies hung low with meat. Her grin widened further at Blackthorn padding quickly to the den.

"The hyenas have been denied, young one." Aalwyn whispered.

"We led those hyenas on a merry chase." Essenhout pranced toward the denning area, where she released an enormous meal before the pups. "They followed us dutifully over hill and glen, never questioning why we failed to show interest in any prey."

"Hyenas lack the instinct to coordinate a hunt or to divine reasoning." Blackthorn's voice was guttural, and he stooped his shoulder slightly toward Aalwyn in deference. "They act as individuals, incapable of synergy."

"Do you suggest that they are not a threat to us?" Aalwyn nudged aside a pup who presented her with a favored bit of undigested hide. "They remain an adversary, even if they do not have our hunting prowess. Their numbers and ability to shadow our kind demand respect and vigilance." Blackthorn moved to lie down but was blocked by Grootboom.

"Distance, Blackthorn," Grootboom seethed. "Your proximity to my litter will bring you suffering." Saliva dripped as his ears flattened back, and Vaalgras was at Grootboom's side in an instant.

Blackthorn dipped his head beneath Grootboom's chin, one paw behind the other to slowly back away. He glanced briefly at Aalwyn before turning to amble into the giraffe thorn acacia.

Grootboom lay down beside Aalwyn, where he nosed the little pup onto its back to make its legs flail in the air.

"Are you certain he felt welcome enough?" Aalwyn looked to him with bemusement.

The largest pup carried a small branch past the others, but when none chased him for his prize, he dropped it to the ground.

"What say you about this old wolf?" Sekelbos gestured irritably to young Vaalgras.

"I am unsure what to make of him." Vaalgras scratched behind his ear and dislodged a tick. "Not a bad hunter."

"We would do well to be quit of him," Sekelbos rumbled, watching Aalwyn nose a pup back onto its feet.

"He is not here to take the alpha position, if that is your concern." Vaalgras followed his gaze with a smirk.

"I am sure the Dark One would begrudge me any legacy—"
Sekelbos averted his eyes. "As our brother Grootboom already has." He looked to Vaalgras. "I came from the litter before either of you. And as such I am in line as alpha." He glared at Aalwyn. "Far more than this new upstart, no matter what his virtues."

"Be not in such a hurry to ascend to leadership." Vaalgras appeared to laugh, muzzle open. He rolled onto his back and worked himself back and forth, scratching himself on the rocks. "We are not all fit for the role."

"The sun leaves us and takes the day and its promise with it—"
Sekelbos's ears twitched with annoyance to the rising trill of
katydids. "Such is the life that I should have had."

The setting sun left the east in darkness that descended rapidly, as
Aalwyn nosed the pups into the den and followed them on her belly.
The other wolves buried their noses in their paws and closed their
eyes. Eyes shone through the coming night—rodents and hares. A
lesser bushbaby poked its head from a leafy nest amid the branches
surveying the clearing with giant globe eyes. Prehensile hands
gripped the tree limbs as it climbed to lap acacia sap from a flaw in
the bark and extracted with nimble fingers a trapped insect. While its
young waited patiently in the nest above, the bushbaby foraged on
the ground at the base of the knobthorn acacia.

Roo-ungh—roo-ungh—a lion call resounded distantly.

Chapter 7

Nearly a meter tall with a wingspan twice that, the massive brown
hooded vulture lifted its naked scarlet head at the edge of the
clearing, staring at the pups in the morning light. The vulture spied a
bit of antelope hide and hopped forward.
Aalwyn dashed snarling from the foot of the acacia, and the vulture
flapped quickly aloft with a lazy glide to the opposite side of the
clearing. Aalwyn rushed again, and the vulture came to a rest again
where it had been before. She looked up to another hooded vulture
soaring impossibly high, gently on the breeze.
"Mother, what disturbs you?" Her largest pup sat by her side.
"The vultures."
"Do they eat us?"
"That's a strange question." She shook her head. "No—they are here
for anything that we do not eat." She yawned and displayed her
serrated teeth. She did not explain that some eagles do eat pups, and
they may look similar to vultures. She looked up to where another
vulture had joined the first in the thermal. "Our den is attracting
attention that we do not need."
A distant *whoop* reached her ears, common in recent days. Her heart
froze when it was answered by another *whoop!* much closer.
She gave a subsonic growl that sent the pups scrambling into the
den. Padding back and forth, she scanned the brush. She made a
larger circle away from the den to the north but found nothing other
than a fleeing scrub hare. She turned toward the den, and the fur on
her back stood on end.
The spotted hyena was relatively young—stout with high shoulders
sloping to less muscular hindquarters, his short coarse hair sandy to
ginger and the dark spots of youth on his back along a short mane

behind the shoulders. She only met Aalwyn's glare once, her eyes focused upon the den.

When the largest pup raised his head from the opening, Aalwyn growled so fiercely that he disappeared immediately.

The hyena opened his salivating mouth and emitted a low moan. Only his scent told Aalwyn that he was male, as the genders differ only by size. Female hyena are somewhat larger than males with nearly identical genitalia.

Aalwyn advanced toward the hyena, her fangs bared. The hyena made a rattling growl. Aalwyn's steady lope accelerated to an open run, and the hyena gave a high giggle—a sign of aggression. The hyena circled around, but Aalwyn cut him off before he could run toward the den. With a shocking burst of speed, Aalwyn dashed close to the hyena and clipped his shoulder. The hyena gave a babble of giggling and growls, displaying a mouthful of conical teeth, and in another rush Aalwyn nearly took the hyena's ear.

The hyena loped toward the south with a deep *whoop*. Another male emerged from the brush, and for a moment they traded quick genital inspections, the sniffing and touching followed by a return to Aalwyn at the entrance to her den.

Aalwyn looked urgently toward the horizon, willing the hunting party home. She could hold out inside the den, but hyena are persistent. Their mouths hung agape, tongues lolling in anticipation, their deep brown marble-like eyes holding no malice—they were hungry, and wild dog pups are easy to kill.

Blackthorn trotted from under the thorn acacia. The hyena suddenly stopped, their teeth bared to one side. They backed and turned to gallop away, but he kept pace with them easily, biting viciously at their heels and hips. The hyena increased speed, until the distant *Combretum* shrubs obscured their forms. Shadows enveloped the scrub as the sun descended into the horizon.

When Blackthorn padded calmly back toward the den, he glanced once at Aalwyn and disappeared into the brush.

The hunters returned soon after covered in blood, and Grootboom and the others whistled and twittered for the pups with birdlike calls. "Fortune has favored you." Aalwyn touched noses with Grootboom.

"The river antelope were unable to escape."

"We may not have much time." She looked to the edge of the clearing where Vaalgras energetically pursued the hooded vulture. "Hyenas were here. Two."

"How fortunate that you managed to chase them away."

"Yes." Aalwyn bent over the meat that he had disgorged for her and the pups. "Fortune was with me as well."

"The hyena den is close—" Grootboom followed the noise of distant *whoops* that rose and carried across the veld from the south. "They are established beyond the grove of mahogany."

Aalwyn nodded and silently cast a glance to the south, where the head of Blackthorn rose over a stand of short grass, then vanished again. Grootboom followed her eyes and pricked up his ears.

Chapter 8

The Chobe River snakes lazily through the bushveld, its wide
breadth leading to a slower flow of water. The elephant bull made
his way to the center of the languid river, trudging in water no
deeper than his knees. His lashes were flecked with dust over eyes
that surveyed the river for lion or hyena, while crocodiles scattered
at his heavy footfalls. The bull gave a deep groan, and the elephant
herd followed him into the river, trunkfuls of now-muddy water
thrown luxuriously across their backs. The matriarch rolled in the
water, careful not to crush her young close by her side. Her baby was
little taller than an eland, but already aware of its stature, and it took
the time to chase a lechwe onto the muck of the shore.
The scent of lechwe became more pronounced.
 "Here is our opportunity." The gravelly voice of Blackthorn rose in
a low rumble like distant thunder. "The two walls must meet."
"Essenhout, Sekelbos—take the flanks to close the escape."
Grootboom twittered his commands to the rest. "The rest stay
together."
Blackthorn cast a glance at Grootboom and joined the wolves in
their advance, creeping through the tall grass over a wide area near
the river. Ears flattened, and muzzles lowered beneath shoulders.
Their paws made no sound on the sand, until the ground was so
waterlogged that they began to sink with each step.
"What is that?" Vaalgras looked from side to side, sniffing.
"Not food." Grootboom followed his gaze to a black bird on a clump
of grass and mud with its needle-shaped head extended on a
serpentine neck, plumage fluttering from wings spread wide to dry in
the slight breeze. "Only a snakebird. Now, silence, *domkop*."

"We must rush before the wind shifts and our approach becomes apparent," Blackthorn muttered to Grootboom.

"Or before Vaalgras chases a damned bird." Grootboom nodded and gave the order.

The elder Essenhout and Sekelbos broke through the edge of the tall grasses, and the lechwe responded with their awkward vertical leaping toward the river, the wolves struggling to keep pace as their paws sank deep into the mud.

The elephants splashed in the shallows with torrents of mud flying in all directions. A group of white-faced whistling ducks, feeding at the river, scattered at their approach. The lechwe paused, bulls snorting and stamping in the thick, wet sand, while Grootboom and Blackthorn rushed ahead of the pack in the shallow of the river. The lechwe realized that they were trapped. Two moved to escape into the river around the elephants, but Vaalgras and Duinemirt closed in. The lechwe panicked and bolted directly back to shore, where Grootboom snapped at one, just missing its throat. Blackthorn pounced on another, unable to bite into the back of its neck. He released it and dove to grip the back leg, closing with a crunch, then let the buck go before it could deliver a lethal kick.

"This one is wounded!"

The wolves closed around the lechwe now loping from the river. The remaining antelope calmed quickly and moved downriver away from the elephants to continue grazing.

The wounded lechwe, leaking blood from his rear leg under the knee joint, pounded on without hesitation. The wolves' twittering behind grew in intensity. His large black eyes rolled as he swept his head and back-bent horns from side to side, Essenhout and Sekelbos keeping just away and allowing their prey to expend his energy. Bounding in leaps with forefeet and hindfeet in pairs, the lechwe struggled on until Grootboom closed his jaws deeply into the flank and dug in his paws. Essenhout gripped the neck and crushed the bones, while Duinemirt dipped underneath and scissored open the abdomen to pull out the still-beating heart. The lechwe sank to the ground, exhaling its final breath.

"Steady on—" Blackthorn rumbled. "There is another fight upon us."

Loping toward them came a pack of spotted hyena uttering deep *whoop*s. Two were male, and so their voices carried little across the veld, but the female gave her own deeper *whoop!* and the effect was electric. Distant calls answered.

"The matriarch." Blackthorn advanced on the hyena, who more than twice outweighed him. "Continue dining. I will deal with them." Grootboom glanced up as each wolf held a limb to dismember the lechwe.

"What does he intend?" Essenhout pulled, her paws anchored to the ground. She felt the connective tissue giving way as the hip left its joint with an audible pop.

"He is distracting them until we finish." Grootboom stopped to watch as he gulped down a mouthful of liver.

Blackthorn rounded on the hyenas, giving chase to first one, then another to confuse them. The alpha hyena stood her ground, and Blackthorn ran straight at her to click his jaws just short of her shoulder, so that she giggled furiously after him. He made a tight circle around her hindquarters and delivered a deep wound to her haunch. She spun about, cackling, to chase him, Blackthorn accelerated with the hyena clamped onto his tail, and she slammed her powerful forelegs into the ground and brought them both to a halt, readying herself for a more substantial bite.

The instant she released him, Blackthorn whirled to find Grootboom on the hyena's flank. The hyena sank her teeth into Grootboom's shoulder, Grootboom stumbled, and the hyenas closed quickly upon him, salivating at the prospect of an unexpected kill.

Blackthorn hoo-called to the ground, unnerving the hyenas, and sprinted hard into the pack, chasing them from the alpha hyena with her teeth still in Grootboom's shoulder. Blackthorn turned as she adjusted her grip and bit into Grootboom with a crippling bite. Grootboom howled in pain, the hyena screamed, and the wolf was unexpectedly released. Blackthorn closed his jaws on the hyena's hind leg with a sickening crack.

When Grootboom dropped to the ground, she tensed to pounce on him. Blackthorn shot to her throat and tore it open, and she shrieked and heaved on the ground. Grootboom was drenched in blood by the time he lifted himself to his feet. The other wolves chased away the hyena, who left their alpha female bleeding to death at the feet of the painted wolves.

"Finish your meals." Blackthorn loped toward the lechwe carcass to take his share. "There will be more trouble to come."

***

"Blackthorn." Grootboom strained with each step across the herringbone grass on their return to the den with the wolves flanking him in protective walls. "You have my gratitude."

"And you have mine." Blackthorn acknowledged with a dip of the head, a subservient gesture.

"From where do you hail?" Grootboom struggled to keep his voice even, as his shoulder throbbed.

"Mountain country far to the north." Blackthorn's obsidian eyes scanned the veld, his brow furrowed. "A lifetime away."

"Was your last pack—" Grootboom hesitated. "—lost to you?"

"Hunt only with great caution in the coming days." Blackthorn's sepulchral rasp was barely audible. He trudged for some time just a step behind Grootboom. "The hyena who fell was their alpha. Their gang will be a hungry chaos."

"Your vision has been of great aid to us." Grootboom peered into the brush they went by. "As well as to my pups."

"Lions have been this way." Blackthorn sniffed the granular soil. "Be on your guard."

It was well after sunset when the pack returned on a path illuminated by moonlight. Blackthorn kept clear of the trees, where the flat crowns of the giraffe thorn acacia left dense blackness at their base, branches extending twisted shadows as though to take hold of those who passed.

Chapter 9

The sun stood high at midday, as though fixed in the air, drenching the bushveld with heat despite the late winter season. The wolf pack lazed in the warmth, as a widowbird flitted past with a rattling call of 'zeh-zeh-zeh'. Half the adults lay sleeping, by all appearances dead until a deep breath was drawn. Grootboom rested uneasily on his side, his wounded shoulder not allowing him a position of comfort.

"You should not be hunting with this injury." Aalwyn licked the wound, clearing away the biting flies. "Especially if we must fight the hyena clan again."

"I am sure you are right." Grootboom winced, adjusting himself before wincing in futility. "And another fight is coming, surely."

"Why did he come to join us, do you think?"

"He is an opaque fellow." Grootboom adjusted his good foreleg and rolled onto his side. "Unwilling to explain what happened to his last pack - if there was one. In any case, I am reluctant to delve - there is little to gain opening old wounds."

"I am sure he has a number of them, with so many seasons behind him." Aalwyn lapped his muzzle.

"How many does he have left, I wonder?" He shook his head rapidly to dislodge the flies.

The pups were clustered about Blackthorn closer to the den. They could not hear him muttering to their brood, but by their occasional outbursts, he seemed to be telling them a story. He murmured, cast his head to the sky, dipped closer to the ground, and abruptly took to his feet. Aalwyn started for a moment, before she realized it was part of the drama. The grey wolf bared his teeth, and the pups were on their feet, scattered, then came back to hear more.

The largest pup bounded over to Aalwyn. "Did you know a monitor lizard ate his brother when he was a pup?" His small paws were against her side, eyes wide with awe and dismay.

"No, my love, I did not." She arched her brow and wondered what else this odd wolf had told them.

"I cannot—" The pup jolted off her, saw the story had resumed, and was back to Blackthorn's side in a flash.

Aalwyn trotted over and joined the group. "Feeding their nightmares, Blackthorn?"

"Nightmares keep us alert, even in sleep." His dark eyes regarded her with what seemed annoyance. "So bear in mind, young ones… even if an animal is strange to you, do not feel safe in its midst. That lizard crept into our den and not a single alarm was raised. Even as my brother's face disappeared down its throat."

Aalwyn furrowed her brow and snuffed.

"Danger awaits you young ones… dangerous though you may be." He gestured to the acacia wood about their den. "Look about you. Every tree and shrub is armed with spikes or loaded with poison. Even the plants do not want us here."

The pups darted their heads about. A few of them began to whimper.

"Be not fearful, however." His low rumble became a chuckle. "Anticipate no quarter from the veld. We fight for every day we inhabit this murderous place, and expect neither gift nor mercy." His teeth shone again in a sinister grin. "And the veld shall expect none from formidable killers like you."

The pup closest to him trembled. Blackthorn nudged her roughly. The fear left her eyes and she bared her teeth in kind. With a squeak she rushed him, and clamped her sharp teeth onto his paw. The rest swarmed over him, as Aalwyn shook her head.

"Now you are in for it."

Blackthorn ignored the onslaught. "We must hunt this evening. It would be wise to keep them close to the den. He peered into the distant trees. "Those hyenas will be back when they sort out their new matriarch."

***

The reedbuck browsed with economical lack of movement under Zambezi teak that towered overhead in a dense spreading crown, its dark brown wood weathered for decades to provide a shield against the sun. The reedbuck's slender body of tawny fur blended with the broken shadow of riverine wood, and he chewed quickly, eyes darting about, scarcely moving his short, upward-curved horns.

The sudden crash through tangled foliage brought a twittering that surrounded him on all sides. Panic flashed in his eyes as Vaalgras and Essenhout ripped open his throat and abdomen, viscera spilling onto the sand and grass.

"Where are you now, scavenger?" Blackthorn paced by the carcass with his black eyes on the kill.

"Your measure of the meat awaits you," Duinemirt twittered to him.

"They should have been upon us by now." Blackthorn took a moment to gulp a mouthful of flesh, his mind elsewhere.

"*Eish,* you worry too much." Sekelbos muttered.

"Have the hyenas left us well enough alone?" Essenhout raised her head.

"Would that it were so." Blackthorn furrowed his brow.

***

The veld was a riot of life. The hunting party made its way swiftly through the brush and across open grasslands out of the cover of the woods. The drier soil here supported fewer trees, where periodic fires often destroyed saplings before they achieved mature canopy. The waves of grass undulated like an ocean, the sugars and cellulose growing inexorably only to be cut down by vast armies of millions of grasshoppers and thousands of herbivores. Even under such an assault, the defiant grass grew forth.

The pack returned to the den with their stark black and white fur flecked with dust and soaked with blood as they disgorged meat for the ravenous pups, while the hooded vultures watched with patience, hopping ever-so-slightly closer.

"As the tick and flea, so they accompany us," Grootboom commented as Aalwyn chased a vulture across the clearing. "It is just as well to leave them alone."

"Death follows them. It brings me anxiety."

"And they follow the death that we bring to the veld." Grootboom yawned widely, resting his injured shoulder in the dirt. "They await the kill that our hunters bring."

"Or our demise." Aalwyn glared.

"Indeed." Grootboom nodded. "They are not particular about whether they pick apart reedbuck or us. Not as we are." He smiled, muzzle open, at two of the pups tussling over a section of reedbuck hip muscle. Each pup held tightly in its small jaws an end of the string of flesh, planted its little paws on the ground, and with great effort pulled the piece apart. "They will try to follow us on our hunts soon enough."

"Are my worries excessive?" Aalwyn allowed herself a smile, shaking her ruff.

"Quite the opposite, my *bokkie*." Grootboom touched noses with her. "Your caution keeps us safe. Our pack is an island surrounded by a bitter void."

The pups tore into a section of hide and began the work of pulling it apart.

"You alone have prepared them for what must come."

Chapter 10

Dusk found the pack hungry but at leisure. A Cape turtledove in the tree purred into the evening savanna its steady, *kuk-coorr-kuk, kuk-coorr-kuk*, as Aalwyn chased down a scrub hare for the pups' meal. His stomach full, the largest pup was barely able to muster the will to bite her foot.

"He has a taste for hunting already," Grootboom said. "Like his father before him."

"Hunting will be precarious if we leave the den and must bivouac the pups from camp to camp." Aalwyn batted the large pup aside, but after a single roll he was back at her paw, gnawing with needle-sharp teeth. She looked around. "Where is Blackthorn?"

"There is movement in the dark." Blackthorn appeared padding from among the acacia trees.

"Do you plan a foray by moonlight?" Vaalgras laughed with a glance up to the night sky.

"Make haste, Aalwyn—call the pups." Blackthorn turned sharply. "A *kraal* for the pups, everyone!"

The air broke with a cacophony of giggling, wails, and whooping. Aalwyn gave a deep growl, and the pups thronged about her feet as the pack formed around them in an impenetrable wall of claw and fang.

A single hyena emerged from the woods, his mouth open with the unmistakable hyena laugh. Fear poured off Aalwyn at the sight of the shadows behind him moving with fur and muzzles.

"We must be swift—" Grootboom circled the *kraal* around Aalwyn and the pups. "The hyenas have found our den. It provides sanctuary no more. Aalwyn?"

Aalwyn nodded, and Grootboom leapt forward away from the hyena, ignoring his shoulder wound, with the pups bounding hesitantly after him. Essenhout, Sekelbos, and Vaalgras ran on either side, and Duinemirt and Aalwyn guarded the rear. The hyena sat on his haunches watching them leave.

The wolves ran quietly, branches snapping and foliage twisting in the dark, their fur brushing leafy bush. The pups moved as quickly as they could, but their pace was slow, and Aalwyn herded them back whenever they drifted in the poor light. The wolves moved away from the Chobe River and deep into the forest of *Combretum* and knobthorn acacia, Blackthorn weaving amid the trees, drifting in and out of view as moonlight glimmered through branches above.

"Our new friend keeps his distance—" Grootboom was wary. "Be prepared. He may abdicate in the face of danger."

Vaalgras nodded and moved closer to the pups with Sekelbos. They had seen immigrant dogs cut their losses.

"Make haste, all—" Grootboom twittered. "Hyenas reign supreme in the darkness. For our pups to live would be extraordinary fortune."

A hyena set upon them abruptly out of the thorn acacia with a cackling eruption, and the air filled with its stench. It seized the largest pup in its teeth, its sharp peal calling out.

"Stay with the others!" Grootboom twittered to Sekelbos as he dashed forward.

The hyena emitted a sharp scream and chuckle, dropped the pup, and lurched around to where Blackthorn had sunk his jaws into the hyena's haunch, dragging it firmly backward. The hyena ripped free, and blood spattered the leaves. The hyena whirled and was struck again. The largest pup had clamped his small, sharp teeth on the hyena's snout, tearing off a piece and withdrawing again to the safety of the pack.

More hyena moved in, intrigued by the scent of blood, loping back and forth against the line of wolves. Black eyes peered, tongues dangling, teeth bared, their lowing calls now a moo in unison.

Grootboom bayed, baring his fangs, and leapt forward to snap at the new alpha female hyena, but he faltered on his wounded shoulder. The hyena giggled madly, feinting in one direction and another, then dove to grab his weak leg close to his scapula. Grootboom hit the ground, snapping ineffectually at her paws.

Aalwyn gave a high, panicked whine, and Blackthorn mobbed the alpha hyena, while Essenhout lunged to pull the hyena's tail entirely off, tearing away flesh at the base of her spine. The hyena loped away, howling in pain, as Blackthorn whirled to blind another. "Take them one at a time!"

The hyena paused at the sound of Blackthorn's guttural call. Then the dark air became thick with shattering noise, sending birds into the air. Essenhout snarled, and Aalwyn—with Vaalgras, Sekelbos, and Duinemirt—closed around the pups and the wounded Grootboom, who struggled to his feet, baying so furiously that spittle and froth flew from his jowls. Essenhout threw herself into the face of the nearest hyena, ripping its ears. Blackthorn chased another into the brush and raced back again to sink his teeth into the flank of a third. Essenhout had a smaller hyena by the scruff and was savaging its neck.

The rest of the hyena retreated into the cacophony of their lowing call with the wolves barking and twittering after them. Eventually the hyena began to drift off, the deep pitch of their call subsiding gradually into the woods.

Grootboom finally stood panting over his pups, his tongue out, his shoulder pouring blood and his eyes ablaze in the dark.

Chapter 11

The wolves escorted Grootboom and the knot of pups to the base of a fever tree.

One—two—three—four—five.

Aalwyn, relieved, tended the large pup, who still mangled the piece he had torn from the hyena's nose. The other pups clambered around Aalwyn's feet, crying from the lacerations of their flight through the tangled brush. She licked their faces, tasting on her large pup the strange blood of hyena.

The night was unnaturally still after the evening's panic, as Essenhout and Duinemirt dug a depression in the soil for the pups. "We camp here and continue on the morrow." Grootboom lapped Aalwyn's muzzle.

"Agreed." Aalwyn licked his face as he settled, careful of his damaged shoulder oozing blood.

Vaalgras and Sekelbos huddled over the pups in their depression with the others around them, conserving body heat and providing shelter. All night, the adults stirred with every slight sound.

They woke to the twilight before daybreak, in no haste to hunt, fatigued as they were. The pups rose and nudged Aalwyn for food. "You seemed to know where the hyena would strike." Grootboom gestured to Blackthorn already on his feet. "You have dealt with them before?"

"I was tracking one of the younger adults." Blackthorn cocked his head. "She seemed impetuous enough to try something unwise." Shaking off the dew, he looked to Essenhout. "You did well. No matter how many hyena you face, remember that they cannot work as a team. Double-attack them, one after the next, and their phalanx will crumble." He lapped Grootboom's wound clean of flies. "These are lessons acquired as the years bleed onward." He nosed the large pup, who smacked his muzzle. "You have a taste for hyena, little one?"

"Disgusting!" The largest pup lolled his tongue, and his snout wrinkled. "But I may grow accustomed."

"This fine warrior—" Blackthorn joined in the twittering laughter. "He has no name?"

Aalwyn shook her head.

"The veld holds no regard for the young or vulnerable." Blackthorn batted the pup with a forepaw, as the pup attempted to bat him back, lost balance, and tumbled into a heap. "No matter how vicious." Blackthorn looked into the crown of the fever tree, where its phosphorescent bark glowed in the growing dawn.

"Why is the tree on fire?" The large pup leapt to his feet.

"It is not—" Grootboom grunted. "It only seems so in the sun. They grow fast and hardy all over."

"I cannot say that I have been anywhere a fever tree has not." Blackthorn put a paw on the root base. "And I dare say that a warrior —" He looked to the largest pup. "—earns the proper name when the time comes."

"*Ja* - they all showed great valor." Aalwyn grinned.

She glanced at Blackthorn, who lowered his head to speak of the coming season in an undertone with Grootboom.

Aalwyn bent and sniffed the earth—this undetermined path. She lifted her muzzle to the messages upon the wind: dried grasses damp with dew, the faint metallic tinge of iron from the soil, the occasionally pungent waft of elephant and their copious dung deposits by the river. She relaxed, as much as any painted wolf can.

"That was most foolish of you, my love." She licked Grootboom's deep shoulder wound.

"There was nothing for it—" Grootboom grimaced with each lap. "The pups were too close and under threat." He cast his eyes on the grass. "That hyena knew I was injured. I underestimated her."

"Our young are safe. One could ask for no greater fortune." She touched noses with him.

A fiery-necked nightjar, a dark brown bird heavily marked with white and black that flitted past so rapidly it was almost invisible, gave its *whill-whill—whrwhrwhrwhr!*

"What memories have you of this place?" Blackthorn growled low to Aalwyn.

"None of our number has ever passed this way." Aalwyn was momentarily startled, still sensitive to alarm. "The pack from which we came originated around the ephemeral river." The Savuti Channel lay to the southwest. "Are you familiar?"

"My mother told me of this place." Blackthorn closed his eyes beyond Grootboom, humming his perpetual rumble. "Elephants knew of a water source that was transient—over the seasons it appeared and disappeared." His strange obsidian eyes opened, seeing far away. "Where once lay a lush paradise, one could find now only barren desert, the riverbed a channel of bone lined with long-dead white trees. Such things take a long time to return to dust."

"We were glad to point our tails toward such a place. Duinemirt, Essenhout, and I are the last of the pack into which we were borne."

"What troubles you, my love?" Grootboom raised his eyes to her. Aalwyn paused, and Blackthorn nodded and sat down. It took Aalwyn a moment to realize that he was waiting for a story.

"Where we were born, the scent of water and live soil hung ever in the air, despite our arid surroundings." Aalwyn glanced at her sisters, who stared absently at the ground. "A dry channel led to a swamp fed by seasonal rains, the water brackish but nourishing to the grasslands. Hill and *kopje* lay beyond the horizon, utterly flat landscape open to a clear and generous sky—never have we seen such antelope as those fattened upon that rich grass. The herds came and went with the seasons, all too easy to follow. Humans wandered the veld, but they were itinerate, never staying long. It was our land —the thorn scrub and occasional broadleaf tree or baobab. My mother gave birth to our litter in an abandoned porcupine den in a stand of giraffe thorn acacia far from the swamp. Under that shade near rocky outcroppings we played all day, fighting over odd bones or hooves. Our father encouraged us—do you remember, Essenhout?"

Essenhout gave a wistful smile and rested her head on her paws. "We realized that the tugging sport trained us for the hunt. And we did hunt, each morning and evening on the good lands of the long grasses. The first antelope to fall under my claws was a steenbok, slight in build and quick as the wind. It bled out under an albizia tree below bits of bark fluttering in the breeze like feathers." Aalwyn scratched a furrow in the ground. "We were lords—over the land entire." She stood again and faced away with her eyes on the distant brush.

"Then we became the hunted." Aalwyn's voice was barely above a whisper. "Half of our adults never returned from a morning foray, and we did not know why until the lion prints appeared. Suddenly they were everywhere. We crossed lion tracks every time we stalked our herds. Our kills were relentlessly stolen. We finally prepared to move, to yield our beloved hunting grounds to the pride."

A distant baboon barked in the dawn twilight, startling the wolves.

"My father was killed by a lion so massive that his mane that seemed to fill the clearing where they fought. Once those teeth found my father's throat, the lion tossed him aside like a scrub hare. Lions do not eat our flesh—they left the dead, and they attacked again without pause. It was not random. They systematically wiped us out."

"They gave chase right to the verge of the marsh," Essenhout joined in.

"There was nowhere to run." Aalwyn nodded. "The lingering smell of lion was on our tongues, our ears filled with their roaring. They were almost serene in their focus as they created a perimeter to press us against the waterline. My mother saw the crocodiles gathering behind us and spoke for the last time: 'Make haste to the east, and do not rest until you catch the sun.' Then she dove at the male lion, followed by our aunts and uncles, while we young raced for our lives without looking back. We never saw what happened—we only know that it did not last long."

"You made your way to safety, such as it is." Blackthorn was on his feet by Aalwyn's side. "One could ask for nothing more."

Grootboom hobbled to Aalwyn and licked her muzzle.

"These wounds never heal." After a moment she responded to Grootboom. "We carry them always."

"They will suffer wounds of their own." Grootboom glanced at the squirming pups. "We all bear them as best we can."

Aalwyn padded through the thorn acacia to defecate and urinate along the pack's boundary. She finished, turned to glance down, and froze.

A lion print lay in the sandy soil, fresh and moist.

Chapter 12

The pack was well on its way before morning light. The pups were happy on the trail, although their short bounding legs allowed the adults only a slow and tireless lope.

The latter part of July sees no rainfall, only dust kicked up by the arid winds tousling the relentlessly drab plains. The wolves crossed lands that dried quickly. The dense herds of the Chobe Riverfront were left behind, along with the humid air and rich green of Natal mahogany and feverberry. Hippo tracks in the mud faded away, as did the throngs of Cape buffalo and imposing presence of elephants pruning the trees.

"A giant stalks the clay lands." Grootboom was intrigued by a whirlwind funnel that stirred the dust.

"There is far less water." Aalwyn observed the clouds.

"Fewer antelope," Blackthorn rasped. "But fewer carnivores as well."

Aalwyn nodded. The lush riverfront became a memory as they crossed into the Ngwezumba Pans.

This large complex of clay basins with its immense volumes of water during the rainy season draws herds from the river to the north. All across the semidesert of Botswana, vast areas seemingly devoid of life are transformed by the wet season. Further to the south the vast salt pans of Makgadikgadi become a shallow brine lake that brims with algae and shrimp, drawing millions of flamingos and their attendant predators. Grasses erupt in a riot of greenery, and all feast upon the bounty. Vast herds of migrating zebra arrive with an uncanny sense of timing to take advantage of the fresh young grass tips. Thousands of wildebeest, gemsbok, and springbok gather to feed. All too soon this fades as the water is quickly evaporated by the burning sun, driving away the migrant zebra and the winged flamingo.

Now in mid winter, quiet covered the grasses around the dry pools, where pumps installed by game rangers to provide water during the lean times lay inoperative. The drought that had struck southern Africa had become more intense every year, and the clay basins quickly lost their residual damp to the morning sun.

The few stubborn survivors left behind eked out a marginal existence through the ever expanding dry season. Small rodents gathered seeds, while desert tolerant antelope such as oryx browsed on dying grasses.

A brown hyena peered at the passing wolf pack. Its shaggy brown coat hung over its powerful, stocky body from its high shoulders toward lower hindquarters. Large pointed ears angled toward the wolves, detecting no aggression. Sniffing the air with its doglike muzzle, it retreated into its burrow, where three cubs and a handful of yearlings dozed during the daytime. Unlike spotted hyena, they were largely silent. The mother and her mate would resume waiting for nightfall to search for dead to scavenge.

Aalwyn closed her eyes against the glare of the sunrise.

Each wolf pup padded next to an adult, working to stay in the shadow. The wolves' tongues lolled out to pant away the heat.

"The pups are exhausted." Aalwyn led the pack off the naked clay into a clump of grass. "Tonight we strike out for game."

"This was a wise move, my love." Grootboom lay down heavily by her side. "We can persist in the arid places. We have often done well."

Blackthorn stepped quietly around the resting wolves with ghostly footfalls.

A sandgrouse, greyish-blue with yellowing and a black band over the neck, browsed for seeds with a throaty, *aw—aw!* Blackthorn shifted his obsidian eyes to the mate with her speckled plumage blending into the grass and shadow. He peered over the tops of grass at other sandgrouse busying themselves with periodic calls of *aw—aw.*

"Essenhout, Sekelbos, Duinemirt—would you mind coming with me?"

The others rose and padded after Blackthorn into the grass.

"What is this, then?" Grootboom looked to Aalwyn, his brow wrinkled.

Aalwyn shook her head.

The wolves paced slowly around the clusters of dried foliage, Blackthorn twittering in a whisper so as not to disturb the easily-startled sandgrouse. As they formed a rough circle, he gave a brief chirp, barely audible, and the wolves slowly closed toward one another, the white tips of their tails barely visible above the grass. Blackthorn gave another chirp, and a sandgrouse fluttered briefly in alarm. Blackthorn pounced and silenced a brief squeal. He raised his head and chirped again, and the wolves closed the circle. Essenhout twittered as she pounced, and another squeal was cut off. The sandgrouse around them ruffled their feathers in alarm. Vaalgras twittered with agitation before pouncing, his hare struggled, and all the sandgrouse fluttered away noisily in a cloud of feathers.

Aalwyn, hunched low, chased a fleeing scrub hare, seized its neck, and broke it with a practiced move. She trotted back to where Blackthorn and the others laid the carcasses of their hares before the yipping pups. The wolves tore open the bellies, and the pups drank the blood greedily for its moisture. Grootboom stripped the bones for the pups, showing them how to find all the meat.

"How were you aware of their presence?" Aalwyn swallowed a mouthful.

"They are seed-hunting birds." Blackthorn watched the pups scarf down the meat. "The plants that bear those seeds provide in kind for hares."

"How did you manage so many?" Grootboom raised his eyebrows.

"A perimeter formation works well: create a line around a small area, and whatever can be flushed will be." Blackthorn looked to Aalwyn. "You were at the only open gap in the line. It has been some time since I learned that trick. It was the same day that I first chased a human."

Grootboom narrowed his eyes.

"Chased a human?" Sekelbos' muzzle hung slack. "Were you *bosbefok*?"

"I suppose I was," Blackthorn rumbled. "Long ago, my pack hunted far north of even the river. We were large in number, to the point of holding our ground to a lion pride. We lived in a wild place of savanna and riverine forest—sighting a human was very rare indeed. Some of us had never even seen a fence. Callow as I was, I resolved to look into the mystery of these upright beasts.

"We encountered a dwelling, unmistakably human, with wood that resembles trees in straight lines and angles. It was in a state of disrepair with, oddly, no livestock. The grass had overgrown much of it. A shiny thing rumbled next to the building with a liquid of some sort leaking from a seam. I had seen these before. Humans poison themselves with the water inside and become uncoordinated, vomiting all about. A baffling species." Blackthorn looked to the sky. "Perhaps primates have this in common. Vervet monkeys eat partially-decayed marula fruit with the same outcome."

Aalwyn glanced at Grootboom, who rested his chin on his paws.

"We converged on the structure, flushing rabbits from the grass tussocks with our perimeter working well. However, as we dined, a figure emerged from the brush by the shiny metal—a living human corpse."

The wolves lifted their heads in alarm, but Grootboom gave Aalwyn a sardonic look.

"He was only poisoned. He saw us—no mistake. I stalked in his direction, and he took off swift as a gazelle with me fast on his heels." Blackthorn paused. "My magnificent hunt ended abruptly when he ran headlong into a wooden box as tall as he. That man went down as though his head had come off. We thought he was dead, so we finished our meal. When he finally found his feet, he opened the door of the wooden box, went inside, shut the door, and stayed. I trotted over to sniff and—*voetsek!*"

The wolves jumped.

"*Ag*, what a stench! Even hyenas are not that foul."

"He rotted that quickly?" Vaalgras glanced around, confused.

"No—that box was where they keep their droppings. He went in, stayed in, and seemed to enjoy the reek."

"They—keep them?"

"They do. Perhaps he voided his bowels continuously for hours. Or perhaps he collapsed in there. There was no other explanation. We rested in the diminishing sun in the shadow of the dwelling. We had never been in such close proximity to humans before, and the older wolves were apprehensive. However, I knew no reason to be concerned about a diseased person unable to stay upright."

"Were there prey about the house?"

"Not concentrated herds." Blackthorn nodded. "But promising enough for a return visit. We prepared for the hunt with our usual rally, and in a pack of our size we made quite a racket. I was particularly enthused, having spotted a small herd of springbok the previous day." He looked at the dirt.

"But as we left the structure, thunder rang out. There was no cloud in the sky nor scent of rain. Just a single clap behind us. I had never heard the sound before. I will never forget it." He paused. "My uncle collapsed next to me, but I did not realize the danger. His mouth went slack, blood left his side in a torrent, and he fell breathing his last. The thunder came again, a high whine past my ear—I felt a sting like a giant insect. I shook my head, and drops of blood sprayed about me. The noise had obscured the voices of my pack as it vanished with a fleetness beyond that of any hunt. Then I knew that they had seen the most dangerous animal of all. I looked back to where my uncle lay motionless in a carmine pool. Beyond him stood a frenzied man with his stick of power. Such sticks have killed many wolves whom I had known since. Never—" Blackthorn advanced on the pups.

Aalwyn raised her hackles.

"—*Never* underestimate humans." Blackthorn's jaw hung open over a streamer of saliva as he lifted his eyes to the wolves. "Give them a wide berth. Or they will *kill us all*."

Grootboom stiffened at Aalwyn's side.

"He means no harm—only to instruct." Aalwyn touched noses with Grootboom. "As though they were his own pups."

Grootboom glared at Blackthorn, but Blackthorn's eyes were on the edge of their makeshift camp.

Chapter 13

"On your feet." Grootboom nosed the pack awake, twittering excitedly. "The *jag* awaits us, and today will be a feast to rival those we had by the river."

He boxed with Sekelbos, then Vaalgras. He landed heavily on his injured shoulder and limped to his feet.

Blackthorn padded over quietly.

"Not you," Grootboom snarled.

Blackthorn circled around to sit patiently at the edge of the encampment.

The pups whined urgently up at Aalwyn, their bellies growling. She lapped one muzzle after another as though preparing them for the adult rally. When Grootboom, Essenhout, Duinemirt, Sekelbos, and Vaalgras sprinted away, the pups bounded gaily after them.

"Not now, young ones." Aalwyn gathered them again. "There is great danger beyond the limits established for you."

"What is out there, Mother?" The largest pup wagged his tail.

"Buffalo and wildebeest with brawn across their shoulders."

"We eat them!"

"Yes, but while they are alive they can stomp you flat under their hooves."

The pups mewled around Aalwyn's feet, staring at the path the wolves had taken, while Blackthorn observed from a distance.

***

Five kilometers from camp, Grootboom groaned with every step as each impact with the ground made him wince.

"Grootboom, are you sure you can hunt this way?"

"Mind yourself, Essenhout. The oribi should be close." Grootboom sniffed the air and twittered to the rest.

"I cannot scent them yet." Vaalgras ran ahead with his nose in the air.

Over the short grasses, a Cape turtledove purred from a squat knobthorn acacia, *kuk-coorrr-uk, kuk-coorrr-uk*. Grootboom stumbled on his wounded leg into a shallow warthog depression overlaid by dried grasses and tumbled forward with an audible *pop*. He rolled, eyes shut tightly and good foreleg flailing.

Duinemirt was by his side in the instant, lapping his clenched muzzle. He relaxed onto his wounded side and planted his good foreleg, hind legs spasming. Uneasily he stood on three legs, growling threats when his weight fell on his dislocated shoulder. He nodded to Sekelbos.

"If we continue this way, we may find the oribi herd."

The wolves took off at a run after Sekelbos over the short grass, their noses searching for the scent of antelope. The injured wolf sensed a presence behind him, rustling through the grasses.

"What is it, Blackthorn?" Grootboom growled, watching them recede into the distance.

"Suffering may be our element, but you are on the verge of a breakdown." Blackthorn padded forward to take a seat. "I had a hunt in mind, but guarding you will do."

"I need no guard." Grootboom pulled back his lip to expose his teeth.

"You need help simply remaining upright, my *boet*." Blackthorn trained his ears on the ambient noise of the surrounding brush. Grootboom stepped experimentally on his injured leg and gave an involuntary moan.

***

"What is their appearance?" Vaalgras panted with excitement after Sekelbos.

"Fawn color above, white belly, black markings about the nose and ears. Oribi are shorter than we are."

"How will we see them in this grass?" Vaalgras indicated the dried tussocks that dominated their view.

"They may jump about." Sekelbos glanced irritably from one wolf to the next.

"Not with us pursuing."

An armored cricket crossed Sekelbos's path, and he stepped on it before it jumped free.

"I have it," Vaalgras twittered and took off with a spirited canter.

"Do you scent them?" Essenhout ran after him.

Vaalgras bounded onward, darted sharply, reversed, and bounded back through a stand of short acacia trees. He stood on hind legs for a moment, then sprinted forward.

Essenhout looked to Duinemirt, who raised her brows.

"Vaalgras—is that what you are pursuing?" Essenhout noted a dust-brown bird fluttering ahead.

"It is a raptor!" Duinemirt tittered.

"You are *bosbefok*," Sekelbos grumbled.

"If that is a raptor, I will eat my own tail," Essenhout said. "It is a greater honeyguide. But why?"

"It will lead us to our prey!"

The course of the drab bird was slow and meandering but clear in direction. Periodically it wavered, gave a chattering *tya*, then resumed fluttering. The wolves had no difficulty keeping up as they ran across the grass and tore through thickets. Essenhout sensed that the bird was performing, although not for them.

Tya—peep—peep—pipe—tya. The bird took a peeping flight into a perch in a dead tree.

The wolves burst from the bush into a small clearing almost on top of a furious black animal with a band of white from head to tail—its cranium small, eyes pitch-black, and teeth bared in a face convulsed with anger, muscles balled in rage as it hissed up at them: a dreaded ratel, the honey badger. Even elephants are loathe to disturb them. The wolves froze.

"*Ratel!*" the vicious honey badger wailed, its rattling call unmistakable. "*Ratel—*"

It snarled unintelligibly with its long claws extended and ignoring the freshly-opened beehive and the bees buzzing around its head. The wolves stepped, one paw behind the other, imperceptibly backward.

The greater honeyguide peered down, waiting patiently for the honey badger to return to the hive and expose the wax and bee larvae. Even human hunters sometimes hack open with a panga knife a beehive shown to them by a honeyguide, leaving exposed the honeycomb. As the wolves slunk away from the clearing, the honey badger turned and ripped into the hive in a cloud of outraged bees.

The wolves returned cowed to Grootboom, who limped slowly in their direction with Blackthorn at his side.

"Why have you not found the oribi?"

"Ratel," said Duinemirt as she explained the failed hunt. She and Essenhout ran forward with Sekelbos at their heels.

Vaalgras hung back, reluctant to face Grootboom.

"*Bliksem.* You chased a damned bird rather than prey?" Grootboom exposed his teeth and snapped at Vaalgras, nearly losing his balance. "You utter cretin." He turned toward the encampment and raised his muzzle to the midday sun. "It will be after sunset when we return. I only hope that Aalwyn is able to protect the pups in the dark."

Vaalgras ran forward with his head below Grootboom's to lick his muzzle. Grootboom snarled and bit Vaalgras's shoulder. Then he turned and led the wolves away at a slow, limping trot.

Chapter 14

Hoo—hoo—hoo—
Aalwyn paused to listen. There should be a return call of the same cadence in a higher pitch from the lost pup. Loping further, she repeated the call, low and plaintive, audible for a kilometer. *Hoo— hoo—hoo—*
She had commanded him to stay, and he had run off into the grass anyway. Now she scanned the brush for the slightest motion. Her search time was limited, as the rest of the pups frisked about the encampment unprotected. She continued, eyes darting, padding further and further with her heart quickening.
Hoo—
She spun about and scurried toward the call, crashing through thick scrub.
Her large pup scampered to her, his motley coloration of black and white beginning to acquire yellow patching and his ears alert and tail shimmying with delight.
"Get back to the others, or I shall clip off your tail." Aalwyn gave a low growl.
He followed her clambering back to the encampment, where her relief turned to panic at the silence there.
Hoo—hoo—hoo!
Hoo—hoo—
The pups came tumbling out of a knot of grass.
"Get them all into camp—sharp, now! This will be your task until you are old enough to have pups of your own as foolish as you."
The large pup chased the others to gather around her feet.
"Take no more chances—" She counted them quickly. "Sharper teeth than mine might find your hide."

"Why do the hyenas hate us?"

"They do not hate us. They are hungry, and you are food."

The pups cowered anxiously around her legs looking up.

"Do not be fearful, my young ones. It is not useful." She licked the smallest pup's muzzle.

The pups licked her muzzle and each other, tonguing the inside of each other's mouths to calm themselves.

"The sun above—" Aalwyn looked up to the burnished orange disc of afternoon. "—heats us and makes the grass grow. The duiker eats the grass—not out of anger, but of necessity. The duiker feeds you, greedy wolves that you are. We feel no emotions for the slain, nor do we revel in the kill—we all fight—for each other and for our place on this land. Our system is complete."

A pair of pups threw themselves together, boxing paws to head and breast.

Aalwyn smiled. "The hyenas that attacked us—they were once pups themselves, every bit as disobedient and untrainable as you."

The smallest pup barked in agreement.

"They hunger for food, love, and adventure, just as you do."

"But they stink." The largest pup was pragmatic.

"Just as you do!" Aalwyn chortled. "I am certain they complained of our musk when we repelled them." She lay down, paws folded one upon another. "We who live on the veld have no malice. The lion kills just as we do—they guard their hunting grounds and massacre any predator in sight. The adder strikes if approached—its venom the only defense it has. The hyena hungers—nothing further."

"Father says that hyenas are cowards."

"They have been known to chase an entire pride of lions from their kill."

The pups were astonished.

"Not the act of cowards." She beamed at them.

"Can we chase lions?"

"Never. It is safer to run. We lack the brute strength to stand our ground." She paused. "But we are the greatest of hunters, and we range to the horizon. That is our place on our veld."

The pups wagged happily.

"Are you afraid of anything, Mother?" twittered the large pup. "No, my child," she lied. "I am not."

Chapter 15

When Aalwyn woke the next morning, she and the pups were still alone. The flat Ngwezumba Pans were easily scanned, but there were no wolves in sight.

Although separation is not unusual for packs that live by long-distance hunts, the pups needed food. She looked at them still slumbering in a pile. If her pack were ever cut down and unable to support so many pups, could she—dare she—abandon them?

Her largest pup rose in a muted mood. He trotted to her and licked her muzzle, begging for meat. The others rose whining.

"Do you recall your father's hunting stories?" Aalwyn called to the large pup.

He nodded.

"Hold the others here. And—" She paused.

He cocked his head.

"If you see a hyena—run."

He passed her warning to the others as she trotted from the clearing. As she left them behind, she could hear them whining their anxiety. August had brought warmer days, and Aalwyn ran full-speed through the grass heavy with seed, until she came to a lone oribi. She charged straight at it, so that it turned and smashed through thick layers of sedge, sprinting on open ground, and left her behind after only a kilometer.

Doubling back, Aalwyn spied a Cape buffalo with its calf feeding some distance from a great herd. She shadowed the mother, robust and muscular, nearly forty times Aalwyn's weight and falling on each step like a sledgehammer upon the clay, grazing with an eye to the edge of the spare acacia forest. The calf, now six months old, nibbled fresh grass, its body ten times Aalwyn's weight and a brownish shade that would fade to black like its mother if it survived. Once long ago, Aalwyn had seen a jackal stray too close to a protective buffalo mother, who had hooked it on her horn and tossed it.

A cheetah sprang from the grass, raising the general alarm of the buffalo gathering. The mother and calf galloped back toward the protection of the herd. The cheetah gave chase to the calf, its lithe body at maximum speed. As the calf banked one way, the cat followed, its broad tail whipping in the same direction as its turn like a rudder. A wall of buffalo gathered toward the cheetah and the calf approached, and the predator gave up its futile chase and retreated. Aalwyn moved on, discouraged.

She crossed a dirt path and within sight was a troop of baboons grazing upon leaves and flowers in the grassy plain. A dozen strong males strode on powerfully-built shoulders, their dog-like muzzles giving them a stoic look. They were on high alert, ready for a quick dash for tree or cliff shelters. An older male to the rear stopped to dig for a bulb. He may have once been dominant but was now subservient to the younger, healthier, and possibly more observant alpha male.

By the time Aalwyn struck him, she was moving at top speed. The baboon spotted her with only a fraction of a second to defend himself, and she gashed his backside open as she took him down. The baboon gave an anguished bark, and his group descended in determined haste, the ground rumbling with the hammer of hands and feet, eyes wide with anger, jaws open in a display of massive fangs. Aalwyn had only seconds. She tore open the old male and spilled his abdominal contents, then backed away, baring her white fangs and black gingiva dripping blood.

The baboons snarled, *bogom—bogom*, in barks that filled the savanna. The baboon young clung to their mothers' backs, pink faces stunned with fright. However, the old male was dead, nothing left to defend. The barking quieted gradually, each baboon shifting its gaze to the grasses until they plodded away with furtive looks while Aalwyn bolted down the precious meat.

***

One of the pups, so young and vulnerable, had slain a field mouse, the body torn in half and the litter playing excitedly with the kill when Aalwyn returned. The pups mobbed her, licking her muzzle so that she disgorged for them the baboon meat. This would sustain them for barely a day. The pack was still absent, and her options weighed heavily on her mind.

Night fell around the nervous pups. The sound of rustling grass reached Aalwyn's sensitive ears, then a shift in the wind brought the familiar musk of wolf to her nose.

The hunters returned dejected.

"Only one hunt without me, and they chased birds." Grootboom flopped next to Aalwyn.

"You cannot hunt with them anymore." She lapped his injured shoulder and watched him adjust his position with great effort.

"I am well aware." Grootboom closed his eyes and lowered his muzzle to the ground. "Even with Blackthorn in the lead, we may not be able to provide for them all."

"Hush!" Aalwyn refused to look at her pups squirming into the depression under Sekelbos and Vaalgras.

Chapter 16

Aalwyn lay on her back with her forepaws against her ribcage,
wriggling with her hind legs to scratch her back against the rocks.
"Are you quite well, love?" She turned to Grootboom, who lay
where he had settled when the hunting party had left for the
morning.
"Quite—" His laconic answer was interrupted by paroxysms of
shivering that stirred the flies in his shoulder wound.
She licked the wound clean of maggots and padded after the pups
straying to the edge of the encampment, Grootboom in sight.
The sandgrouse around them bobbed for seeds of grass, watching the
wolves closely.

***

Essenhout led the charge as the wolves bounded through stands of
northern lala palm, fan leaves providing shade despite the browning
of drought.
"This is the most promising lead thus far," Blackthorn encouraged
her with a low twitter.
The wolves left the tall grass to circle a small band of oribi drinking
from a muddy pool with the air thick with flies.
"This should not be difficult," Sekelbos panted in the heat. "They are
slight in build."
"Do not be so sure," Blackthorn rumbled. "Their swiftness is
shocking."
The oribi were scarcely taller than the wolves, with thin, erect spiked
horns on their streamlined heads. Their bright rufous overcoat and

white under parts were similar to other antelope, and they grazed with great suspicion, speed their protection.

The oribi bull stood hunched with his shoulders just above the grass and his ears flattened when he saw Essenhout leading her column. He sank momentarily to lie prone, then exploded into a run with a whistling eruption, propelled straight-legged into the air in leaps many times his own height. The moment he touched down, his hind legs powered him into another leap, and he continued this pronking over dense brush. The herd followed his lead with whistling and pronking in kind. Each leap covered a dozen meters to provide escape, and declared to any predator in sight the vigor of the prey.

"The first one away is the one to die." Blackthorn accelerated to where the oribi sprinted across open clay. "Close around it!"

"Easier said—" Vaalgras sputtered, dashing after him.

The oribi zagged away, leaving Vaalgras well behind and dodging Sekelbos as he attempted to flank.

"Hold back!" Blackthorn bayed. "We shall chase it to its limit."

The wolves gathered behind him, and the zig-zag sprint wore on, kilometer after kilometer, through thicker *Combretum* shrub and knobthorn acacia tree and brush. Roan antelope browsing on broadleaves were startled as they passed.

The oribi pronked high into the sedge, although with less energy.

"He is tiring—stay close!" Blackthorn pushed himself faster.

The wolves plunged blindly into the bush, cracking branches after the oribi still sprinting ahead. Abruptly it broke to one side, renewing its desperate leaps.

"Give a wide circle to this oke—" Blackthorn slowed. "We are not alone."

There was a rapid bleat, then a series of bleats, a heart-stopping growl, and a thump hitting the ground ahead.

"Easy now." Blackthorn stopped dead.

Their large dish ears swiveled. Something moved and was obscured by the foliage.

"Back away—"

Huhr-humph—huhr-humph—

A wild, deafening call resounded all around them, absolute and unyielding as a mountain. It was a declaration of territory to competing male lions and a call to the lionesses.

The wolves whirled and dashed back the way they had come.

***

The pups jumped and lapped at the mouths of the wolves.

"Not even a bloody pheasant," Sekelbos grumbled.

Blackthorn slumped to the earth on the edge of the encampment.

"The veld is lean." Essenhout lay with a sigh next to Aalwyn. "We are not the only ones vying for prey. We crossed two brother cheetah —their ribs spoke of our prospects. And the lions—"

"They tracked us." Blackthorn rumbled. "Not as though we were difficult to follow."

"You need to hunt with us, Aalwyn." Essenhout sighed.

"Inadvisable, my sister." Aalwyn looked to the pups, who crouched watching the adults with bright eyes. "But unavoidable." She padded over to the largest pup where he lay with his paws in the air and licked his muzzle. He pawed back at her with a whine of pleasure, hooking a claw in her lower lip.

"You are our best chance." Grootboom hobbled to her side. "Our best hunter. I will keep watch." He grunted. "Baboon meat indeed."

"You are ever defiant." Aalwyn touched noses with him. "That is my comfort."

Grootboom settled with Aalwyn by his side, and the pack rested, but their sleep was fitful and uneasy in the twilight.

Huhr-humph—huhr-humph—

Far away, the lions called.

Chapter 17

The hooded vulture's gaze was impassive, blank of emotion with infinite patience in its eyes.

Aalwyn bounded forth instinctively, driving the vulture further from the pups and leaving brown feathers in the grass. It settled on the ground further away, but still within sight, ever watchful.

Blackthorn went from one wolf to the next, twittering and growling in anticipation of the hunt. The enthusiasm of the others was subdued.

"Lions or not," Sekelbos grumbled. "The river calls us to return."

Grootboom limped over to pull himself up his full height and stare Sekelbos down, his hazel eyes rimmed with red. Sekelbos lowered his head in submission, but Grootboom continued to stare until Sekelbos lay on the ground.

"The hunters await you." After a moment, Grootboom returned to Aalwyn. "The *jag* is yours to command."

"I suspect the lions have not strayed from where they were yesterday." Aalwyn looked to the brush where the hooded vulture had already hopped closer. "Perhaps we should travel further."

"I am sure you are right." Grootboom lay down heavily, lapping her muzzle. "We have the utmost confidence in you." He eyed the vulture. "Do not allow the pack to see you indecisive." His eyes met hers. "That is a quality you lack—much to our mutual benefit."

"The hunt shall go forth." Aalwyn nodded.

She padded to the others and took up the excited rally. After weeks with the pups, she was unaccustomed to the displays. She bared her teeth and brushed alongside Essenhout, tongues rolling and the twittering loud. Vaalgras took off running in the direction of the last hunt, while Sekelbos ducked his head below Aalwyn's chin. Aalwyn licked Sekelbos's muzzle in recognition and called to Vaalgras.

"We are going south, further into the clay pans."

"I will let you make a kill—" Grootboom laughed, fangs bared but eyes friendly. "For once, my *bokkie*." He turned to the pups. "And I shall tell you jackals of the time that your father ate an entire giraffe." He kept one eye on the hooded vulture, who watched the pups with mild curiosity.

***

A Caspian plover flitted about over a stretch of grassland, its white underbelly broken by a band of chestnut across the breast. Vaalgras observed its flight and the swift capture of an insect.

Essenhout spotted the oribi as they crested a small rise with a break in the sedge. Eyes darting warily, the oribi grazed, small and slight, alongside a small grouping of handsome black sable antelope.

"Beware the horns—" Blackthorn noted the curved and ridged horns of the sable, tall again as the height of the antelope. "They are more than capable of impaling us."

Aalwyn looked at him as they crept forward with their shoulders low.

"A sable once gave me a fright." Blackthorn met her gaze. "He was a bull, as imposing as he was dark, and hefted a rib in his mouth. For a moment, I mistook him for a carnivore, and I nearly bolted."

"Why would he eat bone?" Vaalgras was incredulous.

"The same reason they lick rocks, I suppose."

"We take the oribi," Aalwyn grunted. "There is one on the edge of the clearing that appears wounded." She peered through the grass. "That hide is worn through in spots. It may have poor nutrition in this marginal place."

"It will not be getting any older." Blackthorn nodded.

Aalwyn gave her orders, and the wolves spread in a broad circle, the twenty minutes seeming to take forever. Any disturbance could spook the herds. Sekelbos and Essenhout took the far station to block escape. A hint of black and gold fur bobbed above the grass here and there as wolves moved quietly into position. Aalwyn nodded to Blackthorn, and they advanced with their ears flattened against their heads and paws placed with caution one before the other. On her twitter, the wolves burst from cover.

The sable antelope bunched together around their calves. The oribi leaped, but the sudden eruption of high-pitched whistles all around confused them. The circle of wolves closed, and the oribi were unable to break through.

"Take down the old one by the acacia tree!" Aalwyn released her loudest chirp.

The wolves descended upon their target, pronking as best it could over the brush while the other oribi scattered. The old antelope galloped faster, hooves striking the loamy dirt, muscle writhing beneath a pale coat, chest heaving and nostrils flaring.

The wolves' excited twittering grew slowly but steadily louder behind their prey.

Aalwyn lunged to catch a wisp of tail. Essenhout gripped a haunch but lost it. The oribi stumbled, and Aalwyn clutched its backside as Blackthorn took the neck and with a titanic rip opened the great vessels so that blood jetted out into the clay pan.

The oribi was pulled quickly to pieces, the skeleton stripped clean before a single vulture wheeled overhead. Aalwyn kept her ears erect for the roar of lion, but the only sound was of antelope hooves beating away into the distance.

* * *

Their bellies filled, the wolves left behind little of the oribi carcass other than bones and hide. The long return underway, they weaved through the acacia trees of the quiet savanna. Few words passed between the sated hunters as they neared their temporary home. Slowing, Aalwyn halted the pack.

Sniff—sniff—

The air seemed wrong, thick and heavy despite the lack of moisture. The scrub around them was still, with not even a bird or insect breaking the silence. The wolves' ears swiveled.

"What—" Vaalgras said, unnerved.

Roo-ah-ruhr—The territorial call of the lion. Sonorous and penetrating, the call was at first high-pitched, then dropped into a guttural noise that reverberated off the forest. This call carried for kilometers—a warning.

Aalwyn's heart dropped.

Roo-ah-ruhr—roo-ah-ruhr— in the direction of the den.

The wolves were paralyzed.

"Do we run?" Sekelbos crouched.

Aalwyn bolted straight forward. Swift and injudicious, crashing through *Combretum* brush in a frenzy, she was struck by another flying body that sent her paws sliding on bare earth.

"Their last hope is your caution." Blackthorn's growl was low.

"I go alone." Aalwyn panted as Blackthorn met her eyes.

She proceeded low to the ground, holding her breath. Fear burned through Aalwyn's veins. The tall grass hid the approach over a slight rise before she emerged from a bushwillow thicket.

The lions were in the wolves' encampment. The lifeless body of Grootboom lay open, tongue lolling in a pool of blood where flies gathered, his forepaws bloodied from his last and greatest fight—lost but not unchallenged. The gaping wounds in his chest and underbelly were ragged—he had been struck many times.

A pair of lionesses searched the far edge of the clearing for tracks, jaws drenched in crimson as they padded back and forth, securing the area. The male lion strode into view, his enormous black mane ruffled with the breeze, his head held high with pride. He strolled past Grootboom's body to the center of the clearing, where he lifted in his teeth the limp body of the smallest pup. He shook his head vigorously and with an audible noise snapped the tiny neck, then slung the small body indifferently onto the other dead pups in a pile.

Too late—I am too late. Aalwyn's panic turned to numbness.

The lion bent his gaze upon her.

Her heart pounded, muscles locked.

She was still in shadow and downwind. He did not see her or smell her pungent musk. His broad face was a fresh wound, vertical claw marks down each side of one eye gouged out. In her mind, Aalwyn saw Grootboom's last bold strike.

I will not give way to a bliksem like you—

The lion seemed to feel no pain or anger. He glanced around, satisfied in the failing sunlight. He padded over to the lionesses grunting.

"There are more—we came too soon." He was annoyed.

"You have won this place." One lioness swiped at him with a short growl. "Be glad of that."

"They are not far—" He returned her strike, drawing blood. "We must take the rest." He glanced again toward Aalwyn, who lay concealed in the shadows. "Hunger can wait a day. We will track them now. Call the rest—we will be rid of these wolves at long last." He raised his head proudly and shook out his mane, raising his voice in a triumphant roar. "*Moordenaar calls.*"

***

My world has ended. And now I walk into the next one.

Aalwyn emerged from the brush after the lions had gone.

Snap—

Behind her a branch broke, and she whirled. Her largest pup stared out of the densest part of the thicket at her, his coat yellowing with maturity. His expression was utterly blank.

"How—did you—" She nudged him gently to assure herself that he was real.

The young wolf looked past her toward the massacre in the encampment.

"We must flee—" Aalwyn hissed with urgency.

"I am watching." He stood for what seemed like hours. "I am remembering."

He has no name.

She led him gradually away to safety, to join what remained of their pack. They had gathered under a stand of trees that appeared to glow with phosphorescent bark. Her face was grim, and none needed to ask what was seen.

"From the hyenas he defended his siblings under the fever tree." She nudged the young wolf, her voice unbroken. "And now he stood his ground here against the pitiless lions." She looked to the crown of the fever tree alight in the declining sun. "Now I shall name him for this tree of fire: *Koorsboom.*"

Part Two:
Zimbabwe

The ancient ones told a story spanning more years than can be counted of the African painted wolf and our triumphs on the bushveld. Today we write a more meager tale of our struggle to persist amidst humans. We do not know how this tale ends. There will not be another.

Chapter 18

Visibility was poor in the irregular bush of the Matebeleland, although the rough terrain was not the reason for the wolves' slow progress. The herds had departed from this stark land, and the only figures moving now were these seven apparitions through the asphyxiating dust.

The drought had left ghostly remains of life. Dust was swept up by the winds, choking the air and rendering the sun impotent. Stands of giraffe thorn acacia interspersed with Governor's plum blended with thickets of grass. The arid lands failed to hold the warmth of daylight as night approached.

Aalwyn trudged with her eyes closed, lashes trapping windblown sand, her black, gold, and white concealed by the nondescript brown of dirt. At long intervals she opened an eye to ensure that Koorsboom was still at her side.

Koorsboom kept his head down in silent pace with the rest. Blackthorn had been restless for weeks, ever since the lions had ravaged the wolf pack. He twittered that "a new scent was emerging," but Sekelbos scoffed at the notion. He continued to grumble at times, though he no longer called for a return to the Chobe River.

Day, then night. The wolves scarcely took notice.

A ribbon of black finally emerged from the dust. The A33 is a busy tar road bringing tourists to the northern parts of the Chobe reserve and Kasane. Heavy trucks of cab and trailer roared along the strip, creating currents that swirled the thick air. These were chased by *bakkies*, smaller trucks with open rears piled high with boxes or more humans. More heavy trucks, then cars, then other vehicles followed in a bewildering column of activity.

"What is that *kak* - is that what gasoline is?" Vaalgras hacked at the new smell.

"The large things reek of petrol and smoke." Blackthorn nodded. "They burn as they move along the black way. Somehow the fire does not consume them. Be cautious—they move more quickly than any cheetah and will strike you down without even slowing." He paused. "Some of them appear to run us down deliberately."

"How can you know the mind of a human?" Sekelbos grumbled.

"I need only see the outcome. A splinter pack I joined long ago was running along a road much like this when the alpha was crushed by one of those things. For hours the pack tried to revive him, and one after another the things struck down the rest of the wolves until only a few remained. Do not make the mistake of trusting these creatures. They are capable of luxurious cruelties."

"Cruelty—or indifference?" Essenhout panted at his side.

"Does it matter?"

Blackthorn padded to the roadside as a gigantic twin-trailer freight lorry thundered by. He wavered in the air current that sucked at him and looked away, far down the ribbon. A series of cars *whoomed* past while the wolves waited behind him.

"Ever taut as a tendon, Koorsboom." Blackthorn glanced down when the pup appeared at his side, paws and legs twitching as though to advance. "This threat is implacable and demands as much suspicion as caution."

Whoom. Whoom. A pause, then another: *whoom.* One car slowed to a stop within sight of the wolves. The dust-covered windows came down, and cylindrical devices extended, making barely audible clicks. Blackthorn tensed, then relaxed as he realized that there were no rifles. He could not identify the devices, only that there was no immediate danger from these humans.

Sekelbos trotted across the black ribbon directly in the path of another car, which wavered as brakes were applied, then steadied while accelerating. *Whoom!*

"Impetuous bastard," Blackthorn growled audibly above the traffic. "We must await an opportunity of quiet." He looked each way and twittered. "Do not delay!" He hurried across the road to the grass on the other side, and each wolf repeated his motions as they crossed.

"There is nothing for it, Koorsboom," Aalwyn cooed to the trembling pup. "Move now if you wish to stay with us."

Koorsboom whimpered as he edged onto the warm, faded asphalt. He began to trot quickly, his claws clicking and nostrils filling with the strange fuel smell of roasted highway. She nosed him off the road onto the far grass just as another truck passed in a deafening blast of horn, and the wolves shook their heads to clear their ears, overloaded with a steady tin ringing.

The dust storm seemed to abate at last. The dirt still reeled before them in eddies, but had lost the ability to blind. The dust curtain fell and revealed distant hills of green and brown foliage on the horizon.

"This is a wild area." Blackthorn padded ahead sniffing the air. "I have no memory of this place—" A pause to sniff again. "There will be no rest here."

Aalwyn nodded, her head hanging low. Blackthorn still deferred to her, but she had given him leadership during her time of mourning.

"Not a track." Essenhout sniffed the earth as she walked. "Not even a hint of our kind."

"Not sure whether that is good news or ill," Duinemirt agreed. "We have neither the numbers nor the will to fight for territory."

"Make no mistake: we are not alone here." Blackthorn stood on his hind legs to half-turn toward the others and fell back down to his forepaws.

"How can you be sure?" Duinemirt cocked her head.

"The scent is faint, but our kind passed this way less than a season hence." Blackthorn put his nose to the dirt. "They will not have given ground—and there are signs of lion." His rasp turned sharp. "Even our droppings will not be welcome."

"*Eish,* he is making this up from moment to moment," Sekelbos whined to Aalwyn.

Aalwyn padded after Blackthorn, watching the dirt before her. Koorsboom nudged her side, but she gave no notice.

In Zimbabwe on the edge of the Kalahari Basin lie the vast thirstlands—arid and depleted, the rolling slight hills of orange-brown dust are marked by exposed rock, and the sand grows maize only with tremendous effort. Marginal for farming at the best of times, the land has become desolate as southern Africa has dried and grown steadily hotter.

The wolves passed a mud hut in the distance behind a stand of Governor's plum trees where a Ndebele family had tilled the soil for a hundred years. A man stood outdoors with a hand over his eyes, while a woman hacked with a paving hoe at desiccated grass knots in the field. Shepherd's trees stood with their rounded green crowns stark against the dead land, trunk and branches greyish white with verdant leaves and round yellow and red berries. It is called the Tree of Life by the Ndebele farmers for the livestock that browse it heavily, woody limbs hacked off for water, and lifesaving shade at the height of summer.

The man gestured to his sons to round up the goats, pointing to the swiftly-moving wolves in the distance with his hands describing in detail how they tear young boys to pieces and eat them alive. If only he had a gun, he motioned, the wolves would all be dead.

The pack filed out of sight as he stood shaking his head—the world would be better off when rid of these vermin of the wild.

Chapter 19

"Lion. This track made within the season." Aalwyn showed
Koorsboom. "See the central pad with toe marks radiating out? Claw
marks indicate a lion in haste."
"How can you tell the age of the mark?" Koorsboom stared.
"I have seen them freshly-made." Her voice was devoid of emotion.
"They weather steadily."
The wolves made their way along the edge of a clay pan holding the
residual moisture of long-departed rains. The grasses were greener
here in Hwange National Park, under towering silver clusterleaf trees
beginning to bud before spring. Coffee bauhinia clung to the dry soil
with its branches growing in chaotic scrambles. Impala had left
gnaw marks on the newly-sprouted leaves and would return to
browse the beans later in the year.
"Do you advise a hunt, Blackthorn?" Essenhout sniffed for any sign
of rain on the wind.
"Not today—we must travel until the lion prints disappear."
Blackthorn trotted ahead, tongue out panting in the heat of day as he
scanned the ground. He glanced back with a sour look. "Every place
with the slightest water lies under claim. And the moisture in the air
carries scent powerfully."
Koorsboom wandered near Aalwyn, afraid to drift too far.
"I doubt the wisdom of leaving this wild place behind." Sekelbos
sidled up to Aalwyn as they passed under a sparse stand of Zambezi
teak.
"What do you suggest?"
"Penetrating inward and fighting for land."
"We are ill-suited for a fight." Aalwyn sighed.

"Essenhout and Vaalgras are more than up to the challenge. And Duinemirt is showing considerable initiative."

"She is showing interest in leaving—or have you not noticed?"

"What do you mean?" Sekelbos stopped.

"She wants a litter." Aalwyn closed her eyes in annoyance. "Which means that she is about to leave us."

"With whom?"

"Vaalgras. If you desire Grootboom's alpha place, I should not have to inform you of the news within our pack."

"I do not presume—" Sekelbos shrank back.

"Have I not heard your complaints to the others? However, I have learned to trust Blackthorn's ability to survive. He made his way alone long before finding us."

Sekelbos padded ahead grumbling to himself.

Aalwyn was glad of the quiet.

The wolves crested a rocky rise above a flat region to the southwest with squat grass and sparse trees interspersed by scrub stretching for a hundred miles in every direction. A hint of water hung in the air, carried from distant boreholes deep in the Hwange National Park operated by rangers through the dry season to sustain the game that draws hunters and tourists. In the distance the landscape rolled over ancient dunes stabilized by grass and scrub brush.

A giraffe emerged from behind a grove of Tamboti wood, bobbing his head as he ambled to an acacia tree. He spiraled his rough tongue around a branch and yanked the leaves into his mouth, undeterred by the sharp thorns. The upper reaches of the acacia, partly denuded of green, released ethylene to neighboring trees so that they would produce bitter tannin poisons to discourage other browsers.

A stand of palm trees stood with massive fan leaves wavering in the slight breeze, the topmost leaves defiantly green in the arid winter and lower fans dried progressively until falling to a greyed pile below. A pair of ostrich browsed on seeds in the grass tussocks, ready to sprint at any moment.

The wolves camped in the shade under the thorned crown of an acacia, at the base of which grew a clump of green creeping Devil's eyelash with its poisonous spined fruits.

Koorsboom lay for comfort next to Aalwyn, and Blackthorn rested alongside them.

"This is a dangerous time for us, Aalwyn," Blackthorn rumbled. "The days between kills exceed our successful hunts. If we begin to starve, the pack will disperse."

"What do you suggest?"

"Only caution. Despite how I detest this area, we must wait for a successful day of hunting." He turned to the valley below with its gathering of mud and thatch huts and a single small fire. "They will not long tolerate our presence."

Aalwyn rolled onto her side.

"Pack cohesion is breaking down. Sekelbos never tires of complaining." Blackthorn's obsidian eyes drifted to the where Duinemirt and Vaalgras lay together. "And there may yet be trouble from those two." He moved slightly closer to Aalwyn, not touching her fur. "I have experienced your loss as my own. As I have lost count of the seasons, so I have forgotten how many good mates have been cut down over so long—like howls into the storm."

Aalwyn did not meet his gaze.

"The time has come for you to take an alpha mate." He regarded the other males. "I fear, however, your choices are limited. Nonetheless, if you do not take one, the others may disperse."

Aalwyn remained quiet, and her body heaved as she rested. Blackthorn stood and moved across the clearing, sniffing the air carefully before lying down.

Cicadas began their trill as the turtledoves purred to the coming night. An echo came through the hills and rock faces, clarity lost over the kilometers, the unmistakable territorial call of a lion.

Chapter 20

Blackthorn awoke startled, but he hid his fangs when he saw that Aalwyn nosed him.

"Is danger upon us?" He was on his paws instantly.

"The hunt will soon be underway."

Aalwyn joined the others in twittering and excited lapping of muzzles. She seemed less than enthused, although she made the noise and the show as expected.

On the open pasture, the wolves paced the grass where it transitioned from thicker brush around a massive herd of wildebeest who glanced constantly at them while ripping mouthfuls of greenery. The blue wildebeest stood twice as tall as the wolves, their coats of dark grey casting a vaguely bluish sheen and horns curved down from their skull to hooks. The wildebeest took long pauses to chew the coarse grass and swallow. Clouds drifted lazily across the sky, flies swarmed in clouds around the flicking tails, and a bull fidgeted and trotted a few steps.

"Their calves appear sure of their footing," Blackthorn observed .

The female wildebeest grazed behind the bulls, calves peeking from behind their mothers, who moved quickly to hide them again. They numbered a few hundred strong, and had been on the move in search of fresh green grass.

"Their rut has been successful."

"A robust phalanx of males." Essenhout spoke with trepidation. "A formidable wall."

"This is folly." Sekelbos shook his head. "We have never hunted prey of this size or number."

"They may stand their ground." Blackthorn was calm. "In which case, we venture elsewhere." He glanced at the distant scrub line.

"We have fortune in our favor—no competition at the moment. We kill here."

The wolves began their approach with ears flat and bodies bunched together to make their own low numbers less evident.

"Shall we attempt to circle them to access the calves?" Vaalgras crouched next to Blackthorn.

"They would only wheel about with us. We must head straight into them."

"What if they do not respond?"

"Then we do not hunt. This is meant as a test." Blackthorn did not mind teaching.

As the wolves drew closer, the wildebeest became visibly nervous. The bulls grouped closer to the wolves, while the mothers shrank back with their calves. The silence was broken by urgent baying, *gnu —gnu—*

When the wolves were within fifty meters, the younger male wildebeest turned to flee but checked themselves. The females stopped feeding. The larger bulls began to stamp.

"Stay alert—here is where their nerve breaks."

Vaalgras nodded. The wolves tensed for the coming sprint. When the wolves were within thirty meters, the bulls snorted to call the females to stay still. When the wolves were within twenty-five meters, a young mother began to gallop with her calf in tow.

"Break around the bulls, and intercept the mother."

The wolves banked around the males, dodging one who lunged at them with his horns. They edged out of range and picked up speed. They swept past the herd toward the female and calf, now both running to the limit of their stamina. Blue wildebeest are fast, but calves only manage half the speed of their mothers. The wildebeest mother hastened into the brush, the wolves fast on their tails and unhindered by acacia thorn. The wildebeest mother ran to a dirt road, hoping to escape. The calf's strength began to wane and the mother pulled away from it.

Essenhout and Vaalgras gripped the calf's shoulders, and Blackthorn rounded the front to hold the snout of the calf, its eyes dilated in terror. Aalwyn burrowed into its abdomen and ripped out the aorta, and the calf died instantly. The wolves dismembered the carcass and rent open the hide. Sekelbos prepared to dive in, but Blackthorn shoved him aside. He gave Koorsboom a nod, and the pup pulled out the viscera and began gulping down the tenderloin muscle behind it. Once he had a significant share and had filled up on the nourishing blood, Aalwyn took her turn. Then the rest of the pack finished while Blackthorn kept watch. He ate last.

Aalwyn shook the blood from her ruff, regarding Blackthorn with a smile.

"We must leave this kill." Blackthorn rose on his back feet and brayed. "Hyenas will not be far by now."

Aalwyn led the wolves to a dusty clearing atop a dry *kopje*, a bald granite dome that stood above the surrounding lowlands. Once they lay down, they were invisible with a commanding view of the valley. They surprised a scrub hare among the rocks, which Vaalgras killed, tossing the body to Koorsboom.

"You chose well, this place of rest." Blackthorn nodded to Aalwyn. "Shall we return after the evening hunt?"

"We may investigate another wildebeest herd nearby—their tracks were not difficult to detect."

"Although we have ventured far, I suspect that our trek has only begun." Blackthorn looked to the west, where the sun faded against the dust of the pans.

"I want a world away from there." Aalwyn looked quickly to the side. "Although our path is full of thorns, I want no more homes for us. The *Dwalen* shall find sanctuary in our trek."

"The *Dwalen*—is that our name now? Wanderers always?"

"So it would seem." She sighed. "May our *Dwaal* never cease. A wolf on the move shall never die."

Blackthorn allowed a cautious smile, unsure of whether that was in jest.

"The sky is bereft of cloud, and the moon will grow fat tonight." Aalwyn looked up. "We hunt again after nightfall." She curled up by a rock still warm from the setting sun.

"I hardly knew my father."

Blackthorn turned, startled at the whisper. "Your stealth is remarkable, young one." His growl was gentle and low. "I never knew mine either. He was killed during a hunt—the lion struck him while they fed, crept upon them silent as a pacific breeze."

"How can I ask my mother about him?"

He sighed with a pause before answering. "You cannot. She will tell you his stories over time." Blackthorn lapped Koorsboom's muzzle. "When one you love suffers trauma, you cannot share it with them or impress them with your understanding. Such gestures reopen wounds best left alone. Be a help to her, perform the tasks you are appointed, and be generous with a listening ear."

"I do not understand," Koorsboom whimpered.

"Anyone who claims to understand is a fool." Blackthorn gnawed his foreleg to dislodge a tick. "Rest now, *boykie*. The night is unforgiving and will put you to the test."

When the wolves hunted after dark, they found no wildebeest. The calls of the lions forced them to return and await the dawn.

Chapter 21

The sun bathed the hillside in ethereal orange, the wildebeest herd stirring and grunting, their heads raised constantly as they grazed on fresh grass. A calf suckled at his nervous mother and drifted off to prance with the other calves. Spontaneously, compulsively, the young broke out in runs, at first clumsily, then bounding in leaps of several feet. The mothers ground their hooves in the dirt, and the calves ran back, identifying their mothers unfailingly by scent and distinctive calls, *gnu—gnu—*

A baboon howled a distant alarm, *bogom!*

At once the herd straightened. The mothers and calves retreated behind the massive bulls, whipping up dust. Visibility lessened, and nerves frayed. A single wildebeest does not stampede, only an entire herd at once. But not yet.

A whisk of tail appeared—brown with a tuft at the end—a lioness. The wildebeest bulls stamped, holding their ground, and maneuvered toward her with a shield of sharp horns.

Suddenly the herd broke together and ran, bulls around the females with their calves. The pounding of hooves shook the earth, and dust blinded and choked them, *gnu—gnu—gnu—gnu* filling the air. The lions lost each other in the impossible cloud and retreated.

Without warning, the wolves tore past the lions and vanished into the dust. They ignored faint sounds in favor of loud thundering, until they came to brush less prone to dust where they zeroed in on three wildebeest that broke free. The herd had ran a kilometer, dispersed for the moment, and regrouped, with the females searching for their calves with urgent calls of *gnu—gnu*, each voice unique. Calves slowly rejoined their mothers. But one calf never found his.

"Blackthorn, I would never have expected you to hunt alongside lions," Essenhout pestered him. "You did realize they were present?"

"Never attempt that again—" Blackthorn rumbled. "Any of you. There was an opportunity, and the lions were in the wrong position for their own hunt. Attacking a herd on a dusty plain from downwind may conceal your scent and approach, but the finishing move will be chaos."

"A necessary gambit." Aalwyn brushed close to him, and licked her chops. "The meat was *lekker,* and we needed it for the way ahead."

Sekelbos glared.

The following morning, the wolves padded through the grass in the general direction of the wildebeest.

"They moved in the night." Blackthorn sniffed fresh prints on the dusty ground. "The lions moved with them."

The pack came over a low rise to find the herd of wildebeest, a blue haze on the plain. They circled the herd at a distance.

"The lion's approach is more sure this time." Aalwyn indicated a swishing tail in the grass. "I am afraid that any kill we make here will be stolen. Along with us."

The wolves pressed eastward but found no more herds of any kind. The arid Matebeleland gave way to sparse grasses and rough savanna. The wolves paused at a waterhole from a recent rain, the water little more than thin mud, to allow Koorsboom to wet his nose.

***

Weeks passed as the wolves survived on scrub hares and rodents caught in the open. When they came upon a recently-killed impala, they scavenged in desperation.

"Why could we not stay around the wildebeest herd?" Koorsboom padded next to Blackthorn.

"Waiting could have been in vain." Blackthorn managed a smile. "Wolves are perfect wanderers. These distances are nothing for us. And that herd will not be around forever." His eyes narrowed at the horizon. "Permanence is a lake shimmering in an arid desert. Neither you nor I leave any mark. Our paw prints are blown with the dust, as are we." He glanced at Koorsboom. "So much the greater that we—against all odds or reason—were ever here and once conquered all."

Chapter 22

A stray goat nibbled on old grass in a dry stream bed that wound its
way from a *kopje* on higher ground. The earth was too rough to farm
and not fertile enough to justify razing with machines. In places the
ground leveled, and the Ndebele set up smallholdings to eke out a
minimal existence, with tiny plots of maize and squash for their
children and the mange-ridden domesticated dogs that skulk in the
shadows of their thatch-covered huts.

Aalwyn knew not what she sought here, only that she was drawn to
the east.

"There is nothing for us in such places," Blackthorn told
Koorsboom. "The antelope are chased away or destroyed."

"So why do we delay?"

"Only to rest, once we are far from their mongrels." Blackthorn eyed
the dogs with disdain. "They are diseased." He glanced up.

"Sekelbos, range ahead and find us a place for the night."

"*Eish,* this tree is fine." Sekelbos jerked his muzzle at a giraffe thorn
acacia within sight the huts.

"It is not." Aalwyn was curt. "Do as he bid."

Sekelbos bounded off in a huff with Vaalgras and Duinemirt at his
heels.

Within an hour, Sekelbos returned without report. Aalwyn did not
press him, but Blackthorn growled and left to scout ahead.

"He presumes too much, this elderly wolf." Sekelbos sidled up to
Aalwyn.

She looked away.

"I have been integral to this pack since inception, Aalwyn. Then this
immigrant arrives and takes the place of my brother?"

"You do not know yourself." Aalwyn's voice was flat. "He is of great help to us."

"I do not trust him."

"If there is a place of safety, he will find it."

"Will we have another story tonight?" Koorsboom yipped.

"I am sure that he will extol the virtues of service—on his behalf," Sekelbos snorted and padded away.

***

The *Combretum* shrubs were thick on all sides, with no visibility. The dried foliage blocked the wind and made the air still and heavy. The wolves clustered within the natural enclosure.

"Sight and sound, Koorsboom. Remember that." Blackthorn sat with forepaws folded.

"You have a parable in mind." Aalwyn lay down close to him.

"Am I that transparent?" Blackthorn allowed himself a smile and shifted his weight, settling into the depression that he had scratched in the ground. He looked off to the edge of their camp where one of the pack lay alone turned away from the rest. "Sekelbos appeared quite comfortable ambling across the black road, if you remember. Were you not, Sekelbos?"

"I had nothing to fear from those things," Sekelbos responded tonelessly.

"Did you now?"

"They ignored me altogether." Sekelbos raised his head to Aalwyn. "Except for the humans in the machine that stopped, who appeared fascinated by me."

"Fascinated." Blackthorn emitted a low growl audible only to Koorsboom and Aalwyn. He scratched behind his torn ear. "Let me relate to you how fascinating they find us. Koorsboom, has your mother told you of the places that are wild yet fenced?"

Koorsboom shook his head.

"There were once vast regions in our world entirely untouched by humans. But they have receded. Even marginal rocky soils are claimed and farmed now, and with those claims come fences. As far as an eagle can see, the fences cut us off."

Essenhout glanced up from where she lay on her back with forepaws folded to her chest.

"The fences do not bother us—we dig under them. Our prey, however, are hemmed in. And some of these fences hold in areas that seem wild."

"Are they not farms?" Essenhout asked.

"Not farms. They have roads and places where humans live, but otherwise they have all the appearance of our own land: bushveld and trees with large quantities of antelope just waiting to be bled." He looked to the wolves. "The pack into which my father was born hunted the wild. There were vast areas, river, hill, and valley devoid of people, far to the north. Stifling heat and tsetse flies, air red with soil that lent a metallic taste to everything. The dull heat of day was a weight that pressed unrelentingly until the sun failed." Blackthorn nodded over the words of his father's story. "And so they happened upon one of the fenced-wild places. Their alpha male saw impala on the other side of a fence and knew that there were riches within." He looked around. "But his disregard for what built those fences doomed their pack." Blackthorn lay down.

"The hunting inside the fence was ferocious— gazelles ran to the horizon, and they took two to three antelope every day. They saw no lions and attracted no hyena. In those times, our kind ran in large packs, and nothing equaled our prowess. Morning and evening, they killed and moved about and killed again. Then one day, down the beaten track came a machine that ground to a halt beside them at a kill." Blackthorn paused. "Two humans looked and murmured to one another like gnus. They pointed things that clicked and continued to click long after the gazelle carcass was nothing but offal. My father lazed in the noon light, basking in not only the triumph of the hunt but what he could only call curiosity." Blackthorn looked to Sekelbos. "He was amused by these humans—'They are fascinated by us,' he said."

Sekelbos turned away.

"That evening was fascinating as well. The machine returned with another in tow, and more humans came upon them. Languid was the way of their first approach, taken and left with leisure. This time they moved with haste, and my father was alarmed, as was the rest of the pack. Fascination was not in their red eyes now. Each human produced a stick, and thunder penetrated hillock and grove. My father managed to lie concealed in a thicket with his mother while the humans strode past them, blast upon blast with light and ash. When that storm ceased, half the pack lay dead in the clearing. One of the alpha humans took something from the crown of his head, tossed it in the air, and made a noise that could only be joy."

"Joy for what?"Vaalgras cocked his head.

"They hate us. The speed of their attack suggested to my father that they were either enraged at our presence or defending the antelope. Perhaps both."

"That is *kak*—it makes little sense."

"Do you have an alternative?" Blackthorn shook his head. "So many of our kind died that day—but they could not have been the first. The humans create these wild areas and then kill the hunters within."

"Do they kill lions as well?"

"I have seen a lion fall to their thunder."

The pack started, and Sekelbos aroused in spite of himself.

"There is scant story to it—a few seasons before I chanced upon you *Dwalen*, I wandered north of the great river. As I examined the banks for a safe way across, I happened upon a lion asleep. I watched as he slept lazily through the entire day. Before sundown, a machine with humans drove up, and one of them stepped out and strode to where the lion lay. The thunder came twice, and the lion died in his sleep. The humans stayed to perform some ritual over the carcass while brandishing their sticks. I did not tarry." Blackthorn looked toward Sekelbos. "And that is how humans express their 'fascination.'"

Sekelbos rolled over sullenly.

"I wonder if they have ill will towards our kind." Essenhout yawned wide before continuing. "Everything they do appears complicated beyond all reason—perhaps their relationship with us is also complicated."

"How is that useful?"

Essenhout rested her head on her forepaws in thought.

"Do humans die?" Koorsboom twittered in excitement.

The wolves looked at one another.

"Maybe they do not," Vaalgras said.

"*Ag.* Of course they do." Blackthorn issued a guttural grunt. "No need to be ludicrous. What is alive eventually ceases to be so. So much about them challenges the mind, with their bizarre machines and sticks of death. However, although their carcasses do not feed anyone and their bones do not gleam in the sun, I am certain that they die as we do—surely they too are eventually brought low." He snorted. "Humans are not great. They fight one another readily. They poison the air and water. They even poison themselves on purpose. And no matter what great powers they possess, they must still eat food and drink water."

Chapter 23

Aalwyn's eyes played over the landscape of arid dust and scrub brush while her ears collected the slightest sounds. She felt the presence of Koorsboom at her side.

"I recall every rock and tree, every aardvark hollow and spoor of the enemy encountered over a lifetime. As will you, my son." The tone of her voice was flat.

"I do remember everything—" Koorsboom lapped her muzzle. "But it was not apparent to me until now."

"The map of your mind will serve you well should you ever need sanctuary or your mate becomes ready for your litter. But there are times when one wishes to forsake memory."

Why did my father die? Could he have fled? Has one of our kind ever defended themselves from a lion?

What did my brothers and sisters feel as they awaited their turn to die?

"You need not protect me from your dark thoughts." Aalwyn stared at an armored cricket at her feet. "We each grapple with our share." Koorsboom was quiet for a moment. "Will you teach me to hunt?"

"When the lands are more forgiving." She mustered a smile. "For now, leave it to those more experienced—there is skill in preying, and skill in avoiding being prey."

***

The wolves scarcely left claw marks upon the hard, dry earth as they ran.

"Is that water in the distance?" Koorsboom moved his tail in a slight wag.

"The light deceives you," Blackthorn did not look up. "There is nothing ahead of us."

The bones of a cow lay spread widely across the ground. Koorsboom stared at the skull that seemed to stare back.

***

Day and night passed, and the wolves' steady lope covered kilometers beyond count. They rested for short periods at the height of the sun and in the darkness of night. Blackthorn was always the first awake, leading with a tireless pace.

"Mother, how does he know where to go?"

"A wolf must be in tune with the dialect of the wild—the chatter of leaf and clamor of bird, the mélange of scents upon the air."

"Are we headed into the desert?" Sekelbos growled to Vaalgras.

"The soil seems to grow more arid." Vaalgras could not speak with confidence.

"This wolf is stubborn, Aalwyn. His obstinacy will be the end of us."

"You know not the difference between obstinacy and conviction," Aalwyn responded without tone. "Leave such things to leadership." She padded quickly ahead to Blackthorn, twittering to Koorsboom to follow.

"We run toward greener places." Blackthorn's voice was gravelly. "But our fortunes will be mixed at best." He let loose a streamer of drool. "Farms. The very land ahead is treacherous."

***

The wolves first encountered smallholdings, patches of land between rocky hills and near-desert with dried and sun-blasted stalks of maize. Domesticated dogs with ribs standing out of their sides gave them vacant stares. Blackthorn led the wolves creeping as though hunting at all times in order to remain invisible. The pack entered a sparse grove of mountain *brachystegia* sprouting the delicate feathery growth of spring leaflets above dried grasses just beginning to show the touch of irregular rain.

"Wait." Blackthorn tensed, muscles rippling under his greyed coat. "One of our kind has passed this way."

Aalwyn sniffed the ground.

The wolves emerged from trees onto a vast farmland in ruin. The fields of grass and hay seemed to stretch beyond the horizon, broken only by the edge of an old maize field where the stalks stood dried and forgotten and filled with weeds and strange white cactus. Overgrown patches of squash and beans tumbled among small trees, and a rusty water pump leaned beneath a thin covering of web and creeper plants. A great house of red brick and grey mortar stood up under a high thatch roof of organized stick-and-stock rather than loose grasses, though worn through in places. The glass of the barred windows were broken out and small holes the size of coins perforated the bricks. Invasive weeds had grown over the foundations, and vines climbed the brick walls. A sliding door hung off its runner. In the fields lay a broken washing machine vomiting forth rags, the frame of an ironing board, a shattered wooden chair, and colorful children's blocks.

Blackthorn growled a warning, but Vaalgras and Duinemirt trotted to the house and nosed among the wonderful objects in the grass.

"There is no smell of human here—" Vaalgras pranced about.

"There are shiny things on the ground." Duinemirt pawed at spent bullet casings.

"If humans once inhabited this place, they have now left it to the wild." Aalwyn paused at Blackthorn's shoulder.

"Are you curious?" Blackthorn scanned the horizon.

"No. I would prefer to avoid it."

"The wolf is here!" Koorsboom twittered rapidly.

From a patch of weeds and large, strong-smelling leaves crept forward a stranger. His coat of white, black, and mostly gold was of a higher gloss than those of the *Dwalen*. He padded toward Vaalgras and Duinemirt with no apparent hostility or hesitation, and they sniffed one another.

"*Eish,* you look rather well!" Sekelbos trotted out to greet him. "What is your name?"

"Mloyi." He shook himself free of burrs. "So peculiar to hear words so familiar. So many seasons have passed alone."

"Have you been here long?"

"I left the wild in the north with my brothers, came to this place, and found it quite agreeable."

"Where are your brothers?" Blackthorn narrowed his eyes.

"Long since departed." Mloyi glanced around. "Not sure where."

"They left? Why?"

"I am unaware. Such things matter little—" Mloyi's tone was clipped. "—in a place filled with food."

Vaalgras and Duinemirt ran in twittering circles around Mloyi.

"Are the antelope far?" Sekelbos drooled.

Essenhout glanced quickly at Blackthorn and Aalwyn.

Koorsboom whimpered, but he stepped forward to join the rally with Vaalgras and Duinemirt. Aalwyn glared, and he returned to her side.

"This is a farm, is it not?" Aalwyn watched Mloyi's reaction.

"I have not seen humans here for some time."

"They left all this alone?"

"You see that I am here." Mloyi gestured to Vaalgras and Duinemirt to stop their rally. "A few seasons ago when the last chill was in the air, there were humans here busying themselves with their industry. But something extraordinary occurred. So strange, these humans."

"What?" Sekelbos shuffled closer.

"A mob came, more humans than I had ever seen in a lifetime and all reeking of anger. An incredible racket filled the air, but we—I could not take my eyes off the throng. They waved metal implements about, while the few who lived on the farm hid inside the house. The air was pierced with thunder over and over again. They closed in on the farm and charged the dwelling, where they pulled the hiders outside, and the mob closed around them. We took quickly to the fields, but we smelt the blood."

"Your brothers were with you?" Aalwyn interrupted.

"I was alone." Mloyi was on his paws, pacing. "When I returned the humans were gone, the house in ruins, and another shack on the farm aflame. No humans have set foot here since."

Vaalgras leapt into a run after a hare that blundered too close, pounced, and broke its neck.

Mloyi emitted a rapid twitter, and Aalwyn realized that he was laughing.

"You shall feel foolish indeed when you see what lives in this place." Mloyi trotted in a circle on his hind legs to box Sekelbos.

Mloyi turned and sprinted past the house with Sekelbos, Vaalgras, and Duinemirt on his tail. Essenhout followed, stopped, and watched a moment before she finally padded after them.

"What is on your mind?" Blackthorn muttered to Aalwyn.

"I am not sure." Aalwyn was disturbed by how quickly the others had left. She looked in frustration at Koorsboom, who had jumped upon the hare and ripped it open. "I dislike the smell of him—I have nothing else to say."

"We have had our share of discouragement." Blackthorn thought for a moment. "We will learn his quality."

"His—or ours?"

Blackthorn met her eyes.

***

Blackthorn's mood remained dark. He and Aalwyn and Koorsboom lay in the shadow of a giant *Euphorbia* candelabra tree, whose bark and succulent leaves had cracked in the brisk wind, oozing toxic milky latex that filled the dry air with a sharp smell. The branches were tipped with red berries that antelope could not eat for the burning white syrup. Time dragged, and none of them truly rested.

The sun was receding when Aalwyn took to her feet with a start. Mloyi approached with the other wolves, padding toward Koorsboom, who looked lean and weak. The wolves were covered in blood that coated their fur in a maroon slick matting as it dried. While their bellies hung low, their steps were lithe and bouncing. Essenhout and Vaalgras hurried to Aalwyn and Koorsboom and regurgitated.

Stunned, Koorsboom gulped down the meat and licked morsels from the dusty soil. Aalwyn ate her share, and Blackthorn took a few cautious bites, eyeing Mloyi.

"Your travels need go no further." Mloyi licked Aalwyn's muzzle gently.

"For feeding my son, you have my gratitude." Aalwyn licked his muzzle back and allowed herself a rare smile.

Vaalgras and Duinemirt stood on their hind legs to box in play, their exhaustion forgotten, while Blackthorn lay down next to Mloyi and prodded him.

"Strange that you have done so well in such a bleak landscape. What was on order? Massive piles of field mice? Puff adders?"

"Only the best." Mloyi beamed and ran a tongue over his black lips. "Cattle."

Chapter 24

The vibrant gold blooms of yellow arum withered during the dry season had left remains like meadow hay. The valley was quiet save the wolves who lingered with their agitated twittering.

"What world do you think we live in?" Blackthorn whirled around Mloyi. "How many cattle have you killed?"

"No need to strip your *moer*, old one. I have felled many." Mloyi was calm, his hazel eyes lively. "And no hyenas—or anything else—deprived me of my gains."

Vaalgras shook drying blood from his fur and looked furtively from one wolf to the other.

"No humans took issue with this?" Blackthorn was seething and baring his fangs. "How could you be so reckless?"

"Should any humans set eyes on me—" Mloyi's arched brow was bemused. "—they will run for their miserable lives." He leapt to his feet, and Blackthorn tensed for battle, but Mloyi remained relaxed, hardly exerted. "I shall enjoy the evening air on the ridge. The view is most pleasing, and one can easily detect the approach of an enemy —if any existed here."

Mloyi ran off with the white of his tail in the air, watched by Sekelbos and Vaalgras.

"What is it about comfort that makes you so contemptuous?" Sekelbos turned irritably to Blackthorn.

"Come, we must find shelter for the evening." Blackthorn's grey fur seemed greyer as he bit his tongue.

Blackthorn led Aalwyn and Koorsboom away from the farm, but the others hesitated. After a moment Sekelbos, Vaalgras, and Duinemirt ran after Mloyi to the ridge, while Essenhout turned and padded after Aalwyn.

Blackthorn hid them under a tangle of acacia and *Combretum*.
"There was no hunt, as such." Essenhout spoke in a subdued twitter.
"After we spotted the cattle from the ridge, we circled around and
selected our kill. But before we could attack, Mloyi simply engaged
one and killed it." Wonder crept into her voice. "He rent the throat
with a practiced slash, and the steer barely responded. The other
cattle ran for a bit, then returned to grazing. Vaalgras thought they
must be plants rooted to the ground."
Koorsboom laughed with a chirp.
"We must be well away from this place by dawn. Although—"
Blackthorn met Aalwyn's gaze, "—you will not wish it."
"I understand your trepidation." Aalwyn nodded. "We need time to
decide where this is headed."
Blackthorn laid his head upon his forepaws and closed his eyes.
"Into the storm," he muttered to himself.

***

"You will be joining them." It was not a question.
"I will be back. We all will." Duinemirt stood in supplication with
bent posture. "The hunt will be brief, and we need so desperately to
feed—"
"Fear no anger, my sister. Our history is too long to be broken
easily." Aalwyn looked down at Duinemirt's head dipping steadily
under her gaze.
"It troubles me—"
"As I have said—"
"—that you will go hungry." Duinemirt drew back.
She paused before responding. "Go well, my sister." Aalwyn kept
her expression blank.
Blackthorn and Koorsboom stood with Aalwyn as the wolves
departed. Koorsboom brushed up to Aalwyn and closed his eyes at
the comfort of her fur.
"I will scout the area." Aalwyn muttered to Blackthorn in a series of
whines. "Perhaps there is antelope here, now that humans are not."

She was away before either could respond and disappeared quickly over the rise.

Koorsboom whimpered up to Blackthorn, his eyes wet and large ears drooped.

"Come, *boykie*." Blackthorn surveyed the fields choked with new growth of a strange cactus. "Let us see how lethal your methods can be."

Koorsboom gave a slight wag of his tail as he followed the old wolf to a cactus. It was not the typical *Euphorbia* seen in southern Africa with regular patterns of spikes and a woody stem. This was a stunted Mexican *rosea,* growing wild in a tangle of green cylindrical arms jutting from a central trunk. The arms bristled with a riot of white spines, dried remains of blossoms at each arm tip. The *rosea* cacti were knotted together like wrestling figures frozen in time.

"Steady on, Koorsboom. Make your way carefully." The cactus grew everywhere.

Blackthorn was forced to stop, turn, and find another way constantly through the maze of cactus. After a tiring afternoon of backtracking, they eventually picked their way to the other side of the field, where they emerged to a breeze wafting the strong, sweet odor of decay. Blackthorn followed the scent to the carcass of a cow rotting from the inside out and swarming with maggots.

"Curious—the body itself is intact. Either this area is devoid of scavengers or—" Blackthorn examined the body tangled in the cactus spines. "—these things are highly poisonous." He glanced at Koorsboom. "*Verstaan jy?*"

"I understand. Poisonous." Koorsboom nodded.

The *rosea* cactus had spread throughout the fields.

"Remember to urinate periodically, Koorsboom." Blackthorn paused to mark the territory. "Only small amounts, so that your mother can find us. This is not our territory. If it were, we would do well to soak the ground."

"We would not want this territory."

Blackthorn nodded. "Astute of you to notice."

"Does my mother *want* to find us again?"

"Of course she does." Blackthorn looked toward the horizon with a sigh. "She is still struggling with the deaths of your father and siblings." He bit his tongue with a serrated canine for a moment. "There are times when being alone can be pleasingly simple."

"Does she wish I were dead?" Koorsboom sniffed lightly at a thick green arm of a cactus.

"No." Blackthorn took a deep breath. "However, if you were dead, our search for a new home range would be easier and she would no longer fear losing you. But her fear is a measure of her love."

A slow sigh escaped Koorsboom.

"A mother's love, like a stone dropped into a cataract, does not alter the river course. It will flow where it must. Wherever we are swept in this life, we find the savanna's callous apathy."

"I am ready, *Oom Blackthorn*."

"*Oom?* Are you certain I have earned the honor of that title?"

The pup nodded. "And I shall kill before this day is done."

Koorsboom looked at up Blackthorn with a new light in his young eyes.

***

As the sun began to bleed into the horizon, fingers of shadow reached across the ruined fields to the mountain *Brachystegia* trees with their large, flat crowns acquiring their coppery spring foliage, subtle cover for the wolves lying underneath.

"Your time will come, *boykie*. Do not feel a failure. I was considerably older when I first cut down prey."

"Time feels short," Koorsboom growled. "How long do I have?"

"For what?" Blackthorn lowered his brow.

"To kill my share."

"None of us knows that. You will learn at the pace of which you are capable. We resume tomorrow." Blackthorn raised his dish-like ears at a slender figure loping in the distance followed by two others. "It seems that your mother has found your aunts."

Essenhout and Duinemirt padded up and greeted Blackthorn with much lapping of muzzles and tonguing of his palate. Koorsboom greeted them in kind, but with some reluctance. A red-eyed dove announced the coming of night, *coo-coo, cuk-coo-coo.*

"How was the hunting?" Aalwyn sat next to Blackthorn.

"Barren place, this." His rumbling was guttural.

"Fat steer today—" Duinemirt danced lightly on her feet as she twittered. "Killed with no difficulty at all by Mloyi and Sekelbos. The blood just poured forth—I thought it would never end!" She shook herself and sprayed the others with dried flecks of crimson. "The liver was large and laden with fat, the best meat we have ever had." She regurgitated a mountain of undigested flesh before Koorsboom, who plunged into the offering.

Aalwyn ate as much as she could tolerate, and Blackthorn ventured a small bite. Koorsboom took his fill, unwilling to meet Aalwyn's gaze. Had he tried, he would have failed.

Chapter 25

Koorsboom looked to Aalwyn, whose voice sounded far away. Her gaze rested upon the bushveld ahead, always ahead, unblinking and awake. Blackthorn sat by her side, his fur dark and greyed, also looking ahead—or perhaps at nothing. Koorsboom wondered for a moment if all adults are dying, to speak so often of death.

"Understand your role here, *boykie*," Blackthorn growled. "We kill and eventually join the killed."

"Over the course of your lifetime, many animals will die on your behalf," Aalwyn joined in. "You will be hunted yourself, and one day you will join your father and siblings in death." She paused for a long time. "Before you die, you must bear young of your own. But this is nothing."

"You must pass on what you learn each day to your own pups, the knowledge crafted throughout our history." Blackthorn leaned in to him. "It has been hard-won and demands absolute respect."

Koorsboom nodded imperceptibly. He followed Aalwyn's eyes along arid scrubland and its dried grasses. A *kopje* towered in the distance, a bald granite dome that had resisted millennia of erosion leveling the softer sedimentary rocks around it into the dusty plain. It was too distant to be the focus of her gaze, but Koorsboom knew not to ask. He was unsure what exactly was happening. Perhaps a test of some sort.

There was no sound except the breeze that tousled their wiry fur. Dust whipped up for a moment, then the wind flagged. Minutes passed—too many? Koorsboom was not sure.

Blackthorn glanced at Aalwyn, her stare blank and withdrawn.

"Scrub hare just there," Koorsboom twittered.

Two hundred meters away, erect ears showed against a low acacia bush, then folded back again.

"Shall we?"

"You shall." She did not speak further.

Koorsboom padded out to the hare without camouflage, his dish-like ears forward and swiveling. His lean body was relaxed and ready to break into a run. He searched the grass for the hare but found nothing.

"His approach has the subtlety of a hyena," Aalwyn commented.

"He makes his mistakes as we made ours." Blackthorn's rumbling became a chuckle.

Ha-da! Ha-da-da-da! Grey-brown feathers fluttered to the ground as an ibis took flight.

Koorsboom looked up in alarm. Then the minutes dragged on as he nosed around stunted acacia shrubs and knots of grass in the bare sandy soil. He glanced back to Aalwyn on the distant ridge, her cold expression unchanged.

He trotted around noticing that most of the bushes around him were fairly small and the open ground between them widely spaced. He sniffed each small bush close to the sighting of the hare, stabbing himself on sharp thorns. He craned his head as high as he could and even stood on hind legs for a moment. Hollows—were there any? None in view. His ears rang slightly with the loud hadeda call and enveloping silence. He sat by the largest shrub where the hare was first sighted and looked closely at a sickle bush sapling growing from its center with feather-like leaves. After the rains, it would flourish with tips of purple and yellow fuzzy blossoms. Sekelbos had been named for it.

"Should we prompt him, Aalwyn?"

"Hunger will provide a drive that nothing else will equal."

Koorsboom stared around with a sour expression. Small, compact, and hazy brown with fawn underbelly, its long ears folded back in danger—the hare must be long gone. Koorsboom batted a branch of the sickle bush sapling. The wood was indeed hard. He reached into the acacia bush with both paws, and a hazy brown shape bolted.

Koorsboom, shocked, pounced and broke the neck of the hare with a single bite.

"Time will tell if this was a fluke." Aalwyn padded to him, followed by Blackthorn. "I will have him lead the next hunt, if we can find an antelope herd."

"The times are lean enough." Blackthorn frowned. "We could all starve if his inexperience causes too many failures."

"Perhaps Mloyi will get us through his transition time."

"Be cautious with Mloyi." Blackthorn suppressed a growl. "He may not own the wondrous answer to survival that he pretends."

"Mloyi is drenched in blood every day, keeping my pup alive. Words of caution alone will not help Koorsboom thrive." Aalwyn picked up her pace to move ahead.

Blackthorn paused quietly and let her go.

***

"There is a danger with cattle, of course, for the novice. Those horns are not adornment." Mloyi ran a forepaw along his muzzle, dislodging dried fragments of meat. "Is your pup well? Adequately fed?"

"Tell me about the cattle. Where have you been hunting?"

Mloyi stretched and arched his rear before settling. His coloration was heavy gold over black, and if not for the blood dried on his fur he would have glowed in the sunlight. Essenhout had taken to calling him Sunset, and he had not corrected her.

"This farm sprawls far into the distance across an expanse of open grassland between tangled fields. One can find cattle wandering everywhere, sometimes alone, other times in small groups. I do not know where they originate, but I would not be surprised if they came from other farms."

"There are more farms?" Koorsboom licked his chops.

"Oh, yes. They are not as large as this one, but they are less— chaotic. I suspect that they are actively tended. It may be their cattle wandering in."

"Only cattle?"

"Some goats perhaps. Once I found a strange bird clicking about with brown feathers and a red crown. It did not have the chance to run far."

"How did you trap it before it took flight?" Aalwyn's voice was full of wonder.

"It did not. It merely fluttered. Humans keep animals unable to defend themselves." Mloyi revealed his fangs as though laughing. "More the better for us."

"You have done well for yourself here." Aalwyn padded to him.

"Hunt with us on the morrow." Mloyi stood and lapped her muzzle. "You will see how we can do so much more than survive."

"What on earth are these plants?" Vaalgras was snuffling and rubbing his nose on the ground. "I touched a single spine, and my face is in torment."

"They grow all over." Mloyi nodded. "Across many areas that were once farms. The humans cut them down and burn them, but they only spread, crowding out the cattle. I have seen them nowhere else but where humans live, so I suspect it is one of their creations." The Mexican cactus had spread from human gardens, planted for ornamental reasons.

"They are a form of succulent." Blackthorn spoke for the first time. "Dangerous things. I found a cow dead in a knot of them."

"If one knows the way through the fields, they offer an advantage." Mloyi smiled slightly. "The people seem to call them *mloyi,* and so the name suits me."

"Our wandering may come to an end here." Sekelbos sidled up to Aalwyn and lapped her muzzle. "There are no enemies, and prey is slain with little effort, leaving the entire day for us to enjoy." His voice was low, a viscous whisper. "I have found under a sickle bush tree an abandoned porcupine den."

Aalwyn licked his muzzle, but Mloyi inserted his powerful body between them. His sleek fur brushed against her, and she pushed imperceptibly into him.

"The ridge beckons, Aalwyn. There is no better way to view the sunset." Mloyi padded toward an acacia on a rise in the grassy fields, where the crown radiated outward in a flat canopy.

Aalwyn followed and sat with Mloyi under the acacia. Together they watched deep red fill the valley as the sun dipped behind distant hills to the west.

"Your malcontent has brought us to this." Sekelbos walked growling to Blackthorn, now dark in the falling twilight. Sekelbos lifted a lip to expose fang. "Did you ruin everything else you touched before coming to us?"

"*Voetsek*." Blackthorn kept his eyes on the ridge. "If you wish to keep your hide."

Sekelbos slunk away to where Duinemirt and Vaalgras lay with their noses in their paws.

"Did I do well with the hare, *Oom*?" Koorsboom lay down next to Blackthorn.

"You exceeded expectations, *boykie*."

"Will you teach me more tomorrow?"

"You will have all of my attentions, Koorsboom." Blackthorn raked the ground with a claw. "All of them."

Chapter 26

These tracks are like ours—but they are not of our pack.
"You may wish to see this!" Koorsboom hoo-called to Blackthorn.
Koorsboom and Blackthorn had strayed far in the afternoon,
patrolling the arid landscape. Once the farms had disappeared behind
them they had both felt at ease. The rough ground heaved from low
gullies to high red rocks, and the wolves glided across it as though
floating.

Blackthorn loped from a gully to peer at the dust.
"Single pad with four toes, claw marks to match." Koorsboom
paused. "I am guessing it is not a hippo." He laughed up at
Blackthorn.
"A canine, of course. One of ours—no dewclaw to signify a
domesticated dog." Blackthorn studied the series of tracks. "They
are alone—" He padded along, followed by Koorsboom. "And they
are weak."
The wolves walked carefully between grass clumps and thorn brush.
"Frequent stops for rest. Here the step and distance vary as though
stumbling."
"Just ahead!" Koorsboom stood on his hind legs excitedly for a
moment.
The scent of wild dog reached them, oddly altered.
"Something is afoot, Koorsboom. Ever taut as a tendon." The stale
taste of the air reminded Blackthorn of bracken despite the aridity,
with a sour and caustic undercurrent.
Three wild dogs lay prone in the distance under a low-hanging
giraffe thorn acacia tree, the still broken only by an occasional tsetse
fly. From far away came the call, *klooee—klooee*, of a martial eagle.

The slight sway of leaves in the imperceptible breeze cast the static setting into sharp relief.

The wild dogs did not stir as Blackthorn and Koorsboom approached. Blackthorn hissed sharply at a new smell.

"Come away—now!" Blackthorn's growl aroused the wild dogs. They held their heads up and peered around vaguely with extraordinary effort. Their eyes were unfocused and clotted with discharge, their mouths drooling copiously. One gained its feet and lumbered toward Koorsboom, placing its paws without coordination until it collapsed in a heap with a high whine.

Help us—

"What is this place?" Koorsboom's stomach crawled.

Blackthorn led him wordlessly to the scratching of a makeshift den, where the frail bodies of pups lay dead and stiffened under the wavering branches.

"An *abattoir*." Blackthorn broke into a trot.

Koorsboom ran close behind, on edge. They passed the bodies of partially-eaten wolves all around the den, black flies thick and insufferable.

"What killed them?"

"The Rage." Blackthorn shut his eyes and muttered to himself.

"*Gaan naai*, I am losing my skills." He paused. "The Rage consumes each host in turn, and before long an entire pack is taken." He burst into a gallop. "Never approach a wolf who is acting unusually. *Never*."

"What happens?" Koorsboom galloped rapidly at his side.

"Eyes and muzzle drip and ooze, a fierce anger consumes one as the mind burns, and the wolf attacks everything in sight. Once the fire burns out, the wolf is left dumb and apathetic—unable to walk, eat, or swallow, until death collects its bounty." Blackthorn growled. "Never again be as stupid as I was just now."

"How do I—"

"I knew. And I should have known." Blackthorn's muttering turned to a rumble as he began to run at speed. "Always trust your judgment. Always give the unexpected its distance."

Forgive me, Aalwyn, if I have been so ignorant as to destroy all that is left of your litter.

The grasses spread out around them as they ran flat-out toward the ruined farm. Blackthorn only stopped panting when he reached the flat spreading canopy of the acacia overlooking the encampment.

"Koorsboom—do not speak of today."

"I watch and remember."

"Your mother already takes a dim view of me." Blackthorn scratched the ground. "I worry for you—"

"I will say nothing."

Chapter 27

This new farm was not quite so overgrown. The grasses were long and neglected, and the poisonous cactus grew along the edges of the land. The great house was derelict—looted and left to ruin. In the yard lay the rusting hulk of a refrigerator and the splintered wooden remains of furniture among creeping ivy.

"Aalwyn has not come with us today." Essenhout lazed in the sun and heat. "I wonder about her thoughts. When last we spoke, she seemed unsure whom to follow."

"Blackthorn is walking on sharp rocks." Sekelbos restrained a smile. "He has yet to guide anyone to a kill larger than a field mouse. She will be back among us soon enough."

Vaalgras and Duinemirt came bounding, as Vaalgras twittered and lapped at Duinemirt's muzzle.

"There are a more cattle over the ridge—these dumb grass-eaters help us constantly to fight our hunger!"

"Working on your alpha status, Vaalgras?" Essenhout got onto her paws and stretched.

"How—" Vaalgras looked to the others. "Whatever do you—"

"You are mating with—"

"What of it?"

"What if you are that big a fool?" Essenhout spoke as though pointing out an interesting shrub. "Between Blackthorn and Mloyi, you two are in for it, should you succeed."

"What would they do to my litter?" Duinemirt stopped prancing.

"Off their hunting grounds? Probably nothing. On their hunting grounds, however—" Essenhout glanced at her calmly. "Come. We must not let a good kill go to waste."

Essenhout led the wolves back to the freshly-killed cow where it lay on its side with its organs spilling onto the grass. Flies buzzed around, and lappet-faced vultures perched upon its hip. A head rose from behind the shoulder.

"Is that—one of us?" Vaalgras tilted his head.

"No." Duinemirt put her ears back and bared her fangs. "It is one of *theirs*."

The dog stood taller than a wolf, with floppy ears contrasted to the erect dish-ears of the wolves. His light brown coat was worn through with the mange, and his eyes were rimmed with red, but he bared his canines and growled deep in his throat.

"Easy now—this one carries a special anger." Essenhout felt her pulse quicken.

The dog ambled to and fro in front of the cattle, shaking his head and spraying drool as his ears flapped. His bark was utterly alien to them, and sounded like a cough, ending with an absurd 'pop'.

"Are they all this agitated?" Essenhout dropped back, ears still flattened, now looking for escape routes.

"This cur has no claim on our meal!" Sekelbos charged with Vaalgras and Duinemirt close on his heels.

The dog chomped empty air and abruptly raced toward them with a speed they did not expect. In an instant he was among them, a whirl of black, white, gold, and brown, a wild snarl like two dogs at once. Sekelbos retreated with bites oozing crimson onto his coat.

Duinemirt nursed deep gashes on her side, while Vaalgras sustained mild scratches. The four retreated far from the fallen cattle. The dog stumbled and ran back to the carcass, where it paced and pawed the air.

"*Bosbefok*—" Sekelbos licked his wounds. "Mad as a hyena mating with a lion!"

"I should have such anger to unleash on command!" Vaalgras licked his own abrasions.

Essenhout paused with her ears alert at their words. For the remainder of the hunt, she did not lick the others despite their attempts to lap muzzles at a rally. They left the strange dog far behind.

Aalwyn found them soon after by following their urine markings, their hunts these days abnormally short.

"Are you well, sister?" Aalwyn lapped Essenhout's muzzle and whined. "Did you kill?" She glanced at Duinemirt.

"Before you greet the others—" Essenhout stopped her. "You must hear what has occurred." She described the peculiar dog and his frantic behavior.

"Are you certain?" Aalwyn looked from one to the other. "His behavior was quite mad?"

"We do not know the dogs that humans keep, so their actions may be exotic. But I am certain there was no reason in his eyes."

Aalwyn's mother had taught her as a pup of the Rage, and none of the wolves knew that they had been vaccinated when they had eaten the plastic packets in the antelope thrown to them off the truck long ago in Botswana. Now she glanced at the others, thinking of the shunning that they could not avoid.

"Duinemirt, my sister," she whimpered softly as she lay down.

Chapter 28

The goat consumed every green leaf possible off the small shrub while its eyes darted about. It took little notice of the wolf nearby, gold dominant over its black and white.

"Perhaps this one will fall later." Mloyi's twitter alarmed the goat slightly. "For now, we pursue more substantial prey."

"You mean to spare it?" Aalwyn cocked her head.

"We live among an embarrassment of riches." Mloyi lapped her muzzle. "You may grow used to it."

The goat stopped eating and shifted weight from one hoof to another, as the column of wild dogs passed and disappeared into a rough thicket of giraffe thorn acacia.

"How do we track cattle?" Vaalgras was bewildered.

"Cattle do not move around enough to track. They leave heavy hoof marks in slowly wandering lines that lead straight to the kill." Mloyi paused. "No method is required."

"Are there lions?"

"Never." Mloyi dashed ahead. "Just there—three cows approaching."

The pack ran after him.

"This place is paradise. Only the agony of choice awaits us."

"A human is with them—" Aalwyn's twitter exploded into alarm. "A human!"

The wolves stopped dead with the thunder of stories echoing in their minds.

"Prepare to flee—"

"Trust in me." Mloyi bounded back to her in a flash, his eyes serene and manner casual. "And you will never hunger."

Mloyi's face tensed, ears flattened, and body straightened. He raced toward the cattle with Sekelbos and Duinemirt close behind. The cows milled about and began to trot away in random directions. Mloyi bore down upon the man who walked with a stick in hand and tattered clothing hanging off his slender frame, his shoes fashioned from old tires and his dark skin covered with dust. When he saw the wolf closing the distance, Aalwyn tensed for deafening thunder. Instead, the man waved his stick and ran without looking back. "*Iganyana*!" he wailed in panic and disappeared without his cows.

"Would you like to select, love?" Mloyi returned to Aalwyn's side. "The closest one?"

Mloyi bounded away and gave chase, such as it was. Sekelbos took hold of the snout, and the cow bellowing with fright while Essenhout pulled a hip from its socket. Mloyi ripped open the underbelly, spilling intestines, and buried his head inside just as Vaalgras yanked the cow over nearly on top of him. Aalwyn padded over last, and as she lowered her head Mloyi glanced up.

"Wait for her." Mloyi's voice was soft. "She is our queen."

The wolves paused for Aalwyn to begin to feed. She seemed distant and lost. Forgetting to avoid Vaalgras and Duinemirt, she picked at the hide and gulped down all the flesh she could stomach. The wolves ate in peace, and the man made no return, leaving behind only the memory of the word that had chilled Aalwyn to the core: "*Iganyana*!"

*　*　*

The wolves moved across the abandoned farm with its vast open areas of green grass, then threaded through weed-filled patches choked with the Mexican *rosea* cactus.

"Observe." Mloyi indicated dried piles of desiccated light green husks and white spines surrounded by robust green cactus. "The humans did this. They hack at the greenery with blades of metal, recoiling in pain whenever they impale themselves upon the plants. And after days of labor, the cactus returns with even greater power." He sniffed. "Humans are failures."

Aalwyn's eyes darted here and there, reacting to every shift in wind. "You are troubled, love, are you not?" Mloyi brushed closely. She pulled away.

"I smell your fear."

"The man—he was speaking."

"As do all things we hunt. They grunt like cattle or wildebeest."

"And if he was speaking to other humans?"

"He is free to try." Mloyi trotted ahead to view a crest over a shallow valley. "More areas here have been left fallow, and the animals wander, both human-type and the wild things we hunt." He sat down and waited for her. "Not far lies a field dominated by the white spines in flower." He dipped his head to her slightly in deference. "Just as you are in flower. Whenever you are ready for another litter, the wealth of this land will provide you with a mighty pack indeed." Aalwyn watched a vulture soar overhead, wings spread wide to glide long distances without effort.

"Whether or not your *Dwalen* stays with us is irrelevant. I alone can provide for all. Here we need neither run nor to subsist on the edge of starvation and disease. No longer."

"Koorsboom." Aalwyn realized that it had been days since she had last spoken his name.

"His concerns are not mine." Mloyi pointed his slender muzzle toward the horizon in the east. "And soon will not be yours." He lapped her muzzle gently. "He seems to prefer the company of one destined to wander always."

"Indeed he does." Aalwyn shook with a chill despite the heat of the ground. She leaned back on her paws and tensed. "And we shall continue our *dwaal*, leaving this place far behind."

"Have you have forgotten already your times of famine?" Mloyi raised his brow.

However, Aalwyn was already well away with her tail in the air, racing toward the wolves resting in the grass.

Mloyi loped after her in time for the end of her speech.

"—and if you hear something, anything—unnatural—run until your paws leave prints of blood."

"Spring is upon us, Aalwyn. " Mloyi cornered her. "Soon the fields will riot with the white wildflowers that coat this valley. You cannot leave now."

"Wolves like us—" Aalwyn looked up at the sky where lappet-faced vultures circled over their last kill. "We are nomadic. To remain rooted is to invite danger. Our *dwaal* is our destiny."

"No danger threatens us here." Mloyi stepped closer.

"I choose my own way." Aalwyn's voice dropped a growl as she closed the distance between them. "No other."

"It seems I have labored under a misapprehension. Your mind has been broken by your wandering, and you are now accustomed to misery. You wish your failed brood to be your last."

"My time will come again once we are far from here."

"You are wrong. Your time has come—and gone." Mloyi turned to Essenhout and Duinemirt with a slight nod and padded away.

"I am returning to Koorsboom." Aalwyn spoke to the milling wolves. "We will be away with the dawn."

"I do not understand." Duinemirt lapped Vaalgras's muzzle as Aalwyn trotted away. "Why are we not staying?"

"I see no reason to flee." Vaalgras shrugged. "We are free to do as we will."

"If you think Sunset over there wants the pair of you living as alphas upon his land, you are truly delusional," Essenhout snorted.

"We could run him off easily enough." Vaalgras tipped his head. Essenhout, Sekelbos, and Duinemirt turned to watch Mloyi seat himself on the distant rise.

"Who wishes it?" Vaalgras looked at the others expectantly. Sekelbos loped off before anyone could answer, and the wolves braced themselves. However, the two wolves sat a long time at leisure in discussion.

"Perhaps there is a way." Vaalgras prodded Duinemirt, indicating the quiet. "We can stay in this land of plenty after all."

Chapter 29

Hard quartz stood out of the rock outcropping on the low ridge, the beige and tan stone marked with vertical white and brown streaks. One small giraffe thorn acacia grew upon the rock itself, its shadow hiding small, stout balls of fur and muscle, the hyrax—rock dassies —that emerged furtively in the sun on short legs of surprising speed. Their feet cupped the rock and adhered to it, moving with caution to browse upon new leaves while the lookout sat peering across the land and the sky.

Thud—thud—thud—The hyrax tensed and put all four feet on the rock, where reverberations echoed through the solid stone.

Thud—thud—thud—thud—The hyrax gave a sharp bark and pulsing cry, *Awk! Uk-uk-uk-uk-uk-uk!* The rock dassies darted back and rapidly disappeared into crevasses and cracks.

Overhead a Verreaux's eagle, black with bold white markings underneath, aborted its dive. It glared at the wolf with baleful eyes, an adult too large to kill.

"Your approach was fine, Koorsboom, but you did not mind your surroundings." Aalwyn panted to his side.

Although Koorsboom was too large to be of concern now, she was still frightened of eagles, known to take wild dog pups. Her footfalls had alerted the dassies.

"I failed." Koorsboom's stomach growled.

"You do well—some prey are beyond us. Only caracals or leopards can hunt hyrax. I was referring to the eagle."

"I am sorry, Mother." Koorsboom looked up at the wheeling raptor and slumped to the ground.

"There are other opportunities all around."

"That was not what I meant." Koorsboom looked through her.

"I understand, young one. In truth, you were never meant to survive." Aalwyn lapped his muzzle and prodded him.

Koorsboom looked at her in shock.

"Most pups die before the change of the season. The world seems set against us, but rarely can offer the chance to endure." She nuzzled him.

Koorsboom softened against her.

"The veld is bitter. And so we force our way with claw and fang." Aalwyn eyed the eagle. "And those who defy us discover the true nature of suffering."

"We are not far from the edge of the farm." Blackthorn padded rapidly through the grass. "We will soon be free."

"What is outside?" Koorsboom gazed up.

"Smaller dwellings inhabited by humans and another large place like this, left to return to the wild."

"Strange that such places would be abandoned, when humans occupy every available patch of dirt." Aalwyn shook her ears.

"I suspect that humans here did great violence to one another. Perhaps fear keeps these dwellings vacant. When a species has no one else to compete with," Blackthorn said soberly, "it competes with itself."

***

The wolves' progress was slow as they picked their way around impassible thickets and cactus patches. Aalwyn kept a gradual pace, peering over every rise and avoiding every shadow. The pup ranged ahead of them, chasing after a fluttering bird.

"How were they when you left?"

"I am unsure. Most seemed at a loss." Aalwyn glanced at Koorsboom chasing a lizard through the grass. "I fear that Sekelbos and Vaalgras may carry the Rage."

Blackthorn stopped, staring with a gurgle stuck in his throat.

"Whatever comes must come." Aalwyn met his gaze. "If they return, stay wide of them." She sighed. "If they wish to stay with that fool, that is their fate. Unfortunately, it will make feeding Koorsboom more difficult."

Koorsboom's slight figure leapt above the grasses and disappeared with a grunt.

"Let alone an entire litter."

"We must await safe haven before even considering that."

Blackthorn glanced at Aalwyn.

He nudged her, and she pushed back.

"However the *Dwalen* decide, we must give Mloyi a wide berth."

"Did he threaten us?"

"He did not need to."

Ahead, Koorsboom lunged at a butterfly fluttering about, and he stumbled. His paws were in the air as he tumbled in the grass.

***

The plain was flooded with moonlight, not a cloud in the sky. Bright light shimmered on Mloyi's gold coat when he stopped and put his nose to the ground. The urine markings left by Aalwyn were strong and clear, meant for her sisters should they wish to rejoin her. Plants in flower, trees releasing pollen or seed, secretions of insect or vertebrate—nothing escapes the notice of a painted wolf.

Mloyi straightened and nodded to those behind him. Two more wolves emerged from the shadows with gold coats like his own, deferring to him.

"Blackthorn will know we are coming. Kill him quickly, and the pup will not stand a chance."

Chapter 30

The trill of cicadas produced a steady dirge broken by the abrupt *hrr-raa!* of a side-striped jackal crying in alarm.

Koorsboom stirred, head up and ears at attention, and saw that Aalwyn was already awake.

"Blackthorn—the veld."

Blackthorn raised his head immediately. On their feet, the wolves rapidly scanned the rolling plains.

"Just there." Aalwyn indicated the unmistakable steady lope of a wolf in silhouette to the west. Her nostrils flared. "We will be attacked."

"What on earth?" Blackthorn was by her side. "There are more."

"You can see in this dark?" Koorsboom was whirling about.

"His approach is an aggressive one. I can scent his anger. A single wolf assaulting us alone in the dark would not be logical. There must be more—and they may be our *Dwalen*." He shook his head.

"Essenhout and Duinemirt would not take part in this." Aalwyn turned and began to run toward the east.

Koorsboom followed, with Blackthorn behind them.

The moon faded, and the world fell into shadow as the wolves maintained a steady lope.

"He is gaining on us," Blackthorn twittered. "The pup is unable to keep the pace."

"I will not hold you back!" Koorsboom streaked ahead.

"Your shorter legs—not your spirit—impede you."

The wolves sprinted without goal as the scent of anger grew stronger with the shifting wind.

"Enough of this pointless flight." Blackthorn stopped suddenly. "I will break whoever emerges from that thicket." He cast a glance to

Koorsboom, now whining gently. "Take him and escape." He touched noses with Aalwyn and lapped her muzzle with care. "Provide for him in all the ways I could not." Blackthorn stepped forward and clawed gashes in the ground, glaring at the veld.

"Only the alpha issues commands." Aalwyn's voice was cold, her muscles steel under her coat of black, white, and gold. "Koorsboom. To me."

Koorsboom padded to her.

"You will now learn to kill your own kind."

Slight movement appeared in relief against the grey landscape of the night as Blackthorn tore at the ground, his drool in a puddle and his obsidian eyes burning into the dark.

"Mloyi approaches." Blackthorn's graveled voice was just above a whisper. "We have been deceived. He was concealing his brothers all along."

Three gold wolves broke through the grass thicket before them.

"Your brothers share your vile scent, Mloyi!" Aalwyn growled.

Mloyi and his brothers bayed as they closed in. Blackthorn leapt before Aalwyn with his fangs glistening, and the wolves' loud twittering became a siren. Blackthorn landed on all four paws and lunged at a neck, blood flashing, to throw Mloyi onto his back. Aalwyn pounced and seized a hind leg in her jaws with a muffled crunch. Mloyi spun off his back onto his forepaws in streamers of drool and dashed at Koorsboom, who sidestepped, taking a portion of Mloyi's ear. Aalwyn bowled Mloyi over and clicked to Koorsboom, and together they knocked over the gold wolves dragging down Blackthorn. Mloyi's brothers leapt free and scampered into the thicket with Blackthorn fast on their tails. Aalwyn whipped her head around to find a fourth wolf watching from a distance.

Her heart fell as she recognized the outline.

Sekelbos.

She twittered to Koorsboom, and they slipped away, the pup hiding in an acacia thicket. She sprinted to Sekelbos sitting under a sparse sourplum tree. Sekelbos started and sidled slightly away as she padded toward him.

"I underestimated you."

"How do you mean?" Sekelbos's eyes cast about.

"A cunning ploy." Aalwyn sat down by his side. "You have enjoyed the hunting here—your coat is looking full, and your girth is robust."

"No cunning is needed to slay cattle."

"But craft is needed to kill a challenger."

Before them in the clearing, Blackthorn had Mloyi but the throat, twisting to release him when one of the gold brothers bit his flank.

"Your gambit to convince Mloyi that we were staying—it seems to have worked."

The growling and high-pitched alarm calls echoed as Blackthorn flung off one gold brother to grapple with the other.

"I did not see the quality of alpha in you, Sekelbos—" Aalwyn's eyes played over the clearing, searching for Koorsboom. "—until now."

"That Blackthorn would kill Mloyi to stay—" Sekelbos's jaw hung open. "I did convince Mloyi of that. I knew they would fight. And once we dispense with the survivors, a land of plenty will be ours."

Aalwyn stared, and Sekelbos met her gaze.

She had no word for betrayal.

She let loose a deep hoo-call, *hoouh! hoouh!* and the wolves below paused to cast their eyes about.

"You have been misled!" Aalwyn leapt forward. "Sekelbos has set the warriors at odds: Blackthorn and Mloyi." She glared around the clearing. "He believed that he would ascend to alpha—" She bared her fangs. "—once he had slain the victor."

"There is no conflict with me - I wish only to leave." Blackthorn shook his head, spraying bloody froth.

"So it would seem." Mloyi looked from Blackthorn to Aalwyn and cast his gaze on Sekelbos. His face slackened as he began to understand.

"There is no love lost between us, Mloyi. However, the reign of the alpha is brief." Aalwyn strode toward Sekelbos as he shrank back. "Even more so when the flesh is riven from your body."

"You have tampered with those more powerful than you." Mloyi and his gold brothers converged upon the traitor. "We shall exact our toll." They pounced as one.

His eyes dilated in terror as Mloyi ripped the fur and tendons from his jaw, and Sekelbos's blood ran in sheets when Mloyi tore his head backward to drop the ragged flesh on the ground. Sekelbos stumbled across the dry soil, falling to his elbows with the side of his head laid bare. His body was still quivering with disbelief when Mloyi climbed over him, drenched in blood, and twittered to his gold brothers.

"You were once an heir, Sekelbos—" Aalwyn's high twitter sounded through the clearing. "*Now you may join the void!*"

"Nothing frightens my mother," Koorsboom whispered to Blackthorn.

"I cannot say the same." Blackthorn spat blood. "Now that I have come to know her."

"Mloyi, we *Dwalen* want nothing more to do with you or your hunting grounds. We return to the wild." Aalwyn bared her fangs in the moonlight.

"Why not stay?" Mloyi panted heavily. "Do you not fear for your pup?"

"My fear for him guides me to leave."

"Go, then, whatever your motives." Mloyi grunted his disappointment and twittered to his brothers, their gold coats dark with blood under the moon. "Do not return, and I shall not pursue. The rest of your *Dwalen*, however, have decided to remain with me." Mloyi hobbled toward her, hind leg dragging. "And if you return, you will find me only too easily."

"I shall never seek you again." Aalwyn glared.

Mloyi and his brothers departed as quickly as their injuries would allow. The sound of katydids rose once again now that the noise of the battle had faded.

Blackthorn growled darkly, "To find him, one would need only to sift through vulture droppings."

"What of the others?" Koorsboom's wet eyes gleamed.

"I do not relinquish my pack so easily." Aalwyn lapped Koorsboom's muzzle. "Rage or no, they will be given one last chance." She trotted off to the west, following the golden wolves at great distance.

"Why do we not kill them for attacking us?" Koorsboom chirped uneasily as he padded after Blackthorn, glancing over his shoulder as Aalwyn disappeared into the shadows of brush.

"The most damaging thing one can do to the unwise—" Blackthorn rasped, spitting blood. "—is to leave them to it."

Chapter 31

The wolves shook the late September dew from their fur, where they clustered in a fallow field next to the rusted hulk of a tractor engulfed in strangling shrubs and grass. The land here sloped gently to a dry riverbed and a thick knot of acacia and sourplum around the dead remains of fruit trees.

Aalwyn crouched on the ridge above with her dish-like ears swiveling to catch the muttering below.

"Today we explore to the east!" Mloyi nosed the wolves awake, and Vaalgras and Duinemirt leapt up eagerly with the rally.

Mloyi stood tall to greet them with his brothers flanking his sides, staring until Vaalgras and Duinemirt dipped their heads beneath his muzzle. Essenhout met Mloyi at eye-level and refused to lick even her pack.

"What ails you, Essenhout?" Mloyi whispered.

"What is to the east that so interests you?"

"Across the riverbed lies another farm. There is no need to deplete our food supply here."

Mloyi set off at a limping trot with the others behind him as Essenhout watched, undecided.

"Leaving so quickly, my sister?" Aalwyn purred over Essenhout's shoulder into the quiet.

"I might have known you would not forsake us." Essenhout lapped Aalwyn's muzzle. "It seems I am the chosen alpha." She frowned.

"Your presumptuous mate is cavalier." Aalwyn nodded. "To put it lightly. Should he chance to face humans, you would do well to goad him."

"With pleasure." Essenhout padded off to follow the golden wolf. "I will do my best to recall the others."

"I'll not leave a trail. Look to the south as you go." Aalwyn retreated into the brush. "There I will be."

***

The cow carcass was already drawing flies, and vultures circled overhead.

"These cattle had never seen our kind." Mloyi lazed with his brothers and the *Dwalen* in the sun. "Not even a run when we came into view." He lay on his back with his tongue lolled out and his injured leg resting.

"You are a great hunter." Vaalgras dipped his muzzle. "We eat well under your care."

Duinemirt licked Vaalgras's muzzle.

Essenhout's ears stood erect as she stared at a distant ridge to the north where a slight whirring came from a far clump of *Brachystegia* trees. There was a blinding flash of light. In the afterglow moved a shiny object along a road on the ridge, belching blue smoke until it disappeared.

Essenhout rested her head on her forepaws.

To the south ran the vague silhouette of Aalwyn ducking into the grass.

***

"Essenhout, eat your fill while the birds allow!" Vaalgras scarfed down a massive tenderloin ripped from the cow's pelvis. He looked up at the hooded vultures. "Soon there will be too many."

Essenhout's stomach slowed its rumbling. She was up on her feet to pace.

"Get back!" Vaalgras leapt at a drab hooded vulture on the cow's rib cage.

The vulture rose with a massive sweep of its wings, and another landed. More vultures soared down, whirling and descending, until the carcass was enveloped in a writhing mass of dirty white and brown feathers.

Essenhout looked up at a column of vultures circling above with the dead cow at the neck of a whirlpool.

"We must finish and be gone." Essenhout padded over to Duinemirt. "Mloyi did not say—"Duinemirt paused chewing a length of muscle. "Silence—" Essenhout hissed. "Aalwyn beckons."

"She has left us." Duinemirt cocked her head.

"Indeed she has." Mloyi shouldered next to Essenhout as Duinemirt cowered. "She has left you behind to continue her starving elsewhere."

Essenhout dipped her head.

"You are clever, Essenhout." Mloyi leaned in toward her. "But not clever enough to undermine me." He bared his teeth. "An unending river of animals runs across these lands."

"I don't understand you." Vaalgras sat down.

"I once viewed humans with trepidation." Mloyi gazed at the *Dwalen* with his gold brothers at his sides. "Then I watched their own dogs take down a cow in the night and devour it. They did nothing—only killed a leopard in retaliation. The fools never thought to suspect one of their own dogs!" Mloyi stood to his full height to gaze across the landscape. "Such a revelation of their nature! Their arrogance and vulgarity are their very undoing. One must be resolute. We shall take one farm after the next. We shall leave one litter after the next." He glared at Essenhout. "No fence nor thunder shall thwart our march of dominance over these cattle that they are too lazy to tend. They have no more control of their animals than they do a river." His eyes narrowed, rimmed with red. "It is time that our kind drank deeply from it."

"Your ambition is mighty indeed." Essenhout's voice was slight, but it pierced the quiet. "The kingdom you envision encounters now its first challenge." She glanced at the distant ridge.

The wolves turned to see three *bakkies* descending. The gold wolves twitched as the engines grew in pitch, the noise enveloping them.

"Will you make your stand against these pathetic monkeys?" Essenhout barked.

The gold brothers turned, their eyes wide with anxiety.

"Will you defend me, the mother of the pups you hope to sire—your great army that will number as blades of grass across the veld?"

"You doubt me?" Mloyi pulled back his lips, eyes narrowed into slits.

"Give me no reason!" Essenhout gave a pealing twitter like a scream.

"To my sides, brothers," Mloyi twittered. "We stand against these ridiculous creatures."

The gold wolves bared their fangs.

"Leave their bodies—" Essenhout backed away as the *bakkies* came up the hill.

"For the vultures?"

"As a warning to the rest."

The first *bakkie* ground to a halt as the gold wolves sprinted forward.

"Make haste or die." Essenhout snapped at the flanks of Vaalgras and Duinemirt, and they bolted for the grass at the edge of the field.

"They attack—"Aalwyn leapt out to run with them.

The *Dwalen* spun about to see Mloyi and his brothers surround a human in blue coveralls emerging from a *bakkie*. With a desperate wail, the blue figure was pinned against the *bakkie* by the circling gold wolves.

"Why does it not run?" The gold brothers paused and twittered.

The next *bakkie* braked, and humans jumped from the rear brandishing sticks of wood and metal. The *Dwalen* winced at the sharp flashes followed by deafening claps that echoed all around. The gold brothers yelped sharply as they stumbled and struck the dirt. Mloyi broke away in a limping dash toward Aalwyn. A crack rang out, he gave a mighty jump and twisted in the air, and he fell with his head plowed into the dust.

"Run as though the veld were afire." Aalwyn leapt forward into the high grasses.

Chapter 32

A capped wheatear sang a warble and chatter as it hopped among tussocks of dried grasses searching for insects, the black stripe around its keen eyes stretching down its neck to a band through white across its breast. The wheatear perched on a termite mound to scan the horizon, gave a sharp *chik-chik*, and fluttered away.

"Lizards and bustards. Nothing that satisfies," Blackthorn rasped. "There will be little near these dwellings but cattle, dogs, cats, and rats. They kill everything else. How do you fare, Koorsboom?"

"I will keep pace." Koorsboom's small body showed the wear of the trail, his ribs standing out. It had been days since any substantial meal.

A faint, hollow whisper came on the breeze.

"Your mother has found our trail." Blackthorn bent his head. He lowered his face to the ground and issued a hollowed hoo-call.

A minute later the call was answered.

"We rest here."

Blackthorn disappeared into the bracken and returned to drop a mangled rabbit at Koorsboom's feet. They settled down to wait as Koorsboom ripped into the hare.

Evening fell, and finally out of the acacia padded Aalwyn leading the *Dwalen*. She bounded forward to touch noses with Blackthorn and lick Koorsboom's face and muzzle.

Koorsboom licked her muzzle with a tongue as dry as stone.

"I will never again leave your side, my son." Aalwyn's voice was a labored croak.

She turned and glared at the *Dwalen*, who passed her slowly, dipping their heads below her muzzle.

"Let it be known—" Aalwyn spoke loudly over the heads of Duinemirt and Vaalgras. "—that these fools may have the Rage. Give them a wide berth."

Vaalgras opened his mouth to protest, but Duinemirt shook her head.

"I thank you for allowing us to return." Essenhout lay down near Aalwyn. "You seemed to know that the humans were coming."

"Was there ever doubt they would?"

"Did the humans kill Sekelbos?" Vaalgras paced anxiously. "We have not seen him. We were told nothing—"

"There was a great deal that Mloyi did not know," Koorsboom chirped.

"They were hunting for us all along, were they not?" Vaalgras chattered without waiting for answers. "Those humans may be upon our trail now, scenting our path—"

"If they were able to follow our scent, Vaalgras—" Blackthorn stood in a threatening motion. "—our kind would have been wiped out long ago." He uttered this and nothing more.

***

When the Cape turtledove purred into the new morning, *kuk-coorr-uk kuk-coorr-uk,* Blackthorn was gone.

Koorsboom woke and trotted the edge of camp, sniffing here, there, here again, retracing his steps.

"What troubles you?" Vaalgras grumbled.

"He did not leave a trace—"

"No concern to us."

"He has always left a trail—" Koorsboom threaded between short Governor's plum trees.

"Calm yourself," Aalwyn chirped.

"I can hunt for you, Mother. If you are hungry."

"That is our job, my son." Aalwyn shook her head to bat away flies. "Yours, for now, is to learn."

"But is he ever returning, Mother?" Koorsboom lay down a respectful distance away.

"Of course." She watched the grass tops waver with a faint scent of rain. "Neither of us would ever leave you."

"We left my brothers and sisters," Koorsboom said hesitantly. "We left my father—"

"That was different." Aalwyn spoke deep in her throat. "Koorsboom, I have been distant from you for too long—ever since that dreadful day. I have allowed my grief for my beloved mate and pups to eat my insides like a wolf in the belly of an antelope. And yet you are here. You are mine. You are my legacy." She broke off. "You resemble your father more with every passing day." She stood and lay down again by his side, lapping his muzzle. "You will be the alpha of your own pack before long. My great malice awaits any who would stop you."

Koorsboom exhaled deeply and buried his head under her shoulder, until her forepaw draped his neck. He closed his eyes and whined with relief.

"Our path is still uncertain." Essenhout crept close to touch Aalwyn's muzzle. "Do you know yet where we are headed?"

"The *Dwalen* will forge ahead until we reach a place of safety."

"If one exists." Vaalgras looked at her at eye-level—not as a subservient. "Duinemirt has had enough of this relentless *dwaal*." Aalwyn growled, and he shrank with a whine.

"I am more than aware of my sister's hardships. Your intention is to depart—with my sister?"

Vaalgras raised his brow and opened his mouth.

"I know what you intend. And you are denied." Aalwyn pulled back her lips to reveal white teeth dripping saliva. "Until Koorsboom is safe, none shall ever defy me again."

"But the alpha must have more pups," Vaalgras managed to stammer. "If you do not mean to, why should we delay?"

"I mean to." Aalwyn snapped just short of his snout. "In my own time. If I wait season after season, you wait too." Her fangs seemed to grow. "And wait and wait and wait."

"What brings your anger upon me?" Vaalgras's eyes darted fearfully.

"Your stupidity. Your carelessness, that I foolishly ignored. Above all, your lack of loyalty. You might well have rotted with the cattle.

Be grateful that I allowed you back. It is only to serve me and my pup. Fail your pack again, Vaalgras, and you will be left for the hyenas." Her eyes went to Duinemirt as she spoke.

"Where did Sekelbos go?" Vaalgras croaked.

"He is—destroyed."

***

Koorsboom patrolled the edge of their clearing, nose high to sniff the wind.

"You are nervous, my son." Aalwyn by his side. "You have good reason."

Koorsboom whined suddenly and took a step back.

The grass parted, and though an opening appeared a forepaw. Sekelbos's muzzle was low to the ground as he crept into the clearing with one eye glancing at Aalwyn. He did not approach, but remained rooted to the spot, saliva mixed with blood dripping steadily from his torn jaw.

"Sekelbos?" Koorsboom whined.

Sekelbos started at the sound of his name and shrank closer to the ground, turning away his face.

"You have returned." Aalwyn stood over him impassively. "Now show who you really are."

Sekelbos slowly showed his face, as Koorsboom gasped. A wide rent left one side of Sekelbos's head bare of fur from jaw to mangled ear. His lips were gone and his teeth exposed in a hideous grin, where flies and maggots crawled over the raw muscle and tissue.

Koorsboom looked up at Aalwyn in fear.

"Come, Koorsboom." Aalwyn turned away. "I will not speak of this." She glanced at him. "The alpha does not take challenge lightly. Koorsboom, the day may come when you are alpha." She paused. "But never the Wolf with the Permanent Smile."

***

Blackthorn returned at sunset with blood on his head and breast, dancing and nearly spinning in the air. While Sekelbos crouched under the acacia, the *Dwalen* pounded after Blackthorn through the brush to an impala with its throat torn apart. The wolves pounced upon the impala and ripped off the hide in sheets, dismembering the carcass in less than a minute.

"You two—" Aalwyn directed. "Eat only off those hindquarters, and only after the rest have finished."

Vaalgras glanced at Duinemirt, but she simply lowered her head and did as she was told.

All made room for Koorsboom, who ate half his weight in muscle and liver set aside for him by Essenhout. Aalwyn and Blackthorn ate next, as alphas do, but also to avoid Vaalgras and Duinemirt.

The wolves rested in the failing light on rocks that radiated heat, the satisfaction of their meal offset by uncertainty. Aalwyn watched Vaalgras and Duinemirt vigilantly. Neither showed symptoms of the Rage, but the virus works slowly from wounded muscle to nerve endings and from there to the brain. Sekelbos remained outcast, lying in the grass with his nose on his forepaws. Blackthorn had met Aalwyn's eyes at the sight of Sekelbos with his infected face, and they had shared a silent nod.

"Tomorrow I will scout ahead for the end to these farms and villages." Blackthorn paced restlessly.

"Humans are everywhere here." Vaalgras sounded wistful. "We are far from our river."

"On human lands, it is only a matter of time before they come after us." Essenhout spoke in a haunted voice. "They have their thunder."

"We will find a way," Blackthorn grunted.

"And if there is no end to the farms and villages?"

Blackthorn stood without comment and walked to the edge of the clearing, where he lay down in exhaustion with his jaw upon the ground. His wounds from the battle with the golden wolves still throbbed.

Sekelbos wandered in the brush, knowing not to intrude. His fevers had subsided and muscle aches faded, and he lay exhausted under a *Combretum* shrub. His glazed eyes stared at nothing.

The moon floated concealed in clouds, the grasses shifted and bristled with small nocturnal rodents. Aalwyn trotted to Blackthorn's side and lay down with a gentle caress to his shoulder.

"I have never expressed my gratitude to you for bringing my family to safety."

"My presence was incidental." Blackthorn sniffed. "Your family is strong."

"That is not what I wish to convey."

"I know what you wish." Blackthorn lifted his head to look into her eyes. "But my time on this veld is short. I have not the will to sire a pup. I could never sire one as fine as Koorsboom."

"Your skill with antelope suggests otherwise." Aalwyn was taken aback. "You are afraid?"

Blackthorn was silent.

"We are both afraid." Aalwyn drew closer. "Every passing day our bodies weaken and our fortunes dwindle."

He could not look her in the eye.

"But tonight, Blackthorn, we live. We cannot be denied our place on this earth." Aalwyn brushed his muzzle with the lightest touch.

"Koorsboom grows to a fine wolf under your guardianship. Your own pups will be mighty indeed. Come, love." She stood. "Come to me at last."

Aalwyn turned and glanced over her shoulder. With some reluctance and suffering the joint pains that he masked, Blackthorn rose. She positioned herself, and they mated finally in the all-consuming fire of sunset as it passed into smoldering twilight.

Chapter 33

Cool winds ran through the dried grasses as distant thunderclouds hung low over the plains. A half-dead acacia tree reached skyward with its bleached white arms. Perched on a high branch, the streaked grey plumage of a white-faced owl appeared with its brilliant orange eyes under grey lids. In the heat of day, only the *Dwalen* were in motion.

Koorsboom had grown considerably since leaving Botswana, although his slight build still reflected a life of low-level starvation. Gold was more apparent now in his black and white fur tossed gently by the breeze. The ruff around his neck had expanded, and his dark eyes had sharpened to scan hills, valleys, and horizons.

The wolves had flagged for many days. Their heads hung low with exhaustion as they padded relentlessly over the hard and rocky ground.

Blackthorn had taken the lead. His face was a grim scowl with gold fur across his brow, his black muzzle obscuring the glare. At his side trotted Koorsboom, who looked up and padded quickly to match Blackthorn's pace. Aalwyn ran on the other side of Koorsboom, neck and neck with the old wolf. Her face was set in an obstinate and impassive mask. Neither of the alphas spoke as the distress of famine took its toll.

Essenhout padded a pace behind Aalwyn. Vaalgras and Duinemirt trailed to one side.

Far behind and almost out of sight lagged Sekelbos with his fur worn through and his tail drooping. He worked his jaw as he cantered, the pain keeping him awake and upright.

"We would have done well to stay further from these farms," Blackthorn muttered.

"You would have done well to find a better option." Aalwyn was curt and did not alter her gaze.

"The farmers are out searching for anything with a meat-shearing tooth."

"*Voetsek jou vrek.* You dying-animal-walking."

"It takes only one good strike from their thunder to kill an alpha." Blackthorn stopped. "That would be the end of the *Dwalen*."

"And it takes a thousand stupid decisions to achieve the same." Aalwyn did not slow.

"Does that mean anything?"

"The decisions are mine to make." Aalwyn turned her head. "I live with them."

"We all live with them." Blackthorn was in front of her in a heartbeat, head and ears down and lips parted.

"Would you like your fur removed?" Aalwyn walked around him.

"You forget yourself." Blackthorn ran alongside her. "Our only food we stole from stolen lands. Starvation can break a pack as powerfully as lions."

"You mention the lion." Aalwyn stopped with her jaws open. "As though I would forget—" She leapt at Blackthorn and clipped his muzzle.

Blackthorn crouched.

Aalwyn flattened her ears against her skull and stared as the setting sun sank behind her.

"Over the next rise, I will find our place of nightly rest. Can I trust you not to question my judgment in the time that it takes to walk so far?"

"Aalwyn—"

"Most appreciated." Aalwyn loped away past Blackthorn. Koorsboom sped up to stay with her. The *Dwalen* followed her through the dried grasses and around acacia and brush, over a rise to a human fence that stretched for many kilometers in both directions. Regular poles with plastic insulators were connected by horizontal wires hung with yellow signs of a human hand with lightning bolts: *Danger—Gevaar—Ingozi.*

Aalwyn loped toward the fence with Blackthorn close behind. A faint buzzing reached their ears, the sharp tinge of ozone in the air.

"This is larger than any we have encountered." Blackthorn sniffed and recoiled. "There is prey on the other side, sure enough, but the scent is of Cape buffalo."

"Most unfortunate." Aalwyn looked north and south into undulating hills.

"Why is the fence so high, Mother?" Koorsboom scampered up.

"They are only as high as the animals imprisoned."

"It hardly seems robust." Koorsboom padded back and forth. "There is a chance that I might squeeze through those wires." He trotted toward the fence.

"*Stop—*" Blackthorn leapt on Koorsboom. "This fence is alive!" He knelt panting on Koorsboom's shoulders, pinning his head to the ground.

"A fence alive?" Vaalgras reached them. "I smell nothing."

"This fence can strike with the force of a leopard." Blackthorn looked to Aalwyn.

Koorsboom squirmed out from under Blackthorn and backed away.

"What are we to do?" Aalwyn examined the fence carefully.

"Even without moving, it wounds. I tell you, Aalwyn, we cannot pass."

***

Essenhout shoveled with her forepaws, the dirt flying in clumps between her legs and onto to ground behind her. She paused to eye the depth of the hole.

"Must we go so deep?"

"Leave plenty of room for passage. It should not even be close." Aalwyn padded past her to Koorsboom working at a hole of his own.

Koorsboom turned to Aalwyn.

"Well done, my son."

He twittered happily and resumed digging.

"This—" Blackthorn brushed alongside Aalwyn, speaking in a rugged whisper. "—is a terrible idea. That fence was built by humans, and they will be none too pleased to find us on the wrong side of it."

"We cannot stop our *dwaal*." Aalwyn lowered her voice. "And we are in need of a kill." She met his eyes. "Here. And now."

"I have walked this earth for so long." Blackthorn raked the gravel. "I have likely traveled twice as far as you. You are unwise to ignore my advice."

"I ignore nothing." Aalwyn bared her fangs. She closed her hazel eyes with a deep sigh and opened them again. "Your advice means the world to me. And to my son." She glanced at Koorsboom chasing a dragonfly. "But your words are advice. It is my word that is final." She strode to Blackthorn, who flinched momentarily until she pressed the full weight of her body against him. "I make no decision lightly, least of all in choosing the sire for my pups."
Blackthorn dipped his head in deference.
"I say—" Essenhout trotted past on the opposite side of the fence. "What a handsome herd of cattle you are!"
Koorsboom dove into Essenhout's newly-dug channel in a flash and joined her with a tail wag.
"After you, my lady." Blackthorn bowed.
Aalwyn ducked through, and the *Dwalen* followed.
As Vaalgras pulled himself out, his tail touched a wire. There was a barely-visible spark, and he shrieked abruptly, spasmed, and lay still.
"Vaalgras!" Duinemirt dashed to his side.
"We were—" Vaalgras rose on shaky legs. "Were we going under the fence soon?"
"We did." Duinemirt lapped his muzzle.
"Right." Vaalgras flapped his ears, looked about, and reoriented himself. "I am fine." He lowered his muzzle, abashed.
Before the *Dwalen* were out of sight, Sekelbos found the hole, shook his head violently, and fell dizzily to the ground. Back up and dripping froth, he slumped down in the shade of a feverberry tree. Staring at a rock, he growled and began to bite at it, chipping his fangs and bleeding once again from his wounded mouth.

***

"And that is that." Blackthorn gestured ahead.
Cape buffalo milled around a watering hole in a mass of muscle and horn on a sea of clipped green grass, tearing at the sweet, tough fibers. The massive bulls formed an unbreachable black cordon with their ears twitching away flies and their resolute eyes upon the wolves. The massive skulls carried central bossing down each side into curving horns shaped as shallow Ws. In gaps between the bulls

appeared lighter cows and reddish calves, the gaps closing as rapidly as they formed.

"I do not see a way—" Blackthorn stopped.

Aalwyn glared at him.

Blackthorn nodded and padded forward toward the herd, the bulls leaving their languid feeding as he appeared and ventured forward. With a snort and a stamp, each bull was joined by another and another, forming a wall. Blackthorn sprinted toward the edge of their line, and the wall moved with him. He trotted back toward the *Dwalen,* where Aalwyn nosed Koorsboom gently.

"Go with him." Aalwyn nodded at Essenhout. "Bring news."

Essenhout and Blackthorn loped away in a large circle around the herd and returned within the hour.

"Opposite us there is a dwelling." Essenhout shook the dust from her fur. "No humans about."

"The metal of the *bakkie* is shiny." Blackthorn nodded. "They are close, and this land is maintained. These humans will not tolerate an attack upon their herd. However, we have found a target."

Koorsboom was on his paws in anticipation.

"It is dangerous." Blackthorn looked to Aalwyn. "A lone bull."

***

The pack maneuvered around the buffalo, careful to stay out of sight of the distant farmhouse and barn.

"Just there." Blackthorn indicated a bull with heavily-scarred central bossing and the tip of one horn broken off. "Steady on—this oke is not to be underestimated."

"What makes them so dangerous?" Essenhout sniffed.

"A bull alone is an outcast. He has lost a critical fight to a younger usurper. And so he is deprived of company and any contact with females." Blackthorn grunted. "He will be ill-tempered."

"You have a gift for understatement." Essenhout laughed.

"This, I hope, is one of your worst ideas—" Vaalgras grumbled.

"The hunt begins." Aalwyn cut him short.

"I will not charge an insane Cape buffalo."

"Your courage does you no credit." Aalwyn's ears folded back as she gestured to Koorsboom. "But we will not need it."

The *Dwalen* fell in behind her, Koorsboom running straight with pride. The large black buffalo pulled dried grass with an audible *rrip!* as his nostrils flared and exhaled heavily. His jaw moved in crushing circles, and the dark globes of his eyes stared.

The wolves drew closer, and the buffalo started with a huff. He stomped powerfully.

"You will get the pup killed." Vaalgras began to drift away.

"On my mark." Aalwyn's tone was flat. "Break away and return."

The buffalo gave another stomp and dropped his wad of grass. With a grunt, he charged, hammering the ground with his pounding hooves.

"*Mark!*"

The wolves scattered with the buffalo in pursuit straight past his herd. The buffalo stopped, huffing, and circled around.

Aalwyn approached again, and the bull chased her. The wolves ran further afield. The buffalo stopped and turned to resume feeding. Blackthorn sprinted forward and snapped at the buffalo's flank. The mighty horns swung around with a loud, rattling groan to graze his fur as Blackthorn made a hairpin turn back toward the pack with the buffalo thundering close behind. A hundred meters at a time, the wolves provoked the buffalo, and he responded. For an hour they worked the bull toward the fence, out of sight of the rest of his herd.

"Take him!" Aalwyn gave a rapid twitter.

The *Dwalen* joined in, their demonic howl startling the buffalo. He neared the fence and turned to run along it, but the wolves blocked his path. He turned the other way, blocked again. With a frustrated grunt, he stumbled into the fence.

He gave a high groan, and his body convulsed as his foreleg spasmed tangled in wires. Mighty head wavering, his throat hung open with a gagging cry. The horns swung about wildly, heaving his bulk away from the fence. He gave a deafening groan and collapsed with an impact that shook the earth under the wolves' feet. The pack was quiet, the only sound a slight crackling from the damaged fence, and the air filled with the rich, ashen scent of burned fur.

Chapter 34

As though hewn from the brown sandstone, Koorsboom blended with the growing shadows on the escarpment.

"What do you see?" Aalwyn clambered up to join him.

"Smoke rising. Just a tendril far from here."

"Well done," Blackthorn rasped, "your eyes are superior to mine. It is not normal for wild things to create such smoke. Wildfire is unlikely. So I suspect human hunters." He bumped against Koorsboom. "We will give them a wide berth. Ever taut as a tendon, young one." He padded forward to make his way down the escarpment.

"The sun has descended a few times since we ran that bull into the fence. The meat was *lekker*, but with the starvation we have endured, it has only just kept us going. We need to make a kill." Aalwyn muttered. "Now that we have entered the wild, one would expect antelope." She looked at the sky. "Clouds approach with the scent of water in the air. The rains must be on the way."

"How do we find a waterhole?"

"Follow a river." Aalwyn lapped Koorsboom's muzzle. "Or depend upon good fortune. Although fortune is a quality we have been lacking."

"Were the deaths of my brothers and sisters to our advantage, Mother?"

Aalwyn froze, a dull ache in her heart.

The young wolf stared at her, longingly.

"As it turns out—yes. Our world is harsh to the vulnerable. If they had not died, they very well might have starved by now."

Koorsboom studied the ground.

"With time, you will leave the ranks of the vulnerable, my son. You will never, however, leave death behind."

The wolves' hunger pangs faded into uneasy rest at sunset, when a light sprinkling of rain raised the aromatic scent of soil and vegetation into the night air.

***

"Our first large prey after the dry season ends, and it has to be zebra." Blackthorn shook his head.

Before them, the soaked plain had been stamped into mud by a herd led by a massive stallion. The black and white stripes made a brilliant display as the other males galloped in circles through clouds of flies, their snorts punctuated by periodic whinnies of *kwa—ha—ha*.

"No foals yet." Aalwyn sighed. "Koorsboom, you will wait this one out."

The *Dwalen* followed her into the lower valley as the zebra calls intensified with overlapping whinnies when the wolves were spotted.

"Charge straight into them?" Vaalgras had been anxious all day.

"If your muzzle has no value to you. Their incisors go through bone like water."

Blackthorn picked up the pace, approaching the bachelors on the fringe of the herd. The zebra stallion trotted about the females to group them together, and as soon as he paused the younger males broke into run, then stopped and faced the wolves.

"Abort the attack," Blackthorn twittered as he returned dejectedly to where Koorsboom waited. "No good ending to that, sure enough."

Aalwyn and Blackthorn took the lead as the *Dwalen* continued their effortless pace away through the brush.

"We may have a long way to go before we eat again. This wild place has a human presence." Blackthorn's voice was gravelly and conspiratorial.

"Farmers?" Koorsboom whined.

"Hunters." The old wolf seemed to bite down on the word.

"Would they eat our kind?"

"Impossible to predict. They may hunt us, or kill us out of fear, or slaughter us for a laugh." Blackthorn snorted. "Far to the north, hunters forced my pack from a wild place with their reckless hunting. In a single season, the prey was gone, no tracks left of any kind, even the waterholes devoid of all but rodents. We found only pairs of ruts dug into the soil for long distances." He glared at the bushveld. "At the end of the ruts lay a vast field of death—wildebeest, antelope, zebra decaying in the sun with their skins ripped away. A macabre tableau."

"There must be many humans to lay waste on such a scale."

"That is what disturbed me most. Only one machine carried a few humans with their thunder sticks. They stacked the dried hides into the machine, climbed on top, and went off." He sighed with exhaustion. "*Ag*, unimaginable waste."

"You are wise to hold off mating further, love."

"I desire you greatly, Aalwyn—but nothing poisons the soul more than the plaintive cry of a pup beyond help." Blackthorn's matted fur seemed to have greyed considerably since leaving the Chobe River.

"*Ja.* Time is all that we have in plenty."

Chapter 35

The brush became thicker and the stands of trees more frequent, the fences less sturdy. The people and cattle became fewer. The predators here were lithe, diminutive black-backed jackals, and the birds were seed-eaters rather than vultures. Frightening Cape buffalo wandered the dry veld in herds with reverberating hoofbeats.

"Rest here, my son." Aalwyn twittered. "We need a hunt, and the sedge is too thick to survey quickly." She led them to a sourplum tree, squat in height and sparsely branched. "We need to undertake patrols."

"Agreed. Short sweeps, then broaden them out depending on what prey we find in this meager place." Blackthorn padded off.

Essenhout trotted after Blackthorn with Vaalgras snapping at Duinemirt on their heels.

"Be on your guard, Koorsboom." Aalwyn lapped his muzzle before padding away into the brush.

Left alone, Koorsboom crept through the grass, leaving urine scent markings as he explored this place. Beyond the stand of black-barked sourplum trees he found what appeared to be a moving rock. With a grin he bent down to sniff the leopard tortoise as it stretched its beak-like mouth toward a low-hanging leaf. His nose bumped the black and brown geometric patterns on the high domed carapace, and the tortoise promptly withdrew its head and legs into its fortress. Nosing the sealed shell about, he wondered if turtles sensed fear as he did.

The sun dipped toward low hills to the west.

"*Kooorz-am-bah*—" The noise broke the calm, and Koorsboom whirled.

A demon emerged from the brush with familiar white, black, and gold fur—but missing its face.

"*Krah*." The exposed muscle and skull oozed pink purulence dotted with flies, the jaw laid bare and hanging slackly open, the throat gurgling.

"Sekelbos—" Koorsboom backed away with his heart pounding. The smell of death poured off Sekelbos as he bent his head low and choked with a pronounced *hruk—hruk—kruk!* and a loud *pop!* Swaying gently, he locked his eyes onto Koorsboom and loped abruptly forward.

Koorsboom ran with Sekelbos after him full-speed through the close, still air. He heard only the bounding pulse in his ears and the labored breathing close behind him. Around a tree Koorsboom clawed, as Sekelbos's claws scrabbled in the gravel behind him. Koorsboom plowed through acacia brush, ignoring the thorns now embedded deep in his skin. Around a grove of musasa trees he raced, loose dirt nearly giving way beneath his frantic footfalls, each step threatening to be his last. He circled back toward the camp, scrambling madly through the sedge, while the heaving and panting behind him descended into honking and wheezing.

Koorsboom began to wheeze as well, his legs still pumping. He broke through a cluster of *Combretum* shrub straight into a black-backed jackal, who bared its teeth to snarl, saw Sekelbos, and recoiled into a dead run. Sekelbos gave a muted whine as his body hit the ground just as Koorsboom nearly collided with Aalwyn.

"What chases you?" She was poised, fangs bared.

Koorsboom stopped and slumped, panting, as Sekelbos rose to his feet. "He has returned." He wheezed. "A *monster.*"

Aalwyn turned her head, her eyes wide with fear.

His deformed face broke into an even wider grin on sighting the pup. Bounding forth, the creature's torn muzzle bubbled with frothy saliva that ran in a stream down his neck, the smell rich and sickening with decay. A rattle erupted from his throat as he sped toward the exhausted Koorsboom. When Sekelbos was nearly upon him, Aalwyn struck back with the full force of her body.

Their jaws locked, skulls tight and quivering, forepaws gripping the hard earth and struggling against one another's weight.

Aalwyn looked into Sekelbos's eyes, and no one looked back. She pushed against this shadow-wolf with every muscle, pushing against the brute force of madness. If she hit the ground it was all over, and the rabid Sekelbos would kill Koorsboom.

Aalwyn released her grip and jumped aside, Sekelbos tumbling into the dirt. She was upon him in an instant, and her jaws ripped open the vessels of his throat. She backed away from the lethal wound. Sekelbos leaped to his feet, streamers of drool and blood flying, muscles in flaps and fur matted with blood as, snarling, he closed his jaws on Aalwyn's flank and ripped a gash in her back. Aalwyn rolled him off and bit a long, deep rent in his belly. He stumbled forward onto his shattered face, and she jumped away breathing rapidly. Sekelbos rose, dragging his intestines, and threw himself straight at her. His eyes rolled, wild with the madness, his throat gurgling a vicious snarl. Aalwyn bit down on his forepaw in mid-air with a stomach-turning crunch. He bounded forward, his full weight grinding into the broken bone, but unable to jump again he stumbled blindly. Aalwyn bit down on his other forepaw, severing it.

Hruk! Hruk—hruk—hruk–bok! Bloody vomit dribbled out of Sekelbos's open face as he fell to his side, and his legs scissored back and forth.

"It would be a mercy to kill him—" Vaalgras gasped from the edge of the clearing where he and Duinemirt stood frozen. The *Dwalen* backed away.

His eyes flashed, jaw slack, throat gurgling. His legs flailed helplessly.

"He is dead already." Aalwyn staggered unsteadily away and slumped finally to the ground.

***

Blackthorn and Essenhout returned to find Koorsboom alone and grim. Vaalgras and Duinemirt lay at a distance, Vaalgras on his feet to pace and then down again over and over.

"What has happened?" Blackthorn licked Koorsboom's muzzle. Koorsboom nodded silently at the stinking body in the field where vultures hovered.

"Where is your mother?" Blackthorn nosed Koorsboom anxiously.

"She has gone away to lick her wounds." Koorsboom shook his head. "That—" He whined faintly. "—was Sekelbos."

"So the Rage has played out its hand." Blackthorn sighed as he lay down by Koorsboom. "I am here for you now, young one."

"And I." Essenhout nodded. "Should my sister succumb—"

Koorsboom shivered.

"—I will die rather than see you harmed."

"You have my gratitude." Aalwyn crept up behind them, and the wolves jumped.

"My love!" Blackthorn's obsidian eyes were huge.

"I could ask for nothing more." Aalwyn settled heavily by his side. "You are all that remains of the *Dwalen*."

***

Resting in the open, basking in the sun, Aalwyn stared ahead of her at nothing. A small shadow raced across the ground before her, and she looked up to see the the white sweep of wings and dark belly plumage of a bateleur overhead. She considered looking for what may have drawn the raptor's attention, but recalled they only hunted for rodents or other birds. She lay her head on her paws again to rest, shuddering as chills raced through her aching muscles. She rolled to one side, and heaved deep breaths as the fever began its work.

***

Days passed, and hunts passed in kind, more often than not failed. Aalwyn continued to languish in the clearing.

Blackthorn watched, afraid to breathe too loudly. He laid his head on his paws to rest, and was startled again to his feet when a hacking cough erupted from her. A rattle in her throat subsided, and her body shuddered and remained still.

The grey wolf was on his feet again, and hurried to her side. He sniffed, and after some hesitation, nudged her body. A slow heaving breath.

He turned to see Koorsboom watching. Blackthorn lay down again, unable to meet the pup's gaze.

"I want to lay by my mother's side."

"As do I, *boykie*. She needs her strength, however, and cannot waste any comforting you."

"If she stops breathing, will you bite her awake?"

"I would not dare." Blackthorn could almost muster a grin. "I would fear her reprisal if she lives."

***

The breeze carried the warmth of spring as it rattled the horned thorn acacia tree above the *Dwalen*. Small green buds appeared, and the leaves would soon obscure the spines that resembled a thousand angry teeth.

"Will she die?" The pup whispered.

Blackthorn did not respond, looking up to a sky through the maze of chalk-white spines.

"What will we do?"

"The seasonal change is upon us." His eyes closed as the sun emerged from behind a bank of clouds. "No matter the intrigues of the veld, the seasons shall come, inexorably." He turned to look at Koorsboom, eyes wet with anxiety.

"I cannot hide my fear, *Oom* Blackthorn." Koorsboom peered into the shade under a tangle of sweet thorn to see his mother lying motionless.

"It is to your credit." The old wolf managed a rasping chuckle. "In my youth I worried about a great many things. That I would be found out. That I was not the bravest, the canniest, or even a passable hunter. So long it took me to discover these things do not matter." His dark eyes bore into the pups'. "When I ceased to worry about *seeming*, far more effort was put into *being*." He shifted his gaze to the sweet thorn ahead.

Aalwyn did not stir.

Shaggy grey fur mixed with the red of iron and blood, torn open and rustled by the wolves underneath. The tongue of the nyala hung out of its mouth, eyes blind to the world.

Koorsboom was first to raise his head, having had his fill. As he smacked and swallowed the hunks of kidney in his throat, he nearly choked. "Mother!"

Blackthorn was away from the kill as the pup spoke. He raced to Aalwyn's side, careful to avoid physical contact.

Before he could react, she lapped his muzzle with a gentle tongue, and twittered before he could recoil. "The fevers have passed." She licked Koorsboom in kind. "However it happened, I am not in the grasp of the Rage." Unknown to the wolves, the vaccination of Aalwyn and Duinemirt held good. She joined in at the kill, her appetite ravenous.

"One question remains." Blackthorn gestured towards Vaalgras, still pacing distant from the nyala, unsure of whether he was welcome. "If the Rage were to come, it would have taken him by now." She mustered a weak smile, tongue out and panting. "Sadly, he is afflicted by a more insidious illness - stupidity."

Chapter 36

As October wore on, every morning sunrise brought heat rising over the low-lying woodlands, with the promised showers rare and rationed by the clouds. The *Dwalen* left the farmlands and returned to wild scrub and twisted trees, unaware that they were entering the Limpopo Transfrontier Park.

The wolves passed an indistinct heap of pale fiber bleached to almond, thick roots radiating from an elevated pile that had once been a trunk, fallen now with sheets like paper hanging from the central husk. The baobab tree had endured for at least three thousand years, resistant to fire, bark-stripping, and disease. In the end, it succumbed to nothing more than time. The defiant wood became a whisper, and its life, outlasting all of recorded history, became a forgotten rumor.

***

"My trust in you is implicit, love. But I am fearful." Blackthorn wrinkled his nose as particles of faded ash reached them with their tale of recent fire.
"Food is worth the risk."
The wolves tensed at a crash, their shoulders hunched into stalking position, as a branch broke with the harsh whisper of disturbed leaves. Blackthorn motioned toward a bush that shook once. He placed one paw after the next, eyes fixed, with only a glance in either direction for signs of lion or hyena. His shoulders pumped gradually as he snaked toward the bush, sniffing the breeze—it was a wildebeest calf that smelled potently of fear.

He twittered, and the wolves joined him in a flash. They surrounded the bush, where a wildebeest calf thrashed against a tether.

"What is this?" Vaalgras was agitated.

"A snare." Blackthorn twittered at high pitch. "Do not approach! Look for the shine of metal."

The wolves stepped cautiously, not understanding.

"This—do you see?" Blackthorn took a steel wire in his teeth and held it taut until the calf whipped it out of his grasp.

"Another—a large loop between branches." Essenhout scratched at a wire suspended between bushes and secured to the base of a small acacia tree.

"I found another!" Koorsboom hopped on all four paws under a twist of wire.

"Careful!" Aalwyn was by his side and touching noses with him.

"Be on your guard," Blackthorn growled. "These are designed to kill. When you are caught, the snare tightens around your neck before you know that it is there."

The calf's eyes bulged, but its glassy stare reflected more exhaustion than fear. Blackthorn pounced, breaking its windpipe and tearing open the throat vessels to kill it instantly.

***

The wolves rested in the open, digesting the wildebeest calf as the trill of katydids filled the air. Every now and then one wolf sat up, looked about, and lay back down again.

"If there are any lion prints in this land, they escape my notice." Essenhout was on edge.

"Or hyena." Aalwyn rolled onto her back to scratch against the rocks.

"Humans may have killed them all," Blackthorn muttered.

"Good for us."

"No, Duinemirt. It simply means that we may be next." Blackthorn looked up at the crescent moon. "We will learn our fate tomorrow."

Nyala berry trees with their towering evergreen crowns provided shade, here among the elliptical leaves of Tamboti trees with their black, cracked bark and the star-shaped white flowers of the groves nearly in bloom. Between the trees, squat shrubs and ever-present acacia stood in the stark contrasts of light and shadow.

The round black eyes of a shy nyala antelope shifted, and its tall ears held still between high, curving horns in spite of the biting flies. Not a muscle twitched where the shaggy mane and vertical white stripes mimicked the lighting. The breeze picked up slightly, bringing more blazing heat with the ripe scent of wolf musk, and the nyala flared its nostrils.

The wolves ran through the grass with their heads low and forward, their ears swept back, and their bodies held with absolute steadiness. Aalwyn moved her head from side to side. The scent of prey had come from this way.

The nyala stood frozen, its heart beating no harder than usual.

The wolves crept over the short grasses into a stand of Tamboti trees, and the nyala resumed ripping leaves from the short brush.

There was no more sound until the wind shifted to carry the scent of nyala to the wolves, and then their twittering reached its ears.

Blackthorn bore down suddenly from one side, Aalwyn from the other, with Essenhout, Duinemirt, and Vaalgras circling. The nyala barely cleared the edge of the grove before Essenhout had its snout, immobilizing the curved horns, while Aalwyn dragged its haunches to the ground. Blackthorn tore free the bowels, and the sheer volume of blood-loss instantly arrested the nyala's heart. Koorsboom dove into the opened belly as Aalwyn uttered a deep growl to the others. Vaalgras and Duinemirt kept their distance until the rest had fed.

***

"This will do." Blackthorn strained under the weight of the nyala hip in his jaws. It was not far to drag the body beneath the canopy of berry trees. "There may not be a great deal of meat left on this oke, but we will reduce it to bone before hunting another."

"Our opportunities have been so rare," Essenhout agreed. "I would not mind digesting bone."

"Can we do that?" Koorsboom paused.

Vaalgras laughed and boxed him, knocking him over. Koorsboom rolled upright, but Aalwyn blocked him from returning the blow in play. Under her withering glare, Vaalgras sank into subservient pose with his ears down, eventually lying on the ground and rolling onto his back. When he attempted to lick her muzzle, she snarled.

"That was hardly necessary, love." Blackthorn rumbled as she joined him. "No harm was intended."

"It was my weakness and distraction that allowed them to stray." She scratched behind an ear. "The command is mine to wield, and none are to forget that ever again." She lapped his muzzle and rubbed her cheek along the side of his greyed head. "Not even you."

Blackthorn flinched as she nipped his torn ear and moved away to lie down next to Koorsboom in the deep shade.

"Her anger is volatile," Essenhout murmured into Blackthorn's bleeding ear. "She does not forgive us for leaving."

"She is our alpha." Blackthorn response was louder than necessary. "What you see is not anger but resolve."

***

The next tendril of smoke was closer, a wispy finger scraping the sky. The polished bones of the nyala had been left far behind, and a scrub hare and visibly-ill red-crested bustard were all that Koorsboom had eaten for days. The forest became more sparse and the sun more powerful.

"Koorsboom." Aalwyn crested a low ridge over vast open area with odd stands of Tamboti wood and isolated acacia trees.

Koorsboom appeared at her side.

"Do you see any signs of prey?"

They patiently scanned the plains for motion, before Aalwyn gave a grunt and descended the ridge. She altered course to the northeast with the finger of ash rising into the dead air ahead.

Chapter 37

"We have not seen damage like this since the river." Essenhout
sniffed a young leadwood tree partially toppled to expose a
byzantine maze of roots and dirt clumps. Its trunk was broken
through, exposing the dark brown hardwood, with its canopy a ruin
of partly-eaten branches. A broad swath of the trees had been razed,
their crowns ripped down and denuded of leaves.
"Might have known that we would see elephants in such dry
conditions. Few animals do well here outside of the wet season."
"I thought this *was* the wet season," Vaalgras grumbled.
"It was a herd of decent size." Blackthorn put his muzzle to the
ground, where impressions like platters showed in the dirt along the
line of cracked trees. "They moved in this direction. Aalwyn, I
suggest we follow."
The trail threaded through Tamboti trees with dense crowns that
burst into sprays of violet flowers overhead.
"The earth is wet." Essenhout hesitated and received a splat from the
branches above.
"The rain tree." Blackthorn passed her. "It bleeds water from beetles
eating into the bark. Stay if you wish to be soaked."
Essenhout gave her coat a vigorous shake.
The slope gave way to a shallow valley where massive grey shapes
moved slowly. A large bull elephant held his trunk upright in a
vertical S, nostrils forward toward high, grey-barked trees with
broad green crowns, the spectacular yellow flowers fallen away
around bulbous oval fruits. The tip of the bull's trunk grasped an
unripe wild mango and released it, then drifted to where the ground
was littered with ripe golden fruit. He trumpeted sharply and feinted
at a gang of vervet monkeys, who scattered out of range. He took a

golden mango delicately with the tip of his trunk and lifted it to his mouth, chewing the pulp and swallowing the stone whole. He gave a long, low groan, and the other elephants joined him in a thrum of pleasure.

"*Ag.*" Blackthorn turned to Aalwyn. "I was hoping that they were headed to a waterhole with antelope."

Each great footstep fell muted, the massive feet bulging on contact as an internal cushion splayed to take the weight.

"Are elephants the same everywhere?" Essenhout moved closer to a female elephant with her ears erect and muscles tensed.

"Do you abandon caution, sister?"

"One cannot but admire these creatures. How can such size be brought to bear so quickly and quietly? A marvel." Essenhout paused. "This one is blinded in one eye—and there are holes above her shoulder—"

The elephant flapped an ear and turned her head, catching sight of the wolf with her one good eye. She charged abruptly with a sharp trumpet, and a bull ran to her side.

Essenhout backpedaled and turned to sprint away while the elephants gave chase. When she vanished into the trees, the elephants slowed and returned to foraging with a wary eye on the wolves.

Essenhout doubled back.

"That one lives in a tempestuous mood." Blackthorn smiled faintly.

"She is healing from an attack. When the human thunder comes, it leaves strange circle-bites in its victims. Elephants can survive them —sometimes."

"They are not in the mood for play."

The elephant matriarch grunted with annoyance and resumed her walk toward the finger of smoke.

"I am so hungry." Koorsboom sidled up to Aalwyn, whining gently.

"We all are, my son. Our hunger may abate soon."

***

The massive central seed of the mango lay on the forest floor, gnawed bare by a vervet monkey.

"Nothing about." Koorsboom sniffed the remains of mango pulp, recoiling at the sharp, acidic scent. "Who would eat this?"

"They likely feel the same about impala organs." Duinemirt looked up into the forest canopy where small black eyes peered down from the branches.

"Come now, before the elephants return," Aalwyn bayed.

In the cool shade of the trees, the *Dwalen* became aware of movement far away, then closer, with a rustle of leaves. The dappled edge of forest poured sunlight onto the wolves, revealing great moving grey shapes between the tree trunks.

A bull elephant eyed Essenhout through branches, a wet patch across his temple and fluid trickling from a pore.

"Aalwyn, that one is in *musth*." Essenhout eyed the elephants nervously as they made their way through the forest on either side of the pack.

"That one is a randy oke. *Musth* renders them aggressive in their breeding season." Blackthorn trotted next to Aalwyn. "I advise a wide berth."

"Have you advised your pup?" Vaalgras snorted, shaking his head as Koorsboom scampered through the trees toward the elephants with his head up and ears alert.

"Bloody hell—" Blackthorn broke into a sprint, stumbled in a warthog hole, and righted himself.

Aalwyn rocketed after Koorsboom just as an engine revved and echoed in the distance. The bull elephant blurted a blast of trumpet while the females jostled together, calves knocked aside and shuffled behind, and the scent of tension rose in the air. Koorsboom slowed to stand on his hind legs.

"Return, Koorsboom!" Aalwyn's twittering was agitated. "Come back!"

"Essenhout plays with the *eles*," Koorsboom ran to her. "I thought it was fun."

"Imbecile—"

The elephants drew in a close semicircle around the wolves with an ear-shattering noise of trumpets.

"*Run!*" Aalwyn jumped forward.

Koorsboom dashed after the *Dwalen* past the massive grey bull, who thundered forward with his ears flapping and trunk elevated. The bull dropped his trunk and whipped it at Koorsboom's hindquarters with a sharp trumpet, and struck a glancing blow. Koorsboom spun around and fell mewling into a heap. Aalwyn gave a high staccato call and dove at the bull elephant's foot. The bull chased her backward away from the others.

"On your feet," Blackthorn hissed to the pup.

Koorsboom leaped up and ran with Blackthorn, while Aalwyn darted between the elephants, narrowly avoiding a swinging trunk and nearly crushed underfoot.

"Make haste!" Aalwyn shot to the waiting *Dwalen*, followed closely by the thundering elephant herd. The wolves sped faster and faster with the bull crashing through the trees just behind them, until Aalwyn gave a burst of panicked speed, the others leaped with her, and they left the furious grey herd in a billowing cloud of dust.

"What was that all about?" Duinemirt twittered.

"We must avoid the titans." Blackthorn rounded the pack and glanced toward smoke rising in the distance. "Something is afoot."

"Elephants live very long—far longer than we." Aalwyn peered anxiously into the brush. "The traumas accumulate over time."

"It was the engine," Blackthorn grunted, boxing the sheepish Koorsboom. "Those *eles* have suffered violence at the hands of humans." He lapped Aalwyn's muzzle. "Are you certain we should be seeking them?"

"Nothing is certain." Aalwyn nodded. "Not this or anything."

Chapter 38

Essenhout came upon Aalwyn standing in a clearing under a fever tree and padded closer. Aalwyn stood over a bizarre shape: head missing, shoulder muscles chopped off at the powerful forelegs, and body stripped of skin down to the hind legs. A black cloud of flies hung over the corpse, maggots and beetles crawling in the rotting meat.

"What is — was that?"

"I suspect it was a leopard." Aalwyn waited a long time. "There are no bite wounds. I have never seen a leopard alive, so I cannot be sure."

"I thought their nature kept them out of reach of humans." Essenhout flared her nostrils at the powerful miasma of decay.

"I imagine it thought the same." Aalwyn muttered.

A breeze picked up with a hint of water, scattering the flies and clearing for the moment the scent of rotting flesh.

"There is a pond not far from here." Essenhout's nostrils flared, her tongue tasting the moisture. "Brackish. Reminds me of the marsh where we were born, so long ago. Do you recall?"

"Every stone, every tree." Aalwyn nodded. Memories of the Savuti marsh of Botswana bloomed forth in her mind.

"Impala seemed to be everywhere." Essenhout took a deep breath. "Springbok pronking like mad. Every day we ate well despite our numbers. As a pup, I believed the world was ours to command. When we joined the coursing, I did not understand why some were called off without comment."

Overhead, a crowned eagle called, *kewee—kewee—kewee*, its black and white underwings striking against the sunlight.

"Then we moved from the den, and I began to understand why our mother was so cautious."

"Before the lions came for us?" Aalwyn's voice was hollow.

"When we moved to marginal land with fewer prey, I thought we sought the challenge. Our lives became harsher, our kills more sporadic. Even after our siblings died, we did not return to the rich hunting grounds."

"It was necessary." Aalwyn sighed. "Even the deaths of the pups."

"Our mother spoke to me." Essenhout paused. "Just before the time when you and Duinemirt and I would venture out on our own." Essenhout nudged Aalwyn. "She said that you would be alpha, not I."

"Why?"

"It was not cunning, daring, or strength that favored you, Aalwyn. It is that you shoulder the burden of choice without hesitation. Right or wrong, you always move forward."

The crowned eagle passed overhead, *kwee—kwee—kwee*.

"We all make our choices on the veld." Essenhout sat down and licked Aalwyn's muzzle. "Merely surviving one season to the next is a triumph."

"East was my choice." Aalwyn turned to the skinned body of the leopard. "Such as it was."

"It is the best choice. However this turns out—even to our ruin, my sister—you are a magnificent alpha."

When a vulture appeared in the sky, Aalwyn turned back to the corpse of the leopard, where flesh-eating beetles scissored the meat and connective tissue from bone. She found herself wondering what possible use could exist for a severed head.

Chapter 39

The acrid smell of smoke grew stronger. Aalwyn growled in a low voice to Koorsboom to hide in the thick *Combretum* brush and nodded to Essenhout, who loped ahead past the stand of rain trees into the clearing.

The humans rested with cans in their hands and cigarettes burning. One leaned over a freshly-killed springbok, using long, smooth strokes of a hunting knife to strip the loose hide from the carcass.

"Use the freezer in the *bakkie*," one human called out, gesturing to the jeep parked near the trees.

The butcher nodded as he wiped his bloody knife on his leg.

Essenhout trotted past with her eyes on the men.

"What's that?" One stood.

"Dog of some sort. I haven't seen that kind before." The hunter lifted his phone and pointed it at Essenhout to click a photograph. "Give the nice dog some meat."

The butcher skinning the springbok hacked sharply through the knee joint of a foreleg and slung it to Essenhout. She froze. No one moved while she sniffed the foreleg, glanced around, and took the leg in her jaws to dash away.

"Strange, that—" The hunter tapped his can with a finger and took another swig before tossing the can into the fire. "It didn't catch the leg in midair and didn't snatch it straight away." He drew deeply on his cigarette and tossed that into the fire as well. "Maybe they're not dogs."

***

"They *what?*" Blackthorn was pacing frantically. "Watch her closely —it may have been poisoned."

"She seems well enough." Aalwyn sniffed Essenhout as she worried the foreleg free of hide and chewed the underlying meat.

Duinemirt scuttled off through the trees with Vaalgras fast on her heels. Within minutes they returned with springbok legs and fell to stripping them of meat.

"Do not allow Koorsboom to eat it, love. I beg of you—"

"We have no choice," Aalwyn sniffed at Blackthorn. "I will not watch him starve." She loped off toward the scent of smoke.

As soon as she entered the clearing, their voices came to her, a murmuring oddly like the voices of wildebeest. There was no anger. One of them laughed with his head back, large and throaty, when he saw her.

"There's a whole pack of them!"

"Last time." The hunter held up his phone and took her photo, the swirls of black, white, and gold of her fur striking.

The butcher tossed her a section of shoulder, which she took quickly into her fangs as she sprinted away.

Behind her, the hunter spoke into his phone, nodded, and tapped more.

"No more feeding the dogs. They are not dogs."

An awkward quiet fell over the camp, no sound but the crackle of the wood in the fire.

***

"There is something amiss." Blackthorn shook his head each time the meat was offered. "The enmity of these creatures does not square with their actions."

"You are incapable of peace, old wolf." Essenhout rested with her head on her forepaws. "My stomach is full for the first time in weeks. Perhaps we can wheedle more meat come the morrow."

"One can hope—" Aalwyn licked Koorsboom's muzzle as he wheezed with satiation.

"Something vexes you—beyond what you have seen of humans in the past." Koorsboom's large eyes looked up at Blackthorn.

"It is not to their advantage to feed us." Blackthorn glowered at him. "Be ready to run on a moment's notice." His livid obsidian eyes softened. "Always be suspicious of comfort, young one."

"We have reason to be content, love." Aalwyn ripped the last shred of meat from the shoulder. "See how Koorsboom's sides bulge."

"I would that you had not fed him of it, Aalwyn."

"Find joy, love. We may yet survive, with these hunters about. Perhaps they will guide us to a herd." Aalwyn cast a pleased eye his way. "Will you join me in the shade of the yellow-flower trees?"

Blackthorn groaned with desire and followed her from the clearing. They touched noses in the shadows, the sunset blazing through the dense foliage.

"My mate," Aalwyn murmured, licking his muzzle and rubbing her cheek on his greyed fur.

"My love."

She turned, he met her, and they mated, while their whining faded gradually into the sounds of the night.

Chapter 40

Blackthorn licked from his chops the blood of the dead hare on the burnt grasses, its body broken, spine shattered, and skin ripped apart. In his mind, he traced the long path from his home mountain range in Zambia far to the north, where he had first seen his own face reflected in an icy tarn. There had been the long journey through the Bangweulu swamp and over savanna to the Chobe River, and now he had traveled for many hundreds of kilometers with the *Dwalen* across Botswana to the Limpopo Park deep in Zimbabwe. His bones ached, and his chest heaved.

A tiny movement on a blade of dried grass revealed a grass mantid with its long, cylindrical head blackened by melanin released after the recent brush fire. The pigment allowed it to blend in with the surrounding burned vegetation. Its forelegs were folded in ambush, each a pincer opened and ready.

"Today we find another source of prey." Turning to Koorsboom, Blackthorn spoke in his familiar rumble. "These humans may be hunters, though none possess our cunning. We yield that cunning at our peril."

"Do you mean the tactics of hunting can be forgotten?" Koorsboom twittered.

"Forgotten or disregarded. The ideas we cherish the most can be so easily misplaced. That wisdom was bought with pain and misery." Blackthorn showed his fangs. "The only currency for those who survive." He raised his muzzle and sniffed. "Our human friends have gone. The scent of ash upon the wind has faded."

Blackthorn stepped with care into the humans' abandoned camp. The air was still with a tiny wisp of smoke still rising from the neglected fire and the coals dark red, the glow almost invisible. The skeleton of the springbok lay blackened by the fire, and Koorsboom awaited Blackthorn's nod before gnawing flesh from the carcass. The *bakkie* was gone, leaving tire ruts through a scattering of smoldering cigarette ends.

"We follow the tracks." Aalwyn's voice came from behind.

"The humans will lead us to more food, perhaps even kill it for us." Koorsboom looked up chewing. "This springbok tastes entirely of smoke." He swallowed and tore another bite.

Blackthorn examined the tire ruts that extended into the veld to disappear around a Tamboti tree. Duinemirt ambled about the camp as they looked for scraps.

Vaalgras strode up to the springbok carcass, shouldering Koorsboom out of the way. He pulled the body and the stake that skewered it off the makeshift spit and onto the ground.

Aalwyn was upon him in a flash, pushing him aside. She snarled with ears back and fangs bared.

"Who is this?" Vaalgras bayed to Duinemirt. "An enemy now?"

"An enemy indeed if you and your mate do not keep your distance." Aalwyn parted her jaws.

Vaalgras bowed his head with reluctance, and he wandered off with Duinemirt.

"It is only a matter of time before they leave." Essenhout was at Aalwyn's side, calming her sister.

"They have been inseparable since we isolated them." Aalwyn shook her head.

"An unavoidable necessity." Essenhout sighed. "Perhaps they would have left regardless."

***

The ruts through the soil and sand faded and returned, as the ground became softer and harder over the course of the long trail.

"Never do these tracks terminate on the black roads that carry the machines," Essenhout mused. "Why would they not make for the nearest way to be with their own kind?"

"This track smells of smoke and tire. We are getting closer." Aalwyn loped more quickly, Essenhout and Koorsboom behind her and Blackthorn running alongside.

The ruts led across open plains dotted with acacia and rain tree, then entered closer forest of Tamboti and *Combretum*. The tracks shifted sharply through an area of broken and toppled trees, smaller trees still rooted with their heartwood exposed in sharp daggers toward the sky. The sun streamed intermittently down upon scattered leafless branches, and the purr of a Cape turtledove called with rolling ease, *kuk coorr-kuk, kuk coorr-kuk*, its grey shape in a giraffe thorn acacia reflecting the dull sky and clouds.

With abrupt violence, the air was split by a deafening buzz. The wolves jolted and ducked, as every bird in the trees took flight. An elephant trumpet was cut short, and more rips tore through the air, followed by explosions. Koorsboom dashed away, and Aalwyn saw with horror that he was running toward the blasts, toward more smaller trumpets and a sudden burst of gunfire.

High whining echoed directly over the wolves as a powerful wind pushed down through the treetops, seesawing leaves from the branches. A gigantic machine appeared and hovered above. It lurched off, taking its windstorm, but the gunfire returned with loud, staccato eruptions in rapid succession and cracks from above, and the rocks scattered the noise into the woods and hills. Aalwyn leapt after Koorsboom, and found him concealed under an acacia.

"Hide yourself, fool!" she hissed, beside herself with terror and rage.

"No, Mother." Koorsboom rounded on her. "We watch and remember—"

The gunfire stopped, its residual echoes shaking the forest. A new, smaller engine gunned to life with a high wheezing buzz and roared down an octave. Koorsboom left the treeline and crawled on his belly to the edge of a ridge, raising his head cautiously. Aalwyn crawled to his side, and her jaw fell open.

Humans were all over the clearing among great, bloody bodies of wrinkled grey. One man straddled the giant head of a bull elephant on the ground, steadying a tusk while another held a roaring machine to bite into the root of the ivory at the elephant's lip and chew through horn and skull. With a quick, high buzz the machine broke free, spattering blood over the humans and dead elephant. Another man secured a metal contraption under the skull of the bull elephant and, working a lever, raised the head off the ground to allow the machine to chew through the other tusk. Nearby, a hunter chopped at the tusk of a female with an axe.

Aalwyn glanced at Koorsboom with her eyes wide with shock. Koorsboom stared in silence as his tongue flicked out, tasting the hint of ash with rust and cinnamon in the air.

A massive hole smoked in the side of the bull elephant, the flesh cooked by the grenade. Two more bulls, ten females, and three calves lay around him, and a small calf shuddered in the crimson waterhole, unable to raise its trunk to take a breath—its body shaking one last time before falling still.

The deafening machine overhead returned with its massive downdraft and lowered to blow up a whirlwind of dust and stir the water into red waves lapping the shores. The humans shouted and waved as they struggled to carry the bloody tusks to the rear of the *bakkie* and toss them with mighty heaves onto the flatbed.

A human stepped from the helicopter as he screwed a broad-brimmed hat onto his head. Crisp khaki safari clothing covered his form, devoid of stain or blemish. He shouted in Portugese, and each man immediately responded. He waved two hunters toward the helicopter, and they ran across the clearing to where he handed them a knife drawn from his hip opposite a holster gleaming with chrome. They drew fabric over their faces and hands and dragged out of the helicopter three large bags, which they heaved to the water's edge and sliced open, letting loose white puffs of powder. They dumped some of the white powder into the water, the rest onto the ground, one bag after another, until the bags were empty. They threw the knife down onto the red dirt and shoveled the white powder carefully over the elephant carcasses, taking care to fill the wounds. The man in the safari hat pointed to the sky and shouted, and the men hustled more quickly, covered in the sweat of heat and fear. Their dark skin collected a light layer of dust, though they took great care not to touch the white powder.

A lappet-faced vulture landed on an elephant carcass, wings parted and head bobbing as it hopped to the cavernous hole in the side. It tore out a bite of flesh, swallowed, and fell over, muscles spasming and chest heaving, and became still. More vultures gathered in the sky above.

The men left their metal implements lying about the clearing among cigarette butts and spent shells as they climbed into the *bakkie*. The helicopter roared deafeningly, and the man in khaki paused at the door to take off his safari hat and wipe his forehead. He glanced around and nodded.

The helicopter scattered gravel and feathers as it lifted off, canted forward, and roared over the tops of the trees. The *bakkie* choked to life and bounced into the bush, digging a fresh pair of ruts. One vulture after another fed and collapsed, until drab brown feathers covered the waterhole. The sky above cleared, removing their timeless African signal of death. The elephant bodies lay as grey as rocks, and the distant mooing of hyena carried through the still air. Wordlessly, Aalwyn rose and left the ridge with Koorsboom at her heels as feathers fluttered all around.

Chapter 41

Dusk surrounded them in the stifling air, and the wolves panted rapidly as they ran.

The steady machine-rattle came behind them, at times closer, others further away. Each time the roar of the *bakkie* reached a crescendo, they heard the humans shouting with excitement.

"Into the brush!" Blackthorn twittered.

Thorns scraped and tore as they crashed through.

"Is there more than one, Aalwyn?"

"Just the big one behind us."

"I will not hold you back," Koorsboom twittered breathlessly.

Aalwyn glanced at Blackthorn and dropped back to run behind Koorsboom, urging him along. The wolves sprinted faster, but the machine was inexhaustible.

Duinemirt ran awkwardly, her increasing girth slowing her. She encouraged Vaalgras, who stumbled as often as not, barely keeping the *Dwalen* in sight. He no longer grumbled, but now only responded to her with snarls. The wolves spread out as they raced toward a steep hillside.

"They cannot follow us there!"

An abrupt yelp broke out behind them, followed by an agonized whine.

Aalwyn stopped dead and whirled around.

"*Keep running!*" Blackthorn howled as he flashed past.

Aalwyn ran back the way she had come, only halting when the headlights bore down upon her. Blackthorn reached her to find her prodding Koorsboom's writhing body, his eyes wide with panic as he lay shuddering on his side with his legs waving uselessly.

"Koorsboom!"

The powerful headlights flooded over them, their bodies casting sharp dark shadows in shards.

"Why can you not speak?"

"Hurt—no, not hurt. He is immobilized—snare—*snare!*" Blackthorn closed his jaws with a loud click and pulled, jostling Koorsboom's body. "Wire—" Blackthorn whipped his head back and forth as he growled, yanking Koorsboom with the wire. "Cannot—" The wire slipped between his teeth, bending but not parting.

A metal bang rang out, followed by another. The humans strode toward the wolves, pointing and mumbling, one carrying a sack.

"Are you sure about this?" The lead human pulled on thick gloves. "Do you know what these things can do?"

"Mister Pereira wants one." He shrugged with resignation. "He is waiting for it and the ivory across the border."

Aalwyn stood over Koorsboom snarling with her fangs bared.

"We must flee." Blackthorn nudged her. "If we stay we cannot help him."

Vaalgras and Duinemirt caught up to them and, confused by the humans, circled in a frenzy.

"What is this *kak*? Leave the dead pup behind!" He sprinted away from the *bakkie* toward the brush, and was jerked to an abrupt standstill not far from Koorsboom. His hind leg hung suspended in midair and pointed awkwardly toward a tree.

"We run now, or die here with Koorsboom." Blackthorn bit sharply but shallowly into Aalwyn's neck just enough to break her focus. His eyes bored into her. "We must do this."

Aalwyn gave a helpless whine, Blackthorn bayed his hoo-calls, and they ran through the grass with Essenhout. As they departed, Duinemirt glanced at Vaalgras one last time before joining her sister. Vaalgras struggled wildly to right himself on three paws, the fourth held tightly in a wire secured to a tree. He watched the humans surround Koorsboom. One produced a tool from his pocket and knelt next to the prone wolf. He worked the tool into the fur of his neck, and after a loud click Koorsboom inhaled in a frothy rattle. Eyes opened wide, he was pushed into the sack and slung over the back of a human, while Vaalgras's eyes darted from one shadowy figure to the next. He clawed deep furrows in the dirt, baffled among shapes and sounds, lost in a cloud of fear.

One of the humans pointed and muttered. He walked toward Vaalgras with his hands out and arms extended, the glare of the *bakkie* headlights obscured. As the fingers moved toward his shoulders, Vaalgras lashed out with his teeth.

The human danced screaming in a circle. He gestured to Vaalgras with one hand clasping the other as red oozed between his palms.

The other human unslung a strap from his shoulder and steadied the wood and metal weapon. A finger slipped into the trigger guard as he brought the butt to his shoulder.

Vaalgras looked from one face to another, writhing helplessly—until suddenly time ceased.

Part Three:
Mozambique

I do not remember my pups.

Chapter 42

"How can you be sure?" Essenhout loped breathlessly after days of running.
"The vehicles, the smoke—and every now and then, a hint of fear pouring off my son." Aalwyn never broke stride despite their pace through the burnt grasses.
Blackthorn by her side had not spoken for two days.
"The smell of dead animal becomes stronger." Essenhout glanced at Duinemirt, who whined at a polite distance. Duinemirt had become plump in the past several days, her appetite ravenous, her drool persistent. She appeared weak and unsure of her footing, but not confused or delirious. She had begun to moan with each step, her abdomen aching steadily.
A small ginger-green bird called from a bare acacia branch with a muffled *hoo—hook, hoo—hook*. The rotund mosque swallow flapped laboriously to swoop just above the burnt grasses and pick off a grasshopper.
Blackthorn's joints ached as he kept pace with Aalwyn, their world reduced to tire ruts in the dust and a fading scent, as they crossed the frontier from Zimbabwe into Mozambique.

***

"Easy. It is still dangerous." Thick gloves reached into the canvas sack, where Koorsboom breathed shallowly as hands steadied the neck of the bag.
"I have it." A chain was fastened around Koorsboom's neck, steel links with a small padlock. "Let it go."

The humans backed away from the rear of the *bakkie* with hands out. Koorsboom lay inert. Eventually he shifted and gave a cautious sniff. He worked his head out of the canvas sack and gaped at the humans. His wide hazel eyes stared around from the Tamboti forest to the *bakkie* in which he lay, and he recoiled at the overwhelming smell of decay from the tusks under the tarp. Flies gathered along the edge of the tarp and crawled on the congealed blood and tissue that remained at the roots of each tusk.

Koorsboom leapt from the tailgate onto the dusty red ground. He hesitated and lurched suddenly forward—choked in midair by the length of chain padlocked to the *bakkie*. Dazed, he jumped back onto his feet and sprang toward a gap between the humans— again choked when he reached the end of the chain. He fell breathlessly and stood again, shaking his head to feel the weight of the chain on his ruff. Slowly he padded away from the *bakkie* until he sensed the restraint. He traced a rough semicircle from the *bakkie*, nosing the links.

"This dog is no fool. Pereira should pay well for this one."

"What will he do with it?"

"Sell it to his buyer from Vietnam, same one who takes the tusks. Maybe the bones and organs will be sold for parties."

"Parties?"

"Of all the animals we take, the ivory and other parts of rare animals are eaten either as medicine or at parties. They believe that it makes you strong."

"Does it?"

"Mister Pereira gets so much money for it—" The human watched Koorsboom pace at the end of the chain. "—it must."

Chapter 43

Even in the middle of wilderness, the Land Rover appeared clean. The windshield had only a slight dusting with no dead bugs trapped in the wipers, and the gleam of yellow paint shone in the sun.

"Do you think he washes it every day?" One of the hunters whispered to another as the vehicle ground to a halt.

"The tusks, are they ready?" The man was out of the yellow Rover and striding toward the hunters, dressed in new jeans, a crisp dress shirt, and safari hat. His Portuguese was clipped, unlike the awkward speech of the Zimbabwean poachers, who primarily spoke Shona.

"Three bulls, the rest females."

"I do not want female tusks!"

"And a dog."

"Adult dog?"

"A pup."

"Better!" The shining black man handed over a wad of *rand*, which the hunter pocketed without negotiations.

The hunter unhooked Koorsboom's chain from the rear of the *bakkie* and held it out to Pereira, who glared until the hunter took the chain to the back of the Rover and pulled Koorsboom into it. Koorsboom whined and resisted. The hunter gave a sharp jerk and tossed a scrap of meat into the back to make him jump.

"Do not throw garbage in my Rover!"

The hunter pretended to retrieve it and closed the rear gate as Koorsboom swallowed the meat.

"What is funny to you?"

"Nothing, *baas*." The hunter bit the insides of his mouth.

"Two weeks, more ivory—more bulls this time!" Pereira tapped his phone, his dress shirt crackling as he moved. He slammed the door of the Rover and pulled away at high speed, making Koorsboom slide and smack against the rear window.

"Do you have any idea what that dog is about to do to that beautiful Land Rover?" The hunter giggled.

***

The *Dwalen* sniffed the ground in the moonlight.

"Here—here!" Essenhout twittered and stood back to box Aalwyn despite herself.

Aalwyn bounded along the dirt road in ruts leading into the brush after the *bakkie*.

"He was here." Blackthorn sprinted around the encampment, the fire now dead and cold and the acrid smell of burning mingled with beer dumped onto the flames. "This is where the smell ends."

Duinemirt trotted into camp, still obediently apart. Her belly hung low, and she had difficulty keeping up.

"Spread out," Aalwyn bayed. "The wind and land will advise us." She loped off with her nose in the air.

"We have not long to find him." Blackthorn looked up to where rain clouds began to obscure the moon.

"Faint scent here!" Aalwyn twittered loudly from a glen of mahogany trees.

The wolves ran along a dirt road patchy with loose sand and overgrown with weeds. Some were flattened but still green, likely by tires. The inauspicious grey trees stood high over them, while ground squirrels and a vervet monkey browsed in the squat bushes.

A sharp buzz erupted, startling in the wilderness, and became sustained before intensifying.

The wolves rounded a curve and found two humans grappling with a small machine biting into a mahogany trunk and spitting out red dust. The machine looked similar to that used on the elephants to remove their tusks. The mighty, vaulted tree cracked, the leaves of the crown rustling and dropping off, until the heavy trunk fell with a tremendous crash. The buzz resumed as the humans lopped off and discarded the branches and began sectioning the trunk. They glanced around them as they worked, visibly nervous as they loaded their stolen cargo.

"It is not them," Aalwyn murmured. "We must give them distance." The *Dwalen* followed her up the road and through a clear-cut suddenly flooded with moonlight, awash in sawdust, ruined branches, and emptied beer bottles.

"This fills me with unease," Essenhout muttered to Aalwyn.

"There is a *vrot* here, a corruption at work. The elephants were ill-tempered—" Aalwyn shook her head. "—and apparently with good reason. If we find my son—"

"We will find your son." Essenhout nodded.

Chapter 44

Pereira stalked back and forth with his phone to his ear.

"I will be waiting!" His shouts carried across the veld, disturbing the birds.

He punched the screen so hard that he cracked the glass. He stormed back to the Land Rover, opened the door, and slammed it on the stench of wolf stool, urine, and vomit.

"You filthy bugger." His hand went to the massive chrome-plated pistol on his hip.

Koorsboom sat in the back of the Rover with his ears up and eyes open in fear.

Clouds obscured the moon as the smell of rain rose from the earth. A drop splatted on Pereira's dress shirt, and he looked wildly around for shelter. He ran for the umbrella of an acacia tree while rain began to fall in sheets, water running in rivulets along the branches. He covered his chrome-plated pistol with both hands and glared at Koorsboom watching through the window of the Rover.

From far away came a machine-like hum that rose above the incessant patter of raindrops onto the roof of the Rover. Pereira stood with one hand cupped over the hammer of the pistol and the other on the handle, his finger curling about the curved steel. A pair of headlights swam into view, wandered, and shuddered to stop against a large rock. The headlights backed up and lurched forward toward the yellow Rover.

The rain stopped as though a tap had been closed, and the roar of the storm left a ringing in Koorsboom's ears, with the relentless patter of drops falling and the renewed call of insects. He rubbed his nose on the window as he looked out, leaving a line of snot.

A human climbed out of a muddy white van as the engine thrummed to a halt, and a passenger in dirty clothing hopped out the other side. The driver peered into the Rover and leapt back with an exclamation.

"Orlando, you took too long." Pereira relaxed his grip on the gun.

"What happened to your Rover? Did you hit a warthog hole again?"

"I am in no mood," Pereira snarled. "Give me the keys."

"Enough of that." The driver fished a keyring out of his pocket with a jangle. "I still need my Caravan."

"It will take a year to scrub the shit out of this." Pereira looked at the other man. "Is he one of yours?"

"My mechanic will take your Rover and clean it." Orlando glanced at Koorsboom. "Do you collect live animals now?"

"Maybe." Pereira glared.

"You plan to sell that thing? Are you afraid of it?"

"I cannot stand the smell."

"The smell of money," Orlando said, teeth gleaming. "But you have seen my lion ranch—a hundred lions on a quarter-hectare, no problem. Wild dogs would die in such a tiny place."

"I could farm them. Show them off to clients. Tourists would watch them kill."

"Let us talk in Mavue in the next couple of days. Drop me at the petrol station on the tar road." Orlando handed over the keys to his Caravan. "You have the beer?" He got into the passenger side.

"Have it cleaned by tomorrow." Pereira threw his Rover keys to the mechanic.

"Yes, *baas*." The mechanic nodded with his head low and hands together.

The engine of the Caravan engaged and tires spun, mud spewing in arcs, as Pereira disappeared into the night.

The mechanic opened the door of the Land Rover and squinted.

"*Yoh!* We need to air you out, my friend." He opened the rest of the doors and the rear gate. "No need to worry." He pulled one end of the chain to make certain that it was fastened to the frame with a padlock. "Yet." He walked away from the Rover.

Koorsboom leapt from the rear gate to the muddy ground and took two long jumps before the chain choked him. Dazed, he got up again on all four paws and shook his head. He took a few halting steps and nosed the chain before sitting down next to the Rover.

The mechanic laughed, striking a match with a rough thumbnail and touching the small flame to a cigarette in his mouth. Koorsboom watched the lit end with fascination.

The mechanic smoked as he cleaned the Rover, until he had a small pile of cigarette butts. He took the chain and tugged, and Koorsboom leaned back in fear. The mechanic tossed a hunk of *biltong* into the Rover, and Koorsboom leapt in after it with his eyes resigned.

The mechanic swung up the rear gate and secured it, turning to a pair of hazel eyes watching from the brush. The head ducked lower, but the large dish-like ears were unmistakable. The man made his way to the driver door and slid inside, nervously watching the sedge. He rolled down the windows, gunned the engine to life, and lit another cigarette as he trundled away over rough ground.

***

The *Dwalen* followed the Land Rover, sprinting forward when the dirt road opened onto level terrain and thumped the Rover over rocks and downed trees.

"We will eventually be forced to hunt," Essenhout murmured.

"We will wait as long as need be." Aalwyn's tone was flat.

"Take care, sister—" Essenhout rasped to her ear. "Duinemirt is staggering and appears weak despite her round shape."

Aalwyn's hazel eyes remained locked on the Rover as it rattled down the road ahead.

Nightfall on the veld brought a deafening racket, with the repetitive high-pitched blasts of cicadas, katydids crackling their three-note call, and firey-necked nightjars crying in plaintive whistles, *wip—wip —whrrhip!* over the subdued *kwow-wow* of freckled nightjars.

The rising whine of another engine joined the sounds of the night. A dirty white car wheezed along the road, tires rattling in the shallow ruts. The stunted grass that grew between the ruts scraped the underbody of the car as it followed the wolves distantly. Two eyes gleamed in the darkness in the driver seat, watching the pack intently as the white tips of their tails caught the moonlight. The headlights were off, as was the radio. His face was grim, asphalt-black skin twisted with malice.

The wolves loped endlessly with their swiveling ears searching constantly for any sound of Koorsboom through the warm night air. Aalwyn was prepared to run forever.

Chapter 45

In the morning, Duinemirt stumbled and fell. After a *thwump* to the grass with a wheeze of forced exhalation, she struggled back to her feet. Her eyes were unfocused, and she wavered gently as blood and mucus dripped from under her tail.

"Essenhout and I will continue the pursuit," Blackthorn twittered. "Aalwyn—"

Aalwyn nodded to Blackthorn, and the *Dwalen* divided.

Aalwyn led Duinemirt, now drooling, into the high grasses of a Tamboti wood grove. At the foot of a towering dark grey tree, Duinemirt slumped onto her side breathing heavily.

"Rest, now, sister. There is much work to be done."

"How far are we from the river?" Duinemirt blinked as her head wavered from side to side.

"You must push, my sister." Aalwyn spoke softly, peering under the base of Duinemirt's tail at the dilating muscles of her birth canal.

"He is dead! Vaalgras, my mate, is dead," Duinemirt moaned. "I cannot live without him—I cannot mother his pups—Aalwyn, I cannot—"

"Push."

A tiny, wet pup slid out, slick with pus laden fluid.

"Vaalgras—my Vaalgras—"

"Take the pup in your teeth—gently now—"

Duinemirt reached back and took hold of the little scruff, lifting the pup forward to lick it clean, open its airway, and prompt a weak cough. She lay on her side with her head on the ground, breathing heavily as the pup mewled. She stopped breathing for a moment, then vomited.

"Come now, sister. Your task has only begun," Aalwyn prompted her.

Again and again, Duinemirt labored to birth another and then another tiny, wet pup, lifting each by its little scruff to lick it clean. Her moaning intensified until, with a gasp, she passed the rest of what her womb contained. The placenta, black with decay, flowed out with the bodies of two stillborn pups. Eventually, she lay exhausted among four blind and helpless pups whining quietly as they mustered the energy to breathe.

Aalwyn gazed at the small, weak pups, and the powerful maternal instinct flooded her. She resisted the urge to nose and caress them. Eyes shut tightly, she gave a heavy exhale and trotted away through the Tamboti grove. A flash of brown leapt from brush to the grey bark of a tree, and Aalwyn pounced on the Cape ground squirrel. "Eat, my sister. Your need for this is most pressing." Aalwyn dropped the body of the squirrel by Duinemirt's gaping mouth. Duinemirt's chest heaved as the pups writhed where they lay. She opened her eyes, recognized food, and ripped a section off the carcass, swallowing small shreds of meat with considerable effort until she licked the bones clean. Her pups crawled and cried at her side, while she lay back with only occasional heaves to show that she was still alive.

Aalwyn stood vigil over Duinemirt with her watchful eyes on the bush. The wolves were hidden among the trees as the sun made its lazy arc overhead and descended into sunset. A black-backed jackal crept past as twilight fell, lifting its nose to the scent of the newborn pups.

***

The glow of morning sun filtered through the Tamboti wood grove with a placid orange light. A Cape turtledove perched on a branch above the wolves with its pale grey plumage and white underside stark against the charcoal bark. *Kuk-coor-uk.*

Aalwyn stared down at the lifeless pups, their little bodies stiffening in the stale morning air while Duinemirt slept on without moving.

Kuk-coorr-uk.

***

Noon heat was radiating down when Duinemirt finally stirred. Aalwyn had returned from an unsuccessful hunt only to find the pups gone.

"The river—have we left it?" Duinemirt opened her eyes crusted with secretions.

"Long behind. And when you are ready, we must go."

Duinemirt flopped down again and fell back asleep. The hours dragged by, while Aalwyn fought the growing desire to leave and find the rest of the *Dwalen*.

***

Aalwyn awoke with a start, her paws out and ready to attack. Duinemirt was roused and alert, seated and no longer wavering.

"Are you well, sister?" Aalwyn asked carefully.

"No—" Duinemirt's voice was broken, her twitter halting. "I had dreams in the darkness—something was after me in the brush but would not reveal itself. I was alone. Everything I knew was gone." She stared blankly.

"I must tell you this," Aalwyn spoke quietly. "It has been a long time since the lions took my mate Grootboom and so many of my young family."

Duinemirt whimpered and closed her eyes, sinking down to lay her nose on her forelegs.

"My young were everything to me while they lived. I brought them onto this veld, and I would have died to keep them here. But, Duinemirt, my sister—" Aalwyn paused. "I do not now remember my pups."

Duinemirt raised her head with her eyes still closed.

"Your pups died," Aalwyn said softly. "They were small and sick and too weak to survive." She paused, taking a deep breath while her sister whined softly. "Their memory will fade, as mine did. And so they must, as you prepare for the next litter." She paused, glancing through the trees to the sunrise. "I recall virtually every tree, stone, and hollow through a lifetime of conflict. And yet the most precious things washed away readily, as though reclaimed by the river." Duinemirt scrabbled back to her feet and crept through the Tamboti wood with a plaintive whine that echoed through the trees.

Aalwyn watched her for a moment and then turned away.

***

Aalwyn traced the faded path of urine markings that Blackthorn had left into a lowveld cut and grasslands. The strength of the scent grew quickly—it had been marked a second time. Blackthorn was waiting for them, somewhere in the savanna ahead.

She hurried back to Duinemirt, careful to conceal the lightness of her steps. Her muted voice did not travel far before Duinemirt appeared from a cluster of sweet thorn acacia trees, wavering as though she might fall over with her hazel eyes rising to Aalwyn's.

"The veld lies ahead, sister," Aalwyn twittered softly. "We shall meet it together."

As they loped away, the verdant green grass rustled in the wind in a high whisper that filled the air like ocean swells.

Chapter 46

Thatch and mud huts stand scattered on the western edge of Mozambique, small villages dotting the landscape between vast open areas of savanna and larger farmholdings of maize and beans along the river. The land is crisscrossed with dirt paths pounded to concrete by generations of feet, among Mopane trees grown for lumber and charcoal and ancient colonial churches standing abandoned with their ornamentation chipped and cracked, roofs caved in, and stone walls crawling with vegetation.

Mavue sits in a remote area on the edge of the Limpopo Transfrontier Park, a widely-spaced town of tradesmen, *spaza* shops, and small gardens. The homes are built of tree poles and boards covered in wire fencing, with small stones piled into the space between boards to create impenetrable rock barriers. Larger homes are constructed of plastered and painted breeze-block, with solid wood roofing and even satellite dishes, Land Rovers, *bakkies,* spare gasoline drums, and garages for storing guns and other armaments. Men in the dank garages clean rifles and hand-thread the barrels for silencers, their eyes always on passing vehicles. They wear new jeans and black slacks, clean buttoned shirts and gold chains. They do not walk—they swagger. Parties are thrown to celebrate their successful hunts, and *bakkies* carrying ivory tusks leave the village just as other *bakkies* arrive with beer and ox meat. Policemen came once to Mavue with warrants for arrest, and were bribed and threatened, and came no more. The poachers are loved and feared throughout the village for the river of money that flows from their pockets.

Now parked outside a pink house with faded curtains stood a yellow Land Rover with doors and windows open, a man scrubbing the interior. Nearby stood a brick *braai,* still black from the grilled meat of the night previous. Scattered beer bottles lay among plastic lawn furniture near a shed. A steel stake was driven into the ground by the shed, and chained to the stake stood a young painted wolf.

Chapter 47

Koorsboom was difficult to see from so far away. Blackthorn spotted him as he paced, stopped, and turned to disappear into the shade of the garage.

"Still present?" Essenhout studied the village from the rise.

"Still present. A human walked past where I presume he lies and threw something. I hope it was food."

"Will we free him come night?"

"Best to wait for Aalwyn." Blackthorn considered. "Should it go ill —she would want to be here."

Essenhout slumped on the rocks. Several humans sat in front of the *spaza* shop, others in front of their houses, while one staggered down the dirt road.

"That one is poisoned. Or infected with the Rage." Essenhout exhaled. "Do humans get the Rage?"

"Possibly." Blackthorn nodded. He glanced at Essenhout. "Your sister Duinemirt became sick, but I do not suspect the Rage."

"What then?"

He examined the ground before him. "Whatever is consuming her - it started in her womb. It happens in new mothers."

Essenhout shook her head and was silent for some time. "Still present?"

***

Aalwyn loped slowly and awkwardly, as behind her came stumbles and a crash into a bush branch. She paused to look back at Duinemirt struggling to her feet. Duinemirt's trot was sluggish but this was from exhaustion rather than disease. She was starving, as they all were, and had yet to recover her strength. Aalwyn was reassured. Her heart could not remain cold, and after each fall she lapped Duinemirt's muzzle and caressed her face.

"Time is with you, sister. As am I."

Duinemirt only hastened her steps for a moment before dropping back to her lethargic amble.

At nightfall, Aalwyn rested while Duinemirt snored loudly, snuffling mucus. A Pel's fishing owl gave a sharp wail like a jackal, and Duinemirt awakened with a start.

"We are safe." Aalwyn spoke quietly. "Be at ease in your sleep."

"I dreamt of the river." Duinemirt yawned widely. "Powerful and dark as it flowed through the trees past grassy banks. It held secrets beyond the crocodiles on its muddy bottom. We all swam in after a waterbuck, and the water swept us away. We washed up in a desert." She shook her head, throwing strings of saliva.

"The river for us was life." Aalwyn nodded. "And the ending of life."

"The dream frightened me."

"The river brought us the antelope dependent upon its waters."

"And it brought us to the lions." Duinemirt's tone was far away. "You and Grootboom seemed to have found the perfect home."

"Grootboom." Aalwyn felt a clawing in her chest. "I have not thought of him for some time. The sound of his call still echoes in my mind."

"Did you feel a failure when your pups died?"

"It is never far from the surface."

"Does it ever cease?"

"Never." Aalwyn gazed up at the moon. "Though I have allowed some of the memories to fade, I preserve that feeling." Her jaw clenched, the muscles rippling aside her head. "Perhaps, in some way, the pups to come shall benefit from that scar."

"I feel myself recovering from sickness, now that the birth is behind me. I so wish to have succumbed."

"Death will come for you in its own time, my sister. Until then, stoicism is our way."

The moon was enveloped in cloud, throwing them into darkness before revealing them again.

"I cannot be stoic." Duinemirt's head sagged. "Those pups—*my* pups—chasing through wood and over the grasses—theirs was the veld. But their veld is cruel and indifferent. My wound is a poisoned cactus thorn buried deep."

"Do not nurture your pain. It will blind and distract you. You owe this to the pack."

"To whom—to my pups?" Duinemirt's brow furrowed, her eyes glassy. "They are gone to jackal and vulture. Who else is there?"

"Your pups to come." Aalwyn approached. "Koorsboom, imprisoned and helpless. Your family, whose strength lies in amity." Aalwyn dipped her head beneath Duinemirt's to catch her eye. "There is no wolf. There is only the *Dwalen*. Only our fangs and claws united show the veld our quality." She turned to the moon. "Sleep, sister. We continue our *dwaal* at sunrise."

Chapter 48

Koorsboom crouched close to the ground with his eyes casting about for escape. His steel chain held, but instinct forced him low as he watched the human pace before him.

"I am investing in this myself!" Pereira shouted. "Bring the clients, and they will see his value." He listened. "No, he will not be moved —not yet! He is—" He glared at Koorsboom with a look of revulsion. "—difficult to transport. Yes, very good. Meet me here, and we will arrange transportation to Maputo." He grinned.

As Pereira pocketed his phone, a figure in stinking rags slumped against a tree at the edge of the garden. He saw the man's eyes, piercing, almost glowing in the darkness, his skin pitch-black. The gaze of the drifter returned to the ground. Pereira snatched up an empty bottle and threw it where the figure was reclining. The glass shattered upon the tree, but the figure had already vanished.

He peered into the dark, but lost interest as an engine whine reached his ears. He walked around to the front of his house as a blue Land Rover pulled up next to his soiled yellow vehicle. "Orlando!" Koorsboom withdrew as much as he could into grass, which afforded little cover.

***

"This night, we take him," Blackthorn rumbled. "I feel it. Do you?"
"I feel something." Essenhout paused. "I do not know what. The insects are muted, and the birds have fled."

No turtledove had called in the morning, nor fiery-necked nightjar at dusk.

"It is our only chance." Blackthorn kept his eyes on Koorsboom.

***

The village faded into darkness among small, flickering fires and the roar of the rare gasoline generator. Humans ambled the streets shouting at one another or at nobody. Gradually voices rose. A radio blared, a DJ nattered, guitar-picking began. Laughter burst out at the *spaza* shop.

Blackthorn and Essenhout crept to the edge of the village not far from the pink house with faded curtains.

"The clouds obscure the moon," Blackthorn chirped. "Still, it requires only one errant human to destroy us all."

"There is nothing for it." A voice came out of the night from behind his shoulder.

"Aalwyn, you could be a cat." Blackthorn jumped.

They lapped one another's muzzles, rubbing faces and lovingly tonguing each other's mouths.

"What of your sister?"

"Duinemirt was wracked by a sickness in her womb. She gave birth, and is somehow recovering. She is resting safely not far away." Blackthorn met her eye, and she shook her head.

"The pups are no more."

As the wolves padded down the dirt road into town, Aalwyn glared at the mud and thatch huts, wood structures, and eventually breeze-block houses. They were not widely spaced, and she felt constricted. "We will be seen." She shook her head balefully.

"Unless their attention is drawn elsewhere." Blackthorn nodded.

They threaded swiftly and silently past a mud hut. A light emanated from a doorway ahead, and a human emerged wrapped in purple, whipping a cloth about before hanging it on a barely-visible line tied to a tree. The wolves froze and shrank into the grasses. The figure paused and squinted in their direction. She dried her fingers in the air as she returned to the hut and pulled a blanket over the doorway behind her.

Blackthorn glanced furtively behind as the wolves trotted on. They passed dark wooden houses and a human drinking from a bottle.

They made a wide circle, keeping to brush and trees. The faded curtains came into view.

"*Ag*—" Blackthorn froze solid with a hiss. "*They have us.*"

Aalwyn turned her head and locked eyes with a human who crouched in the bush as though defecating. His ebony skin was obscured, his imposing figure clad in rags. He reeked of stale beer, the alcohol soaking his clothing. He removed his tattered shirt, which was dropped to the ground. From a rucksack he pulled on a green jacket with epaulets and a patch over a breast pocket. A beret was fastened to his head. At his hip jangled a collection of black plastic zip-ties. His eyes were grim in appearance, his face an angry mask. He hefted a wood and steel rifle in his hands, and as this appeared, the wolves' hearts beat in a panic.

The human adjusted his beret as he slid the rifle onto his back. He reached into a sack at his side, produced a dark object, and fixed it to the end of a great stick that he lifted to his shoulder.

"*On my mark.*" Blackthorn crouched.

The human took a step forward. The wolves jerked but did not run. Aalwyn's brow furrowed as the man stepped urgently around them.

"He has no interest in us." Aalwyn exhaled.

"How—"

"His eyes were elsewhere—he only caught us unaware."

"We can't—"

Aalwyn turned and led the wolves silently after the human with her ears folded back and head down.

The human made a wide circle approaching the house. His strides were long and urgent, yet utterly silent. He seemed to give a slight nod to Koorsboom as he passed the pup, his tongue making a soft clucking sound.

Koorsboom stood, the chain clinking. He looked wildly about, then became calm as the man passed.

"He is—*helping* us," Aalwyn twittered almost inaudibly.

The man strode to a stand of brush on the edge of the house. A pin on his beret, emblazoned with the insignia of the Zimbabwe Parks and Wildlife Authority, reflected light from the house. He made a final adjustment to the bizarre stick in his hands.

The wolves ran to Koorsboom and surrounded him. Aalwyn twittered quietly in tender greeting.

"What is happening, Mother?"

"I do not know. Be ready."

"This does not move." Essenhout dug at the steel stake until she struck concrete.

Two voices rose in words unlike those of the villagers. The cadence was sharp and quick and coming closer.

***

"You have a driver on the way, Orlando?"

"Same guy. You plan a show in Maputo for my clients?"

"Maybe we get a few in a cage and let in an impala. Have you seen these things hunt?"

"A long time ago. These dogs are powerful and cruel—their body parts will be very popular, I think." The human nodded, arms folded as he leaned against his blue Land Rover. "You are a damned clever man."

Their hands clasped as a series of distinct clicks sounded in the darkness. There was a pause while the human in the beret hoisted the bizarre stick. The initial hiss of the rocket grenade became an ear-ripping exhale as the air tore apart, and with a monumental blast the blue Land Rover flew onto its side, scattering shrapnel and blowing out every window in the pink house. The men were thrown dazed and heaving to the ground, and the human in the beret rushed from the shadows to kneel by their sides, voices all around rising in confusion and alarm.

Pereira spit saliva and dirt as the human in the beret raised him and rapidly fastened his wrists across his chest and his ankles together with the plastic zip-ties. He bent and fastened the wrists and ankles of the other man and slugged them both in the face with his black, scarred fists. He paused over their unconscious bodies. Then with a quick motion, he opened the rocket launcher and flipped out the firing pin, tossing the great stick into the burning wreckage of the Rover.

Nearly at a run, he dragged the bound humans by their ankles, digging shallow furrows behind them as their heads thumped over the ground and rocks. He passed the garden behind the pink house and glanced at the wolves standing tensed over Koorsboom.

Aalwyn met his eyes, and he gave the slightest grin before his face returned to its grim, determined mask.

Aalwyn took Koorsboom's chain in her mouth, adjusted her hold, and with her tongue selected a link close to his neck. She took a deep breath, closed her eyes, and bit down. Slowly and with care, her jaw set until every muscle on her skull became taut. Her eyes closed tightly, and her temples knotted. Seconds passed. The other wolves watched in silence and did not breathe as pain began to erupt in her lower jaw. She gave a low rumble, and her head began to vibrate with a fine tremor, her ears flat against her head.

Crack!

Blood streamed from the corner of her mouth as she gulped air in a deep sigh and released the broke pieces of the chain.

Koorsboom crouched stunned, then leapt up with the chain loose and whipping about his neck. He boxed Aalwyn, who bent low with her eyes closed. As he danced, the chain loosened and dropped.

"Are you able to run, my love?" Blackthorn lapped Aalwyn's muzzle dripping blood.

"We break to the northeast—" She spoke with difficulty. "And leave this *vrot* behind."

Part Four:
Gorongosa

Death is always with us, as it ever must be. It greets us each day and shepherds our vast journey. Death was our reason for bringing you here—my son, my heritage—our drive for immortality. And so you must carry on just as we did. Else dust shall be the only inheritance of us all,
and none shall ever know of the African painted wolf.

Chapter 49

"The land is changing—you can see it in the earth." Blackthorn clawed the ground to loosen a clump of wet soil and green grass. "The rains have begun, and the dirt is accustomed to water here. We are out of the thirstlands."

The *Dwalen* had left the Limpopo Transfrontier Park for rural Mozambique, where the level, arid savanna gave way to moist, uneven ground and then mountainsides of exposed granite. The green wilderness grew deeper, with miombo wood and tough grasses upon which duiker and bushpig grazed. Exploring higher elevations, the pack found densely wooded areas. *Brachystegia* trees with their fissured and cracked grey bark stood draped in vines amid the ferns and flowers of the dim forest floor. Lush cycads grew their brilliant emerald 'fruit' cones in the center of radiating, sprawling leaf branches. Samango monkeys with resplendent grey faces climbed gnarled and twisted evergreen tree fuchsia among ripe fruits and sleeping fruit bats.

As they ascended the highlands, the *Dwalen* came to short and bitter grasses grazed upon by rock dassies, who gave sharp cries and vanished into the rocks as the wolves passed. On the plateaued summits, the green became pale among the vibrant peach-colored blossoms of Chimanimani aloes.

"There is no suitable prey here." Aalwyn paused on a rocky outcropping with Blackthorn at her shoulder.

"This is no place for our kind." Blackthorn nodded and turned. "Still, this direction is most promising."

They pushed on to downward slopes. The pack surprised red duiker, hiding in the shadows of the miombo trees. Their dark coloration and black snouts made for effective camouflage, but the pack was too close to be deceived.

"I see you." Blackthorn shot forward and pounced on the small antelope.

The wolves tore the red duiker to pieces, feasting on the rich, grass-fed meat, and rested under the broad crown of a palm tree finally at ease.

"Duiker do not move in herds." Essenhout laid her nose on her forepaws. "Our choices here are limited." She raised her head to a Samango monkey in the lush canopy above. "Yet I realize how desperately I have missed the wild."

"We will go further north skirting the base of the mountain." Aalwyn shook her coat.

"You weary me, love." Blackthorn gave a disgruntled rasp.

"I am glad to be the source of your unrest. There is more to come."

"No roads, no structures, no snares. Not the slightest hint of human." Blackthorn reached his paws out and stretched his spine before collapsing onto the grass. His arthritic joints ached.

When he opened his eyes, Aalwyn was watching him. A slight smile crossed his face, lips parted and fangs exposed.

***

The *Dwalen* padded through virgin forest and wet savanna and crossed a major road with sparse traffic.

Weeks passed. Occasional farms were encountered, and those occupied and cultivated were given cautious distance. One abandoned smallholding was crossed, completely overgrown. Paws lightly ambled through a shallow crater, now filled with grass and weeds. The shrapnel from the exploded mine was long buried, all evidence of past warfare swallowed whole by nature.

They came into Gorongosa, where miombo trees among patches of grasslands and riverine woodland would flourish under daily deluges of rain in the wet season to come. There were no fences demarcating the border of the wildlife reserve, only wild trees and brush growing in thick tangles. Aalwyn lay down in the last rays of sun under the intense yellow and greenish glow of a fever tree.

"This is home. Do you feel it?"

"Indeed." Blackthorn lay down by her side.

"None too soon. The true labor is yet to come." Aalwyn looked over her shoulder at her mate. "If our pups are as stubborn as you."

Blackthorn raised his head, at first uncomprehending, then on his paws next to her. "How soon?"

"Before the rains come in earnest." Her teeth glinted white.

Blackthorn touched noses with her, eyes closed, and brushed past her to rouse the pack.

"Up, you lazy okes!" Blackthorn boxed Koorsboom and knocked him flat.

Koorsboom rolled to his feet with his ears erect and paws out.

"There is work to be done—" Blackthorn glanced at Aalwyn. "—before our new pups join us!"

The *Dwalen* erupted in a cacophony of twittering. The wolves leapt in the air and scurried about in boisterous play. Essenhout and Blackthorn stood on hind legs and appeared to dance. Only Duinemirt lay alone brooding.

"Will I have brothers or sisters?" Koorsboom lapped Aalwyn's muzzle.

"So many of both that you cannot count."

The glow of the fever tree faded with the sun, and the sound of fiery-necked nightjars blended in symphony with the katydids.

Chapter 50

The granite monolith of Mount Gorongosa towers over central Mozambique, source of the great rains and rivers that course over rocks through verdant ravines to the soaked wetlands and plains around Lake Urema. In the wet season, Lake Urema swells to twenty times its dry season size, and is alive with water birds and hippo. The vast lake drains into the Pungue River and courses for a hundred kilometers to the port city of Beira on the Indian Ocean.

During the monsoon season, clouds heavy with water are released upon the mountain, shrouding it in mist. The ravines echo with the *kok—kok—kok--kok—kok* of the Livingstone's Turaco, flashing with purple-blue, green, and rose-pink plumage. Rounded mossy boulders sit in the shade of trees along the rivulets that cascade down the mountainside. Leaves of vibrant green would tremble under the cautious weight of a gecko who moved hand and foot-grips with precision along a branch of a Panga tree.

This year, however, the rains were late, as November brought rising temperatures. Down the flanks of the mountain, rock outcroppings gave way to plains and dust devils winding through the parched landscape. Patchy fires had burned the grasslands, now already covered in a faint lining of renewed green. A warthog perched on short knees with forelegs pointing rear nosed in the dirt for tubers. *Thud.*

The warthog was on its feet suddenly frozen, as the *Dwalen* emerged from the forest on light footfalls. The wolves accelerated at the sight, surrounding the warthog as it loosed a squeal and drove at Essenhout, who jumped back quickly. Another parry and dodge, and Blackthorn drew the warthog his way.

"Watch your legs—it can shatter a bone. Shift the circle to keep it from breaking through." Blackthorn studied the warthog. "When it tires, we strike!"

"It moves more quickly than we," Essenhout panted. "Has it a weakness?" She leapt into the air as the warthog drove at her with steps that shook the ground.

Koorsboom crouched with the white tip of his tail up. He feinted and backed off as the warthog wheeled to face him.

"Distance, Koorsboom," Aalwyn twittered. "Take no chances!"

Koorsboom cocked his head. He noticed the warthog always wheeled predictably in one direction. As it turned, he bounded forward and bit deeply into its flank, and the warthog gave a piston-kick that nearly shattered his scapula.

Aalwyn pounced on the snout above the lethal incisors as the warthog bucked her. Essenhout let go of the forelimb to dive underneath and eviscerate the belly. The muscles slacked, and the wolves each took a limb and pulled. In seconds, the warthog was skinned, muscle ripped from tendon insertion points, intestines pulled away, and organs swallowed. The wolves separated the spine and yanked the ribcage to pieces.

"We must finish and leave. I smell something—" Blackthorn glanced up from the bowels. "*Lion!*"

"*Evade!*" Aalwyn sprinted away with Koorsboom fast on her heels. The *Dwalen* dashed to the edge of miombo wood and melted into the shadows, where Blackthorn paused to look back.

A medium-sized male with a sandy gold mane roared over the remains of the warthog with his lionesses all around.

"They found us quickly!" Koorsboom twittered from behind Blackthorn.

"I suspect they recognize our musk, and may be tracking our hunts. This male is not terribly aggressive, which is good fortune for us." Blackthorn looked to the gathering of clouds above. "We need only spread out the coursing—so tracking us becomes more work than they can bear." He lapped Aalwyn's muzzle and looked at her belly. "You are nearly scraping the ground—and not with fresh kill."

"It shall be tonight," Aalwyn panted.

A patter of rain fell on the leaves of the fever tree, and its smooth iridescent bark shimmered in the sunset over the abandoned aardvark den.

"The rains will make it difficult to track our spoor," Blackthorn rumbled. "Soon they will make it impossible. Is the earth inside dry to your satisfaction?"

The aardvark den went deep into the root system of the fever tree before rising into the hillside. In the darkness Aalwyn gave a pleased nod. She found it bone-dry and devoid of mold.

"Our *dwaal* concludes here." Aalwyn emerged shaking the dirt from her fur. "This is home." She glanced at Koorsboom. "At long last—" She trudged panting back into the den on footfalls uncharacteristically heavy.

"So it ends." Duinemirt examined the clouds.

"We commence patrol with first light." Blackthorn followed Aalwyn into the den. "I will return with something bleeding fresh." His greyed fur had acquired color and depth since the wolves had arrived in Gorongosa.

"Be ready with the hunt."

"I am always yours." Blackthorn licked her muzzle and ducked out of the den. For the next three weeks, he would stand guard at the entrance over Aalwyn and his hidden newborn pups.

As the evening wore on, her contractions intensified, rippling powerfully through her and bringing secretions from her birth canal. She pushed. Into utter darkness a wet pup emerged. She touched it with her nose and gripped it tenderly about the shoulders with her jaws. She lifted it between her forepaws and licked it clean, concentrating with care on the little face and muzzle and freeing its airway. Its tiny mouth opened on sharp, shallow, rapid breaths and an ultrasonic whine.

She pushed, and another small, wet pup emerged. She lifted it between her teeth, licked it clean, and settled it mewling, blind, and helpless with the other against her side. She pushed again, and again, and again, and as each pup emerged into the dark, she learned its scent. Each subtle whine was a unique voice that she would remember always. At last she lay panting and exhausted with the squirming pile of pups crawling over each other against her side, rooting frantically, their tiny mouths drawing the milk from her body.

Seven.

Here, then, was Aalwyn's life, her love—the heirs to her veld and her world entire.

Chapter 51

Blackthorn pretended to doze at the mouth of the den with a fear bordering on panic.

"What ails you?" Koorsboom sniffed him with eyes wide with alarm.

"A sensation that you will come to know when you have made the same mistake I have." Blackthorn sighed.

"Becoming a father?"

He grunted, with a hint of a knowing smile. "Fatherhood is a test for which we are born to fail." Blackthorn rose and boxed Koorsboom. Koorsboom was on his own hind legs batting back with force.

"Many a weaverbird constructs his fragile nest on slight branches, beckoning a female to lay her eggs. And these eggs are lost to snake or a long fall from a poorly designed nest. With time, they figure out how to stay out of reach of the snake, and build a nest that keeps the eggs safe. If the parents do not learn quickly, it is the innocent who suffer." Blackthorn raised his eyes to the horizon. "We all fail at the greatness required of us."

"Until we no longer fail?"

"Quite right." Blackthorn sniffed the air. "Come. Let us—you and I —feed your sisters and brothers for the first time."

***

The waterlogged soil deadened the thunder of the bushbuck's hoofbeats, while Koorsboom tore across the grasslands in pursuit. The bushbuck darted back, then forth to escape, while the young hunter kept a slight distance, cutting across these arcs with ease. Behind Koorsboom came a giant open-top *bakkie* with tourists thrown violently around inside. Each bounce shocked the frame and the metal struts squealed against rattling bolts until the *bakkie* left the ground entirely to cross a ditch. As it crunched back down and the tires spun to regain momentum, there was a spirited *woo-hoo!* from one of the occupants.

Each change in direction by the buck was answered by the wolf with a measured correction, and the prey tired more each time. With a high twitter, Koorsboom closed the distance, and the bushbuck rasped for breath as it bounded over brush and around trees.

"Hoo!" The pup called, his jaw close to the ground as he loped. Blackthorn raced out of the sedge before them at full speed and collided with the bushbuck head-on. He seized it by the throat and dug in with his paws, and the inertia of the bushbuck carried it over his head and cartwheeled it crashing to the ground in a spatter of blood from the opened jugular.

The humans inside the *bakkie* erupted with excited twittering of their own. "Did you see that?"

"Are you filming?"

"I don't believe it!"

The vehicle ground to a halt beside the kill.

"My friends, we will have our sundowner here." The driver worked to remove the foil from the neck of a wine bottle. "Unless there are any objections."

Cameras whirred in a venerated silence as Koorsboom and Blackthorn took hold of the bushbuck's legs and tore it apart.

***

Jogging briskly to the aardvark den, the *Dwalen* came to the fever tree radiant in the morning light, where Blackthorn entered the den with caution.

"You have had a productive hunt, I see," Aalwyn twittered almost serenely.

Blackthorn regurgitated a fountain of meat and gore, and she choked it down with incredible speed, her hunger insatiable.

"We may hunt twice more today."

Aalwyn nodded and lay back on her side with the pups tugging furiously for milk. Two jostled briefly over the same teat with muffled but enthusiastic grunting, and Aalwyn looked up to meet Blackthorn's gaze. He opened his mouth, paused, and left the den without another word.

***

Lake Urema lay as a placid mirror upon the veld, swelling from the recent rains. The plain was losing its aridity, and the moist ground slowly yielded to impassible mud. Cormorants expanded their range into the vast shallows while herons hunted in the growing reed beds. White storks with black-tipped wings glided on air currents overhead, their long yellow bills cutting air. As they dropped to approach the surface of the lake, each bill opened and carefully skimmed the water, so that the birds were always on the verge of stalling and splashing. Some flapped tremendously to circle around again, while others snapped their bills on small fish and rose to return to the nest.

The great mountain of Gorongosa stood over Lake Urema in painstakingly-crafted beauty, with its patient trees and grasses exploding into a riot of color and greenery. Wildlife swarmed the plains below, as though a tableaux from a million years ago.

Chapter 52

The body and windows of the *bakkie* were splattered with mud when the man parked it off the dirt road in a small clearing between stands of miombo wood. Clothed in khaki, he opened the rear of the *bakkie* and pulled out bales of wire.

"Another successful hunt?" Another person clad in a khaki uniform climbed from what appeared to be a small grave, stabbing a shovel into the ground.

"Yes—even less to find than last week. The snares are more haphazard and fewer in number. This is all I have for the whole month." The human at the *bakkie* hefted a snarl of wires. "It's anybody's guess what makes the difference. The income-generating project at the northeast boundary village has been making a profit. The education programs have hit the northeast and west. Revenue sharing with villages may have been the key to it all, though."

"Any progress works for me. There will always be a demand for bushmeat, however."

The men lifted the bale of snares into the hole in the ground and smoothed dirt over them.

"We must find some use for all this metal. Recyclers are too far away."

"We could turn it back into fencing if we start a breeding program."

"It would make for lousy fencing. We can't just sell it back to villagers—it would immediately be turned into snares again."

A large *bakkie* pulled up alongside them, covered in mud and caked dust with a huge gated container in the back.

"Here he comes! My lovely."

"Has he been collared?"

"In place. You can't see it for all that fur. We'll be outfitted with receivers to track him, with more on the way."

The humans crossed to the large *bakkie* and unlocked the rear doors, while the driver climbed out with a shining smile in his wide, dark face.

"Do we have a grant for the study yet?"

Carefully they edged the huge, heavy container onto the tailgate.

"Still being written. There should be no problem. There's considerable interest in breeding with greater genetic variability. In the past couple of years, the number of cubs born here has been mediocre, and it's been blamed on inbreeding. New males from far away is just what we need."

"It could be some time, if he has difficulty finding mates."

"This one will have no trouble. He's a clever chappie."

The humans climbed into the cab of the *bakkie* while the driver clambered to the top of the huge container and reached down to pull up the gate.

A massive golden lion leapt out on soft, heavy paws. He strode forth swishing his tail, magnificent in the noon sunshine. Shaking his head, the black mane cascading down his neck and chest rustled in the wind. He turned his heavy head slightly to survey the clearing, and his tongue swept over the nose of his broad muzzle. He paused, huge and solid under his tawny coat, and gazed around through his single unblinking yellow eye.

Chapter 53

The skies were dour, obstinate grey and the day as night, while the downpour hammered relentlessly across the plain. Blackthorn, Essenhout, and Koorsboom were scouting for new dens in case of flooding. Aalwyn lay unmoving under the fever tree, its glowing light extinguished, with her eyes on the hole and her dish-like ears raised to the mewling of the pups underground.

***

The weeks wore on, and the punishing sun shone down on the waterlogged savanna. The *Dwalen* hunted every morning and late every afternoon when the heat lessened. Blackthorn and Essenhout avoided the nearby bushbuck and waterbuck, preferring to hunt further from the den.

Koorsboom trotted after them past a termite mound where a matabele ant crawled over the trail with its antennae waving, fixed upon the scent of termite larvae from a tiny vent.

"What is the matter with Duinemirt?"

Essenhout bounded ahead.

"Pups cannot be expected to survive—" Blackthorn turned. "Not here with a killer behind every rock and tree. So many tests to pass, few of which are foreseeable or even fair." He looked at Koorsboom. "Some tests come before you are even born."

Koorsboom followed him through acacia shrubs to a semipermanent waterhole, a shimmering mirror edged by green grass. Cattle egrets and cormorants called across the water. A spotted hyena dug furiously at the edge of the pool, provoking a wild splash. He lunged with sharp teeth into the water to pull back a mud-covered catfish so heavy that the hyena could barely lope away with it in its teeth. A herd of elephants ambled through a cloud of rising birds to the waterhole, where the bull plowed with his calves in tow into the deepest water. Submerged to his belly, he dipped his trunk into the cool water and drank his fill. He raised the trunk overhead and splashed water across his back, showering the tender calves.

"You are born, and your parents are unable to feed you or are outwitted or overpowered by predators." Blackthorn sighed. "Ill fortune or drought—the world that provides is also hellbent against us. We walk the edge of a precipice all our lives. I suspect that Duinemirt is falling. She cannot cope with the loss of Vaalgras and her pups, and the veld feels nothing for her suffering. We must, above all, be cold to our tragedies."

"Should we not mourn?" Koorsboom whined.

"Mourn if you must—but do not expect the veld to provide you the time or space."

The elephants made a show of splashing through the waterhole, leaving behind swirls of muddied water. On the green verge a hush fell over them all at once, as the bull reached into the grass with his long trunk and revealed a bleached white elephant skull. The tip of his trunk caressed it softly, rounding over the dome and across the voids of the eye sockets. A pair of females reached out and touched it gently with furtive noises among themselves. When a calf stepped close to investigate, the nearest female made way so that the calf too could touch the skull. The females loosed trumpeting calls when the tips of their trunks found the single hole through the spongy bone just above one eye. They recognized that wound.

The bull searched with his trunk through the grass, lifting a massive scapula. He trumpeted and moved forward, and each elephant filed past the skull to run the tip of a trunk over it.

"Koorsboom! Like a bit of fun with this lot?" Essenhout padded out of the acacia brush around the waterhole.

"We leave them alone," Blackthorn rebuked her sharply. "This is a sacred moment for them."

Essenhout lowered her head.

When the *Dwalen* returned to the den that afternoon, they found Duinemirt gone. No one spoke of it, and there was no search for her.

***

Their next kill was stolen by hyena.

The wolves had found a common duiker in the miombo forest north of the den, the small, sleek body brought down in a flash of teeth. While Koorsboom swallowed all the meat he could, Essenhout and Blackthorn turned on a hyena scout and chased it off, its yellow, spotted coat muddied and loping posture ungainly.

Whoop! whoop! whoop! The hyena was answered by *whoops* not far off, and soon five hyena returned. Essenhout and Blackthorn chased off two at a time, but the others continued to swoop in to harass Koorsboom until Blackthorn raised his muzzle and twittered their retreat. Essenhout and Koorsboom padded unhappily after him through the grass and scrub brush with their heads down.

"Lion." Koorsboom stopped at a deformed track barely visible in the soft ground.

Blackthorn and Essenhout bounded back to where Koorsboom stared down.

"Well done." Essenhout regarded Koorsboom with pride. "Walked right past it, I did."

"Lioness, same as before. We have counted three now. No males as yet—not in our territory." Blackthorn scanned the brush. "I suspect that these okes have never before encountered our kind."

Essenhout raised her eyes anxiously. Blackthorn turned abruptly, and the *Dwalen* raced back to the den, missing in their haste the hyena that followed at a distance.

Chapter 54

Whoop!
Aalwyn jolted awake, knocking the pups off their suckling. Her eyes went to the den entrance as she waited. Sharp twitters and responding giggles came from outside, until Essenhout's shape darkened the hole. The fever tree shaded the entrance upon its small hill, surrounded by a clearing of fresh green grasses that waved in the wind. To the north stood a copse of miombo trees, a long finger of forest stretching down from the distant mountain. Gorongosa was a welcome change with its wild, tangled woods and savanna bounding with antelope.
"Hyenas—they have found our den."
Aalwyn grunted.
The whooping continued outside, with Blackthorn's twitter and Koorsboom's response. Loud barks broke out among alarmed giggles. There was the noise of scuffling, growling, and harsh laughter, and then the noise subsided.
"I saw them off." Blackthorn put his head into the den. "But it will be a struggle. This lot was interested in the leg that Essenhout brought back for you."
"Has Duinemirt returned?"
He shook his head and wordlessly regurgitated the meat of the kill.

***

The following day Koorsboom tumbled into the den twittering wildly.
"I killed a hyena!" He shook his head, and the blood on his ears flecked the walls of the den.

"You only injured it." Essenhout's voice was muted form outside.
"I slashed its throat open!"
"Injured!" Essenhout padded away from the den muttering.
"There are so many pups—" Koorsboom stood over the tiny, feeding pups in wonder.
Aalwyn growled a low rumble, and Koorsboom moved backward. He scampered out into the sunlight, knocking dirt into Aalwyn's face.
She felt a pang. The months had hardened Koorsboom on their endless *dwaal* across arid scrublands and through human-occupied farms, harassed by hyena and disease, living on hares or even mouthfuls of grass. And now her pup was taking on hyena. The newborn pups were now plump with protein-rich milk, and she winced at the sharp little teeth.
Seven names. Can I find seven?
The walls of the den were dark earth, the air stale with the urine and waste of her young always in her nose.
This litter will not meet the fate of the last—

***

Blonde mane over broad shoulders blending with the tawny sands, the lion stretched upon the soft ground in a bed of rumpled grasses among his three lionesses. The ground was littered with odd bones and scraps, marked by scuffing and urine scent. His cubs tussled and scampered in mock charges, and one broke off to stalk its mother's tail swishing at biting flies. The cub put up a paw to snag the tail, the lioness whipped it aside, and the cub flopped onto its chin. *Thwump.* The cub was up again. *Thwump.* The male rolled over and slept on his side.
A figure approached in the distance with large steps and a brisk pace. Even at a kilometer, there was no mistaking that it was a male. The black, shimmering mane shifted as he marched, brawn musculature on display. His scent reached the pride, and the lion and lionesses were on their feet.

Standing tall to maximize his silhouette, the approaching lion gave his territorial call, a higher-pitched *urh!* dropping to *rhoorh!* as it resonated through his frame.

Urh-rhoorh—The lionesses looked expectantly to their male. They glanced at one another, the mother snarled, and her cubs gathered about her. She began to withdraw slowly with her gaze on the approaching stranger. *Urh-rhoorh—urh-rhoorh—*

The male threw back his blonde mane and rushed forward to meet the stranger on hind legs, their roars resounding across the plain. Their broad paws and hooked claws tore out and ripped through coat and flesh, as the echoes of their roars came back from the distant hills. The fight lasted less than a minute, until the stranger laid open the nose of the other. Gushing blood, he stepped back, and his face twisted into a snarl. The stranger was larger, stronger, and his strikes were utterly decisive. Turning, the loser bounded away over the grass while his lionesses and cubs watched him go.

Urh-rhoorh—The victorious stranger roared in exultation.

He padded over to the lionesses, who shrank back. His single yellow eye glared with pupil dilated until he found the mother with her cubs gathered behind her. In giant leaps he caught up to her and met her roar. She did not yield her offspring to the victor. He struck her face, deep gashes spraying blood, and she clawed his muzzle until he drew back. He gave another blow to the side of her head, and she lunged forward to lock her fangs upon his face. He knocked her aside, his jaws closed on her neck, and he ripped free, releasing a torrent of blood. She fell heaving into the flowering grasses with her paws twitching and eventually lay still.

The cubs stared at him with curiosity and anxiety. The giant male lion pounced and seized one in his jaws, shaking it violently until it went limp and he tossed it aside. The cubs stood motionless, numb with terror as each waited for the male to reach them. One by one he caught them, gripped their necks, biting and shaking, and tossed the lifeless bodies into the grass as the lionesses watched with narrowed eyes.

At last he stood defiantly over the dead bodies of the lioness and her cubs with a final territorial roar, *urh-rhoorh—*

"Moordenaar calls."

Chapter 55

"The line remains unbroken." Blackthorn glared across the veld. "Such as it is. Three wolves do not make for a formidable defense. On your feet, Koorsboom."

Koorsboom leapt up to follow him.

"The last foray by hyena came too close. We must never again let them catch sight of our den."

"We bring the attack to them!" Koorsboom raced ahead.

"The wish is parent to the thought." Blackthorn allowed himself a smile and sprinted after Koorsboom with Essenhout on his tail.

The plain was moist and glittering green to the far horizon. Over a rise, they found a lone male hyena who lowered his head when they appeared.

"He was on his way to us." Blackthorn ran straight at him, and the hyena ran at a brisk lope that accelerated as Blackthorn's jaws snapped at his tail. The wolves dropped back and let the hyena escape.

"And if we encounter the rest of them?"

"We chase the first female," Koorsboom answered.

"Quite right. Nobody cares about a male—least of all other hyenas." Blackthorn gave a resounding laugh. "When the females are intimidated, they will give us a wider berth."

***

The rolling land transitioned from grass to mud and back again, and over the next rise the wolves found the hyena clan. They were upwind near a den that had once been a warthog hole, little more than a depression in the ground. In a pool nearby severed limbs from a recent hunt were stored under the surface of the cool water where vultures could not steal them.

A handful of hyena clustered around a zebra, its black and white stark against the mud. It had blundered into the hyena clan's den, and there was no escape. Three held the zebra, and whenever one released its grip the zebra attempted to stand and was pulled down again. Its head waved barely upright while the hyena tore into its belly and pulled out lengths of viscera, until the zebra collapsed and disappeared in a tangle of spotted brown fur.

In the center of the clearing stood the hyena matriarch, a hulk of rippling muscle full of testosterone barking at a diminutive male who had approached her pup. The small male held his hind leg briefly in the air for her to sniff, then yelped and ran away, while she lovingly licked her pup's little face. She settled on her side, and the pup resumed suckling as she scanned the horizon.

Whoop!

When she saw the *Dwalen*, the matriarch gave her call, and the hyena clan stopped everything, even the suckling pup. Her eyes narrowed in silence upon the wolves, until suddenly the hyena clan erupted in a chaotic overlapping of whooping calls, while she lay still next to her pup with another female as bodyguard.

The rest of the clan advanced on the wolves, their whoops mixed with anxious giggling from the males. One male broke forth and loped quickly across the distance, his tongue out and froth dripping from the corner of his mouth, his eyes wide with excitement.

"Koorsboom—flank. Essenhout—opposite forepaw."

The wolves dashed forward, and within seconds they collided with the ambitious male. Blackthorn twittered his orders as Koorsboom dashed out just beyond snapping range and lunged in to lock his teeth on the hyena's flank. Essenhout closed her jaws on the hyena's forepaw and crunched down, while Blackthorn clamped onto an ear and ripped it free with the scalp. The hyena squealed in agony and scrambled away.

The matriarch gave a deep *whoop!* and the others descended on the wolves chattering and cackling.

"We cannot repel this army." Essenhout turned.

"They are no army," Blackthorn was quick to answer. "Only individuals. We must—"

"Attack the alpha." Koorsboom bounded forth into the approaching mob.

"No, you fool-" Blackthorn was fast on his heels. The hyena moved to surround Koorsboom. He took a sharp turn and curved around in a line straight toward the matriarch. The hair rose on her back, and she stood, outweighing him fivefold. Her fearsome conical teeth were revealed, and her jaws widened with drool streaming. Her pup squealed in alarm, and a high-pitched cackle rose in her throat as Koorsboom closed in.

"Bloody hell—" Blackthorn croaked.

Koorsboom planted his hind legs and sprang - not at the matriarch, but at the female bodyguard with forepaws extended and claws out. His jaws ripped into her neck and shoulder as she bumbled onto her back, spattering the pup with blood. Koorsboom sprinted away again with the alpha female fast on his tail.

Twittering rapidly, Blackthorn and Essenhout dashed toward her pup, and the matriarch returned in a panic to protect the future queen of her clan. The wolves veered away from the den and circled around, while the shaken mother comforted her yelping offspring. The rest of the clan quickly lost their interest in the pack as they left.

"I did not expect you to strike such fear into that behemoth." Blackthorn boxed Koorsboom, who slapped him back. "You canny *bliksem.*"

Blackthorn galloped away from the hyena den with Koorsboom and Essenhout behind.

They returned swiftly to the aardvark den under the fever tree, over rolling hills and cutting between miombo forest and palm trees. Pride-of-the-Cape bushes climbed into the trees, blooming with bright red florets, and hare's ears opened their white blossoms, while blue sourplum shrubs opened greenish-white flowers flickering with butterflies. They doubled back again and again to be certain that they were not followed through the thick green brush.

"Have we frightened the hyena for good?" Koorsboom arched his brow as he trotted at Blackthorn's side.

"Of course not. Hyena do not frighten easily. Your gambit has made them uneasy, that is all. They will not be so daring in days to come." Blackthorn glanced at Koorsboom. "We will need that advantage."

Chapter 56

The dung beetle, a stolid hunter in impenetrable black armor, examined the fibrous elephant droppings. It cut carefully into the muffin and shaped with its claws a ball of dung many times its own size, walking the ball with its hind legs the long way through the crisscross of dead grass and leaf litter to the beetle burrow. Hundreds of its kind worked at the long line of fresh droppings left by the herd that marched ahead.

The elephants paused to drink at a new waterhole that had appeared with the rains, startled when the surface erupted in a massive, undulating black cloud of Red-billed Quelea. Tens of thousands shot up and folded over and around them like a curtain in a gale, parting and whipping through the air to descend again on a more distant pool. The elephants flapped their ears in warning as they lifted trunkfuls of water to their dry mouths and threw water over their backs.

The green grasses waved in the breeze where dragonflies hovered, and an armored katydid stopped its march between grass tussocks to browse on a crushed insect.

Duinemirt ran her eyes over the grass, but she saw nothing. Her muscles twitched as she walked, making her recoil, as in her mind the Chobe River snaked through trees to arid sands and desiccated grasses under the night calls of cicada and nightjars. She remembered tiny, furry bodies, blind and helpless, but no faces. Her pups had had no names. These memories flowed through her mind, over and again, without ceasing. Even these images were buried in a fog. There was no hunger, and no desire to hunt, her ribs standing out in starvation.

She shook her head, ears flopping down and erect again. The fog lifted suddenly as she stopped her aimless walking.

A lion print lay in the mud with water leaking slowly into the base, the center pad as large as her head. There were no claw marks, so the lion had been in no hurry. A familiar scent rose about her, and her mind raced back the Chobe River and the clay Ngwezumba Pans. She did not feel the blow that tumbled her numbly to the ground. Hot, dank breath washed over her with the smell of a corpse.

"You are familiar—" The voice rumbled deep and resounding. Perhaps it had never left her mind. "I remember your coat—I tracked your pack so long ago." He planted a broad paw upon her body. "However we came to share the same land again, I am pleased to continue the massacre. And you rats believed you escaped my wrath." Saliva pattered on the wolf's fur.

"Do as you must," Duinemirt whined, her tone flat and fading. "And be on your way."

"The hunting of your pack began with one alpha." Moordenaar shook his mane over Duinemirt, and gripped her head with the other paw. "It shall end with the other."

Chapter 57

The pups blinked up at the leaves of the fever tree filtering the glare of the sun. When the last pup emerged from the den, the wolves pounced on them, licking each with fevered excitement, their tongues lapping and slapping the pups nearly off their feet.

"I cannot believe that I was ever this small." Koorsboom remembered being battered about while he licked clean a mewling pup. "Mother, what is his name?"

Aalwyn glanced at Blackthorn.

"Young brother, you have many hunts ahead." Koorsboom nosed the tiny pup between his paws. "You are a predator, the nexus between life and death on the veld."

With a soft sigh, the pup whined up with his wet eyes blinking and sank his needle-sharp teeth in Koorsboom's nose.

***

The pups sprawled on Aalwyn, mewling with hunger as she breathed deeply the sweet smell of fresh air under the shining fever tree. The sun lay low on the horizon among clouds that shattered it into burnished orange and red. Over the rising carpet of thick grasses, three wolves emerged from the miombo forest along the plain, and Aalwyn leapt to her feet.

"My little ones, you are about to forget that I ever provided you with milk."

Koorsboom sprinted toward them, his belly sloshing. As he reached the clearing, he regurgitated a feast before the shocked pups, who first stared and then salivated at the salty, rusty smell of meat. The pups seized the largest pieces and pulled them in half. There was no wrestling for food—all was shared.

Blackthorn and Essenhout regurgitated their share, and as Aalwyn gulped down hide she looked uneasily at Blackthorn.

He nodded.

"Do not tell the young ones why," Blackthorn whispered to Essenhout. "Tomorrow we start the wide patrols." He stared at the distant line of forest. "Duinemirt has been gone far too long."

Chapter 58

The miombo wood towered over the wolves with the muted light through the canopy turning to gold and white swirls in the shadows. The grey trunks stood straight, branches gnarled and twisted to leafy bundles, and greenery filled the forest floor where Blackthorn moved his muzzle to brush aside the long grasses, his obsidian eyes everywhere.

"The foliage deadens the sound." Blackthorn's dish-like ears swiveled. "Nothing save the hush of grass."

"Even the doves are silent," Essenhout twittered quietly.

It had been three days, and there was still no sign of Duinemirt.

"In the night, no birds call."

"There—a reedbuck!" Blackthorn increased his pace. "At least we can end with a hunt today."

The shoulder of a reedbuck appeared through the dense brush where it browsed upon the leaves within reach, ill at ease and looking constantly about. Its marble-like eyes caught sight of the wolves, and in a flash it bounded over brush and around the trees.

The *Dwalen* gave chase but quickly lost sight of it, while the sun appeared to sink into the distant mountains to the west.

"As though it knew we were coming."

"The herd of bushbuck from the day previous—they are gone."

Blackthorn passed a pool and sniffed at hoof prints stamped into the grass and moist dirt. "This dung midden was made not two days ago." He frowned. "Herds move a bit but do not disappear entirely."

"We will cross the same earth if we return to Aalwyn now."

Essenhout shook her head, spraying moisture from the ruff under her chin. "If we stay out tonight, we can make a wider circle with the day."

"We will need a kill come the morrow," Blackthorn grunted.

***

Aalwyn watched the edge of the wood as evening fell. The pups pawed her, whining for meat, while the sun descended behind rain clouds and left them in grey twilight.

"Shall I hunt, Mother?" Koorsboom yipped at a pup gnawing his forepaw. "I am certain to find something."

"Not tonight."

Darkness crept between the trees with their branches like fingers, the grasses away from the den entrance grown now above the height of Aalwyn's shoulders. She walked down from the clearing around the den to the veld, cautious of hidden puff adders in the grass. When she returned, the pups mewled and pawed until darkness came and they fell asleep under a starless sky. Aalwyn lay awake with her eyes playing futilely over the grasses and more distant treeline.

"Do you hear insects?" Koorsboom twittered softly so as not to disturb the pups.

"No."

"The katydids and cicadas are not calling—"

"Nor the nightjar. Perhaps the rising heat has fatigued them."

Aalwyn looked up.

Koorsboom loped off to the edge of grasses, where a pup had wandered into the brush.

"Koorsboom!" Aalwyn was on her feet suddenly, growling to the rest of her litter.

They woke and tumbled over each other into the den, where she stood alert above the entrance, unable to run and unable to remain still. Breezes rustled the tall grass as she waited. A pup put a paw on the lip of the entrance, and she growled harshly.

A sound came from the black edge of the clearing—a pup yelping in pain.

Aalwyn barreled into the grass, twittering to Koorsboom, who did not twitter back. She lurched through the grass, poking her nose around tussocks, and sniffed as she trotted further from the den with the night sounds all around blocked by the thick greenery. Her heart rose in a panic until her own beating pulse was all she heard.

From behind came a thump. Aalwyn whirled, and Koorsboom stood before her with the wandering pup in his jaws. His voice was muffled as he gestured with his head toward the den, and together they sprinted back. Three other pups had emerged, and she herded them in again as Koorsboom pushed his pup into the hole. "Adventurous lot."

Aalwyn touched noses with Koorsboom. Her ears strained for any noise, even the distant trumpet of elephant. Nothing. She lay down. No moon rose that night, the sky hidden in clouds.

***

Whooooop!

Was she awakened? Had she been asleep? Aalwyn's eyes darted around, adjusting. Koorsboom lay on the ground snoring softly. She ducked her head into the den and counted rapidly: *one—two—three—four—five—six—*

She raised her head to a hyena standing before her. The hyena grinned with the small, round form of a pup in its teeth draining blood in rivulets.

Aalwyn shook her head, casting sleep aside. Darkness yawned before her and she became aware of a low ringing in her ears over the muted rustling of grass. There was no hyena.

Seven.

There were seven small bodies sleeping together in the den.

Have I the Rage now? Is my mind fogged?

She paced the clearing, the treeline invisible in the dark.

Illusions of hyena are as dangerous as the real.

Aalwyn settled against the cool earth with Duinemirt on her mind. A hollow *whoop!* sounded in the distance, answered more faintly by another. She put her muzzle on forepaws and closed her eyes.

They are far away.

Chapter 59

Aalwyn was on her paws instantly, glaring into the grasses as they parted around the hyena matriarch. She faced Aalwyn with a low, humming growl, fangs exposed, ears twitching, and head bowed at the end of her long neck, while her powerful shoulders shifted her weight from side to side.

Whoop! The hyena took a step toward Aalwyn.

Aalwyn curled back her lips over a steady growl. She was unable to move, and felt her paws fastened to the ground. The matriarch snuffled heavily through her nasal secretions, drool pouring from the tips of her fangs. With another step, she closed the distance as her forequarters seemed to grow.

Another step. Shadows drifted over her as red-rimmed eyes locked onto Aalwyn's. She seemed as far as the horizon, then she was upon Aalwyn with her breath heavy and strangely familiar as she sniffed and licked Aalwyn's face with a wet tongue.

Aalwyn shuddered awake in terror.

"Mother?" Koorsboom lapped her muzzle. "Are you well?"

"Did you sleep through the night?" She leapt up, still shaky, and sat to scratch a tick behind her ear. The sun peered through trees to the east. Dew sparkled on tips of leaf and bud.

"No. The silence woke me."

Aalwyn peered into the den to find the pups yawning and stretching with soft noises.

"Shall I attempt a hunt, Mother?"

Aalwyn surveyed the plains with its treeline devoid of familiar silhouettes, the greenery higher than ever and the twisted brush grotesque. No sawing from crickets nor call from animal met her ears. Her heart still pounded from the nightmare, and she felt no reassurance with the morning light.

"We will all hunt."

Aalwyn gave a sharp growl, and the pups gathered at the edge of the den entrance, yipping to themselves. Koorsboom rumbled, and they fell as silent as stone. When Aalwyn and Koorsboom ambled to the edge of the short, stunted grass in the shade of the fever tree, the twittering pups filed after them into the taller sedge. As the grasses closed behind their tails the clearing around the den fell silent.

***

Their progress was slow. Aalwyn and Koorsboom trudged through thick greenery with endless waves brushing under and past them.

"Have you been scent-marking, Mother?"

"Yes." Aalwyn yawned. "The trail was left clearly."

"I see no reedbuck. They should be common around waterholes such as this." Aalwyn trotted away from the muddy, abandoned pool into the grasses and wended toward the miombo wood with the pups tripping upon grass stalks. A twig snapped, and Aalwyn whirled, as the little rogue pup emerged from the foliage with Koorsboom in the rear.

"The wind has died down," he twittered with a nod.

Aalwyn came to a wider clearing where the sedge parted and the stunted grass thinned out around a great baobab tree, its massive center formed of several trunks wound together the width of several elephants. The outermost trunk looped over and ran parallel to the earth with its leafy branches low, as though falling gradually over a thousand years. The light-brown bark varied with the dust, and the knot of roots at its base vaulted to stubby branches against the sky clustered with green leaves.

"Rest here." Aalwyn sat down.

The pups flopped at her feet, and Koorsboom nosed each, twittering gently. Quiet descended as the wolves lay panting with the pups around Aalwyn. Koorsboom looked up at the white clouds where a single lappet-faced vulture glided upon a thermal in the sun.

"Can the baobab trees grow into mountains?"

"Perhaps." Aalwyn examined the tree. "They may be just as old as —"

There was a rustle in the shadow at the base of the baobab tree, and a knobby root stirred.

Aalwyn leapt to her feet with her hackles raised.

His broad tawny paws stepped over the baobab roots, and he shook his black mane as he came into the light.

"Hunting dogs is hardly worth the effort—" The booming voice echoed off the broad baobab trunk. "Finding the den would have been the only challenge. But here you have brought them all to me." He took his steps at leisure, a lip pulled up in a sneer, exposing a fang. A deep, rumbling chuckle emerged from his broad chest, a sound like distant thunder.

"Stay close—" Aalwyn growled urgently, her heart beating rapidly as she glanced wildly around. The wide clearing of the baobab contained only stunted grass and dust. The pups whined at her feet.

Hrur-rhoor—The lion threw back his massive head with a roar that echoed from everywhere at once. "You have failed the veld. Moordenaar does not mourn your passing—"

Hrur-rhoor!—Two lionesses emerged from around the great baobab. Aalwyn trembled above her frightened pups.

"Ever taut as a tendon," Koorsboom whispered to himself, eyes shut tight. He seemed to stand straighter as he opened his eyes again and bellowed. "You mourn nothing—" He stepped forward, voice rising. "Pestilential king!"

The lionesses stopped.

"I have no love for the taste of dog." Moordenaar glared with his one yellow eye. "But I anticipate it eagerly now."

"And I look forward to disembowelling you." Koorsboom bared his teeth over his high-pitched, staccato twitter.

"Run, you imbecile!" Aalwyn's hissing voice caught in her throat.

"The pups are our legacy." Koorsboom did not turn away. "But I am trivial. Keep them safe, Mother." And he was off and sprinting straight toward Moordenaar with his twitter rising into demonic fury.

No wolf had ever attacked a lion before. The lionesses took a step backward, and even Moordenaar paused. Koorsboom stood for an instant at the foot of Moordenaar—then jumped aside in a flash as the mighty paw slashed out. Koorsboom dove forward snapping at Moordenaar's brow, with another jump backward from another swipe. Sprinting quickly behind the lion, Koorsboom bit deeply, drawing blood upon the golden fur.

Moordenaar lunged at him, jaws wide, and caught only the tuft of the tail as Koorsboom darted in again and ripped a section of hide from the lion's face just above his one remaining eye. He caught Koorsboom's shoulder and sent him tumbling, leaping in for the death blow—but Koorsboom was already on his feet racing toward the lionesses, snapping and dodging their claws. Moordenaar barreled through the lionesses and knocked them to the ground as he swiped viciously at Koorsboom in his rage. The pup banked around the baobab trunk with his enemy close behind, breathing heavily in guttural roars. Blood trickled into his yellow eye as he gave chase. Growling, Aalwyn hurried the pups into the thick grasses along the verge of the miombo wood and bounded desperately away with the pups on her heels.

Koorsboom wheeled around the male lion, who snarled in fury with every failed strike. His black, white, and gold fur appeared to dance as he outraced his tormentor. "Have our pups evaded you, diseased parasite?" The pup turned and crouched with his eyes wide with maniacal glee.

"I shall dine on them shortly—and you are invited." Moordenaar surged forward with his powerful paws flying.

Koorsboom dug in his claws as he vaulted sideways, his shoulder scraped with long, bloody tracks. Moordenaar's other paw slammed full-strength into Koorsboom's body, knocking him into a heap, where he paused breathing heavily.

"Your mediocrity is a stain upon the veld." Moordenaar bared his jaws. He unleashed another roar.

Koorsboom struggled upright just as Moordenaar lunged again—and was sent reeling. Koorsboom panted with his eyes wide on the grey shape that materialized from the grasses.

"*Speak well of this veld, which you join in death—*" Blackthorn slashed out, ripping free a section of Moordenaar's hide, while Essenhout snapped in his face to draw him away from Koorsboom. "*My pups shall leave droppings of your remains for seasons to come.*"

"Do you expect to live?" Moordenaar snarled and shook his massive black mane, as rivulets of blood partially blinded his eye. "On *my* land! You are the witless scourge of which it must be purified." He gave chase, throwing clumps of earth and rocks behind him with every lunge after the dark wolf. "Your young are vulture-feed!" He took a swipe at Blackthorn as Essenhout snapped at his hindquarters to distract him.

"It is my call that brings on the night, my will that raises the morning sun. I am the land come alive." Moordenaar was on hind legs with forepaws out, grasping and dodging, while his mane fluttered and his powerful muscles writhed beneath the tawny coat. "*I am the veld!*" Essenhout crouched twittering to one side where Koorsboom scrambled out of the way. Moordenaar leapt at Blackthorn and landed a massive blow to his shoulder, shattering the foreleg and throwing him on the ground.

"Did you expect anything but death?" Moordenaar raked Blackthorn's back, splintering his ribs and puncturing his lungs. Essenhout howled as Blackthorn's grey chest heaved, his muzzle choked with red froth and his eyes rolling and attempting to focus.

"*I—expect—you to follow me.*" Blackthorn heaved himself onto his intact foreleg and clamped his jaws upon a broad forepaw, crunching down with his obsidian eyes glittering.

The lion's roar ripped across the savanna.

Blackthorn was tossed back and forth, his teeth locked together, as Moordenaar shook his paw. He closed his mighty jaws on Blackthorn's back and pulverized the spine until the wolf's hind legs went limp. Moordenaar gave another swipe and threw Blackthorn's quivering body aside, blood streaming from the mouth to collect in a pool on the earth under the fallen grey head.

His one yellow eye burning in fury, the black-maned lion hobbled on his crushed paw away from Blackthorn. Koorsboom snarled, ears back and fangs bared, his eyes so fierce with rage that they bled. "Your feeble alpha is dead," Moordenaar sneered. "As are all who defy me. I killed your father on the riverfront while the rest of your litter watched—I killed one of your pack only yesterday—" He stepped forward on his crippled paw. "And you should have fled me to the sea." A final roar was loosed—"*Moordenaar calls—*"

A flying body struck Moordenaar's head so that he staggered, with a torrent of blood pouring down his ruined face. Aalwyn spun about, fangs dripping carmine as she spat out the bloody remains of Moordenaar's scalp and eye.

"*And Aalwyn answers—*"

Moordenaar flailed wildly with his paws swiping at nothing, calling out to the lionesses.

"*Join your fallen king!*" Aalwyn bayed at them. "*Come forth to us!*"

The lionesses looked to one another and bounded away through the grasses, blending with the tawny savanna until they disappeared.

"Our pups may yet have a taste for lion meat—" Koorsboom gave a high, raving twitter. "It is time to find out!"

Moordenaar held up his remaining paw in feeble defense as Aalwyn snatched it in her teeth and crushed every bone. Koorsboom clamped his jaws upon Moordenaar's belly, and the bowels poured onto the ground in a rusty pool that flooded the clearing. Each wolf braced against the ground, and pulling on the limbs, dismembered the mighty predator. The pups bounded out of the grasses lapping greedily at the blood and pulling the meat from the bones.

Aalwyn's footfalls were heavy as she stepped toward Blackthorn, his obsidian eyes not quite lifeless. He became aware of her presence and cleared his throat. He strained to lift his head as she licked his muzzle tenderly.

"My love—" Blackthorn panted up to her. "Wait a season for their names."

EPILOGUE

Perhaps one day the rains will fail and the veld fall silent. For now, though, the soil is rich and life plentiful. Antelope range the plains, and the land is crisscrossed with burgeoning herds of elephant. Rolling lands of grass cascade from the thick forest that trickles with the rivers from the high mountain of Gorongosa. There are fires, vast armies of grasshopper and cicada, and insatiable antelope. But nothing ever destroys the veld.

During the early winter months, construction had begun on a *boma*, an enclosure of steel cage covered with wood and grass thatch. Now a *bakkie* backed up to the *boma*, and workers in khaki uniforms offloaded sleeping forms. Within hours the sedative wore off and the wolves raised their heads, their eyes swimming into focus upon this new and beautiful land.

Koorsboom and Essenhout found them on a wide patrol.

"From where do you hail?" Koorsboom, now as robust as an adult, pushed his nose between the vertical boards of the *boma*.

"The land of the great river—far, far away." A young female stepped to the wall into light streaming through the incomplete roof. Her coat was the same coloration as Koorsboom's, with a distinctive black shape along her side resembling the African Western Coast and Cape, the coastline and currents of the mighty Benguela.

"We have met before." Essenhout shoved her nose between the boards. "Long ago, we found your pack, you just a pup—"

"Olien, my mother called me. I remember you. You hunted with a younger version of yourself and told us that you wished us no harm."

"You—" Koorsboom's ears swiveled. "You are from our own home river. And you are beautiful."

When the wolves were released by rangers a week later, Koorsboom and Essenhout met them in a tangle of boxing and twittering, a flurry of motion until they leapt away as one for the hunt.

Aalwyn growled at the sight of so many wolves fast approaching, but she relaxed when Essenhout appeared in the lead.

"From the *boma*?" Aalwyn lapped Essenhout's muzzle. "How are they?"

Essenhout smiled and regurgitated a load of meat for the seven pups, who bounded from the brush as Koorsboom and Olien stepped forward with their contributions.

"Have you found a mate already, my son?" Aalwyn licked Koorsboom's muzzle.

"Perhaps." Koorsboom grinned with his tongue lolling out, and Olien stood on hind legs to box him to the ground.

Two pups pulled a section of hide between them, the larger ripping the prize free and running in circles around the other.

"Steady, Blackthorn, my love." Aalwyn touched noses with the young pup. "Now that we have come home to our veld, there will be plenty." She looked out over the pack assembled in the clearing under the burning fever tree. "For us all."

THE END

Resources

This novel was written to reflect as accurately as possible the behaviors of the African Wild Dog or Painted Wolf. In addition to my experiences with these complicated and elusive hunters, the following sources have been essential to understanding more about their tactics, movements, and family structure. Other resources have been useful to get the correct details on plant life, herbivores, and everything that makes an ecological system work.
The mistakes are mine alone.

The African Wild Dog - Behavior, Ecology, and Conservation by Scott and Nancy Creel c2002
Running Wild - Dispelling the Myths of the African Wild Dog by John McNutt and Lesley Boggs c1996
Painted Wolves - Wild Dogs of the Serengeti-Mara by Jonathon Scott c1991
A Window on Eternity by E.O. Wilson c2014
The Behavior Guide to African Mammals by Richard Estes c2012
The Safari Companion by Richard Estes c1999
African Wild Dogs on the Front Line by Brendan Whittington-Jones c2015
The Antelope of Africa by Willem Frost c2014
The Field Guide to Insects of South Africa by Mike Picker c 2004
Sasol Birds of Southern Africa by Ian Sinclair, et al c2014
Snakes of Southern Africa by Johan Marais c2004 Field Guide to Trees of Southern Africa by Braam van Wyk c2013

Organizations protecting and researching the African Painted Wolf:

Painted Dog Conservation - **painteddog.org**
Peter Blinston, managing director

Endangered Wildlife Trust - **ewt.org.za**
Dr. Harriet Davies-Mostert, head of conservation

Wildlife ACT - **wildlifeact.com**
African Wild Dog monitoring and research

African Wild Dog Conservancy - **awdconservancy.org**
Dr. Bob Robbins, director

African Wildlife Foundation - **awf.org**

African Wild Dog Conservation Malawi -
wilddogconservationmalawi.org

African Wildlife Conservation Fund -
africanwildlifeconservationfund.org
Dr. Peter Lindsey, Africa director

Made in the USA
Lexington, KY
01 March 2018